Praise for *Africa, Africa!*

"A sparkling cluster of often poignant tales, told with insight and compassion. They paint an exuberant palette of Africa and its people, overflowing with grace, color and vitality, yet caught in a struggle for dignity and identity in an age that destroys stabilizing traditions. Hunter treads gently but surely between dream and reality. A highly readable, entertaining book."
——David Anable, President, International Center for Journalists

"*Africa, Africa!* is a finely honed collection of stories that evoke the magic of a mysterious and beautiful continent. Fred Hunter introduces us to people and places that are enchanting and dangerous, to a series of deep pools in which we glimpse universal humanity reflected. As you finish one story, you want to start the next."
——Robert Swanson, former writer/producer *Murder, She Wrote*

"From Madagascar to Burkina Faso, Hunter's stories chronicle Africa's unfailing influence on the human spirit, its subtle effect on characters' lives. *Africa, Africa!* offers readers front row seats in observing how Africa marks those who travel it."
——Julie Knight Stokol, former Peace Corps volunteer, Mali

"Frederic Hunter's *Africa, Africa!* stories make old Africa hands want to drop everything and head back for the life of daily adventure Hunter depicts so knowledgeably. Newcomers to the continent will find insight to help them face its many baffling enigmas."
——Richard Matheron, former US Ambassador to Swaziland

About the Author

Frederic Hunter has written for many mediums. His plays include *The Hemingway Play, Disposable Woman,* and *Subway.* His adaptation for PBS of his own *Hemingway Play* won a Writers Guild Award nomination. Also for PBS he adapted Ring Lardner's "The Golden Honeymoon" and wrote *Lincoln and the War Within* under a grant from the National Endowment for the Humanities. Other television projects include *The Beate Klarsfeld Story* for ABC, *A Nightmare in the Daylight* for CBS, and *The Devil in Vienna* for the Disney Channel.

Hunter served as a US Information Service officer in the Congo and spent four years as the Africa correspondent for *The Christian Science Monitor,* later returning to edit its Home Forum. His essay "Fathers and Sons" was published in Cune's anthology, *An Ear to the Ground.*

At present, Hunter works as a screenwriter and lives in Santa Barbara with his wife, Donanne.

Contact the author: murugi@fredhunter.net.

For more information: www.fredhunter.net.

Africa, Africa!

FIFTEEN STORIES

Africa, Africa!

FIFTEEN STORIES
by Frederic Hunter

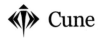 Cune

Africa, Africa!

Cune Press, Seattle, 2000.

ISBN (Paper) 1-885942-18-4
ISBN (Cloth) 1-885942-17-6

Credits: "Equateur" was first published in *The Christian Science Monitor*. Sections of "At the Edge of the Jungle," "Dr. Kleckner," "Night Vigil," "Laban and Murugi," "North of Nairobi," and "Africa, Africa!" appeared originally in *The Christian Science Monitor* in somewhat different form. All are used with permission.

Cover Art: Ian Miller
    Contact by mail: 827 W. Valley Hwy, Suite 48, Kent, WA 98032; or email: shimiller@imajis.com; or phone: (253) 854-6755.

Copies of *Africa, Africa!* are available for purchase online at www.cunepress.com or toll free at (800) 445-8032.

Cune is a project of the Allied Arts Foundation. Make tax-deductible contributions to "Cune Project/Allied Arts" and mail to Cune Press, PO Box 31024, Seattle, WA 98103. Contact Cune by fax: (206) 782-1330; or email: cune@cunepress.com. Visit Cune Magazine online at www.cunepress.com.

 Cune

Cune is a literary press and an online magazine founded in May 1994 to explore innovative ways of bringing superior writing to public attention. Our name is derived from "cuneiform."

FOR DONANDY

AFRICA IN 2000

(The shaded countries are those visited by the stories.)

CONTENTS

At the Edge of the Jungle:
An Introduction

THE COUNTRY WAS CALLED THE CONGO THEN, as it is
now once again. I was living in the Equateur, the remote
northwestern region of the country, in Coquilhatville. It was a
tiny place, now known as Mbandaka, a river port squatting at
the confluence of the mighty, tawny Congo, so wide that some
days you could not see the opposite bank, and a tributary called
the Ruki. A Belgian explorer-adminstrator Camille Coquilhat had
opened a Congo Free State trading post there in the 1890s.

Coq existed outside of time; its only realities were the sky,
the river, and the jungle. Living there, it was hard later to comprehend reports of rebel advances somewhere out in that vast,
swampy, and river-laced jungle. It was hard to believe that Coq
was a place those rebels would want to capture on their path to
Léopoldville, the capital.

But it was.

Although in 1964 it was a shrinking island of civilization, Coq had only a few years earlier served as the capital of the Equateur, one of the Belgian Congo's six colonial provinces. So it was deemed important enough by the United States government to merit an "American presence." Not a diplomatic mission, mind you, just a US Information Service post, an American Cultural Center.

I arrived in the Congo from a training tour in Brussels just at the time the married officer assigned to Coquilhatville flatly refused to accept the posting. He would not take his wife to that isolated and pestiferous place.

So I was sent instead. My job was to open the post.

I was wretchedly lonely for days. Every evening during the first weeks when I walked from the rundown hotel to the town's one restaurant, I mentally composed an angry letter to my USIS boss in Léopoldville. In it I announced my resignation.

But I didn't resign. Eventually I managed to convert an empty house, already leased by the Embassy, into a lending library, a reading room, and a film collection. Six months later when the post was established and Coq seemed habitable, I was instructed to welcome an officer more senior than myself. He would direct the Cultural Center's work.

About the time he and his wife arrived, news began to filter into the Equateur of strange happenings in Kwilu Province, east of Léopoldville, rumblings of insurrection. The disturbances quickly spread to the Kivu, on the eastern border. They threatened the Kivu's principal town, Bukavu, where I had served for six weeks after first arriving in the Congo. The insurgents placed it under siege.

They moved swiftly through the forests, picking up adherents; many were teenagers seeking adventure. Towns whose names I had trouble finding on the map began to fall to the rebels. US military personnel arrived to install a single-side-band radio in the center; our code name was "River Rat."

Then Stanleyville fell. The famous Stanleyville, now known as Kisangani—and familiar to readers of Joseph Conrad's *Heart of Darkness* as Kurtz's Inner Station. An American missionary was killed. We heard rumors of consular and CIA officers trapped in the town.

The rebels started their trek toward Léopoldville—and toward us in Coq. Would they come by river? Or overland? There was only one road into and out of Coquilhatville. If they came along that road and crossed the Ruki at the Ingende ferry, only six hours drive from town, what would happen? Would the *Armée Nationale Congolaise* protect us? Or would the soldiers flee, as they were doing elsewhere, fearing that the rebels were invincible, protected by a magic that turned bullets into droplets of water? If the rebels crossed the Ruki, would we be trapped?

Our days grew increasingly tense. We curtailed my twice-monthly film trips into the bush. It became impossible to accomplish any real work. US military flights landed every two or three days at the Coq airport. Everyone was edgy. Acquaintances in the town, ex-colonials, found reasons to go to Léopoldville—"I haven't seen a dentist in donkeys' years"— and did not return. Panic began to grip Coquilhatville. My boss and his wife talked frequently about leaving. "If we aren't accomplishing things," he'd say, "is there any reason to stay?"

Then one morning I was told that we were evacuating. It was about 10:30 AM. By 3:00 PM we were gone.

The next day at the Embassy one of the American secretaries joshingly remarked to me, "You guys certainly turned tail the minute things got rough."

So I went back.

It struck me even then as a curious thing to do. Despite the secretary's taunt, it was dangerous in Coq. But the Ambassador was agreeable to my returning. Perhaps he wanted a "presence" in the town, some American eyes and ears. But I like to think he realized that I stood at a personal crossroads. Unlike my superior, I had spent a year building something in the town and I wasn't yet prepared to turn my back on it. Returning or walking away: one act or the other would define for me my manhood.

A week had passed when I returned. The rebels were a lot closer to the town; panic was more palpably in the air. Like humidity you could feel it.

I checked in at the Center. I had dinner with Jules André, my best friend in town, a Belgian electrician whose wife Thérèse and three children I had helped evacuate to Léopoldville. He was very depressed. He talked of setting his house ablaze before the rebels came. He wondered if his life's work would be lost.

That night the rebels crossed the Ruki at the Ingende ferry. By the time I awoke in the morning looters were at work in the town center. The single-side-band radio had been evacuated to Léopoldville, but I managed to secure an open phone line to the Embassy—no easy feat—and telexed a plea for a plane. A C-130 arrived in the early afternoon. It had a cargo bay large enough to accommodate a house. We loaded refugees onto the cargo floor and took off.

When I got back to Léopoldville, I was escorted briefly into the presence of the Ambassador. I made my report. He said simply, "Well, we're outa that place."

The story of my year in Coquilhatville can be told so fast that it sounds exciting. But the living of it was slow. And the rebel approach, though fast, excited only dread and emptiness in the stomach.

In the interior of Africa life progresses in slow motion. Often time seems not to move at all. And no wonder. It's hot there. And so humid that a light skin of sweat always clothes your own skin. In that heat nothing wants to move at all. Moreover, on the Equator, against which Coquilhatville nestled, the length of the days hardly varies. Seasons do not change as they do in the temperate zones.

In some expatriates these conditions—heat, stillness, boredom—invite lethargy. Vigor seeps out of them in much the way that water seeps out of a mangrove swamp at low tide. They begin to smoke. They drink—frequently too much and much too frequently. They experiment with drugs. Heat and languor turn their thoughts to sex; they plot dalliances and seek seductions, sometimes failing, sometimes not.

Other expats are not undone by heat, stillness, boredom. If they are new to the life, they are busy responding to other conditions: the strangeness of the locals, the vividness of the surroundings, their own outsider status and the fact and intensity of their youth. All these sharpen their senses.

For some of that latter category, especially if they are impressionable, the old truism holds true. "We are outa that place." But that place is not out of us.

Thirty-five years later Coquilhatville is still working its way out of me.

When my Congo tour concluded, USIS assigned me to Karachi, Pakistan. The posting sounded interesting. And yet. . . . Four continents in five years: North America, Europe, Africa, southern Asia. I had lived and worked at three posts in the Congo:

Coquilhatville, Bukavu, Léopoldville. I had encountered a complex society there as ex-colonials adjusted to a new, less influential status, as various tribes of Congolese tried to forge a nation out of disorder. I had encountered similar, yet different complexities in Belgium where the Flemish-Walloon rivalry seemed never to stop. And in my own country white Americans were just beginning to come to grips—thanks to sit-ins and Freedom Rides—with complexities of their own.

If I was to serve overseas, to live with discontinuity, I would need a balancing continuity in my life, perhaps a marriage, perhaps a family that could move with me whenever I was transferred. Four continents in five years: that was one thing. Four sets of friends in transit: that was something very different. Mulling over the Karachi assignment, I resigned from USIS and returned home to Los Angeles.

Heat, stillness, life in slow motion: these left me ill-prepared for the speed of American living, the bombardment of diversions, the incredible affluence. I tried to write about the Congo, but I could not do it well. As a means of readjusting to America (so I told myself), I took a masters degree in African Studies at UCLA. It was, in fact, an attempt to come to terms with where I'd been, what I'd seen. That had also been the goal in trying to write.

I could not write well about the Congo because I knew too little. In the mid-1960s all of America knew too little about Africa. Part of the nation's racial problem stemmed from that ignorance.

Most Americans at that time thought that Africa had no history, at least none before the colonial penetration. So it was illuminating to learn about Sundiata who organized the Mali Empire over a vast stretch of inland West Africa in the thirteenth century at about the time of the Magna Carta. And about his grandson the philanthropic Mansa Musa who took a pilgrimage to Mecca a century later. With him went an entourage of five hundred slaves carrying staffs of gold and eighty to one hundred camel loads of gold, each weighing about three hundred pounds. (As he passed through Cairo, the city was agog!) And about Muhammed Askia, devout usurper of the Songhai Empire's throne who made a similar visit to Mecca almost two centuries later, accompanied by five hundred cavalry and one thousand infantry and carrying three hundred thousand pieces of gold. And about Shaka Zulu and Dingaan and the fabled city of Zimbabwe, which Europeans insisted that Africans could not have built.

I also studied anthropology and political science. In an early class a young professor spoke of the elite-mass gap and the urban-rural gap, basic concepts, but ones I had never before heard articulated in such comprehensible terms. What I had observed in the Congo began to make sense.

During this time I met Donanne, the daughter of a newly retired Foreign Service couple: Miss Right. I doggedly pursued her. She said, "Yes." We got married.

A year later I sent an essay about our first year of marriage to The Home Forum of *The Christian Science Monitor.* It was accepted. The Home Forum editor and I began to correspond. Then the Monitor's editor wrote me. The paper was in need of someone to cover Africa. No staffer would take the job. Would I? I was unemployed and newly married. Of course, I would!

Sometimes, if you are very fortunate, that place which is still in you—it was all of Africa now, not just Coquilhatville—is a place you get to return to. And with your wife! That was my case when I covered Africa for *The Monitor.*

Gradually the stories presented here began to write themselves. They came as stories, as fiction, because my imagination needed room to exercise itself. And because I wanted to work with materials in my memory, materials that did not fit into news reports. "Equateur," the earliest of these pieces, first appeared on *The Monitor*'s Home Forum page, which publishes literary essays.

Two of the Congo stories—which I have embellished as "Lenoir" and "Card Players"—were told me by Jules André. At night in Coq, when the river flowed silently just beyond the lights from the lamps *chez André*, when the nearby jungle never let us forget its presence, Jules and Thérèse often had me to dinner. And sometimes Jules would tell tales.

On those nights far across the Congo, in Bukavu, other Americans would be speculating about the Mwami of Kabare, a feudal potentate (so they thought) ensconced in mountains high above the town. He was up there, they were sure, plotting mischief against Bukavu. "Waiting for the Mwami" gives an account of my visit to the Mwami in the company of an American correspondent.

The stories "Night Vigil" and "Laban and Murugi" look at the domestic life of a journalist and his wife living in Kenya. "Madagascar" and "North of Nairobi" portray journalists at work. "A Newsman Scratches an Itch" takes us to South Africa.

Sharpened senses. These are a journalist's equipment. Some of the stories stem from them. In my mind's eye I can still see the African woman I watched on the streets of Bobo-Dioulasso. Beauty incarnate. How she floated! She became the pivotal character of "Dr. Kleckner." I recall Sunday lunch with a British couple at a hotel on the Zomba plateau in Malawi. And I'm still grateful for the kindness of embassy people in Bamako, Mali, when

Donanne and I arrived at the airport without visas. They people the story called "Pepper." Jenny Gooch, whose husband Toby ran the Oxfam office in Nairobi, told me the story of "The Barking Dog." "Elizabeth Who Disappeared" takes us back to the Congo. So, in a strange way, does "Africa, Africa!"

When I served as *The Monitor*'s Africa man, I conceived of the job as being an advocate for the continent. Of course, I could not sugarcoat my reportage. But I wanted to show Africa as more than exotic and savage and dysfunctional, which was the impression most reportage offered. I found Africa beautiful. Its people delighted me. I had a hunch that my readers could learn from them.

I still believe that. That's another reason for writing these stories.

By and large they depict Westerners encountering Africa—its people, its mysteries, its beauty and bafflements. Often those encounters change the Westerners, leading some to wisdom, others to heartache and pain.

But if stories and news reports are to help Westerners learn from Africa, then its advocates need to define the special gift that Africans contribute to the world. Not merely music. Not merely art. Or laughter. Or social particularities. These are universal gifts; every culture offers them.

I wanted to suggest the sweetness of the African temperament, the African capacity for patience and palaver, for working things out in a non-violent way. I knew that many readers—and possibly editors—considered this sentimental mush. They had, after all, been schooled to equate Africa with savagery.

In the past decade Africa has seen myriad civil wars, the Hutu-Tutsi massacres, and ethnic killings. Even if these are accepted as evidence of the cost of modernizing traditional societies, it's hard to argue that they do not confirm the presence in Africa of savagery and unspeakable horror.

But overseas it's equally hard to deny that school and workplace shootings and daily killings in America do not confirm that American society is obsessed with violence and awash in blood.

Despite contrary evidence, I am convinced that the sweetness of the African temperament exists. If it did not, the decolonization of Africa could not have been accomplished with so little bloodshed. I feel certain that the African capacity for patience and palaver has something to give the world, once the Northern Hemisphere is ready to learn from the southern one, once the technically-gifted West is ready to learn from soul-gifted others.

Watching Africans lined up to vote in South Africa's first all-citizens elections confirmed in me this certainty. Television pictures showed first-time voters, many of them quite elderly, waiting in quiet, miles-long queues. Their faces showed their amiableness and forbearance, their humility and humanity. "We don't mind waiting," they said. "People have died for this." And I could not help but think that sometimes the meek really do inherit the earth.

"We are out of that place." But that place is not out of us. Once we evacuated Coquilhatville—I am back in 1964 now—there was no reason for me to return. Yes, my call for a plane helped a few refugees escape, but escape from what? As it turned out the rebels never entered Coq. No savagery occurred there. No lives were lost.

Why did I go back? To claim something I could not leave

behind. When a C-130 evacuated me the second time, I brought that something with me. When I served as a reporter in Africa, it was with me. It's with me now.

And even now a longing for the continent occasionally overwhelms me. For me Africa will always be a place whose perplexities baffle and charms delight even while its lessons continue to teach me.

WAITING FOR THE MWAMI

AS THE VAN LEFT BUKAVU and the peninsulas stretching out into Lake Kivu, Eric felt pleased with the prospect of adventure. Night rain had washed the haze from the air. The day was clear and sunny. Out on the road Kabare women trudged down from the hills, balancing baskets of strawberries on the straight columns formed by their backs and heads.

Wedged between two companions on the van's torn seat, Eric breathed deeply of the rain-washed air; he surveyed the patterns of the cloths tied about the women's bodies. As the van climbed toward the *chefferie* of Kabare, he noticed the green fluttering of banana leaves, the burnt umber of the earth. He watched the lake shimmer and the mountains stretch away in receding blues all the way to the Ruwenzoris.

"We've got a great day for this," he said to Mark who peered intently out the window. For the sake of Déogratias who was driving and spoke no English, he added, *"Quel jour, eh?"*

Mark studied the huts visible through the banana leaves. There were two types: one rectangular, mud and wattle with pitched frond-thatched roofs, the other conical. How to describe these to American readers? "Like squat cones?" "Like a thick fur coat of banana fronds?" Hmm. His editors would balk at that. They wanted news. Space was always tight for color pieces like this.

But it was some story. An interview with an African king, demigod to some, autocrat to others. Mark had already worked out his lead, "Being received by the Mwami of Kabare, absolute ruler of a quarter million tribesmen here, is like stepping four hundred years back into 1563." He would make the Mwami a traditionalist rogue, a charming anachronism, and sprinkle gems of his wisdom throughout the piece.

But the fight for space in the paper was as rugged as the fight for space in the jungle. Mme Nhu, the Vietnamese dragon lady, was in New York, demanding coverage. MacMillan had just re-signed in Britain. The Congo story was also being covered from the UN. Unless the Mwami said startling things, editors would think the piece thin for the paper. Bastards. They'd bury it on page twenty. Next to the Gimbels ads.

As he drove, Déogratias waved to the Kabare women; they stopped to watch the van pass, their whole bodies turning. Déo did not know the women, but they knew him. He was, *"Cinéma,"* who worked for the white men, who controlled an entire room-ful of their equipment and gave film shows in the communes. Déo waved in a gesture of noblesse oblige. He did not admire muscular work-hardened bodies or bovine stares. The women he preferred were rounded and laughing.

"Déo, mon ami," Mark said. "During this interview, there may be stuff I don't get. You'll walk me through it afterwards, okay?"

"Bien sur, Monsieur," Déo said, grinning. *"Bien entendu."* Pleased with himself, he tooted the horn at an old man hobbling

across the road. The Consul and Eric, his boss, were treating this famous journalist from New York with such deference that he, too, wanted to render whatever service he could. Perhaps the man needed an assistant. Or a representative in the Kivu. Perhaps Déo should inquire discreetly if he needed a woman. What man did not need a woman?

They left the lakeshore and moved up into the hills. Eric appraised Mark. They were about the same age, not yet thirty. Mark might be younger. But seemed older. That came with the position. Eric wondered if he were jealous of Mark. Well, why not? Great job, great perks. Everyone deferred to him, hung on his words, suggested sources, checked his coverage to see if he'd used their help. The guy had a bedmate in Léopoldville, a hot Belgian girl Eric had dated twice down there; he'd wondered about seducing her. Mark already had, he knew. Maybe that too came with the position. Mark was like a prince, visiting the far reaches of America's empire. The Consul had met his plane, briefed him, visited his hotel, arranged dinners for him, taken charge of his weekend activities, even kept him informed of cable traffic. The Consul had told Eric, "Any help you can give this reporter or his paper, you be damn sure you give it."

The Consul had set up the interview with the reclusive Mwami of Kabare. He'd sent a messenger to the office of the *chefferie*, requesting that the Mwami show Mark Stern the hospitality of the region. He had further suggested that the Mwami offer this hospitality at ten the following morning. Nice having all that help, Eric thought. He wondered if Mark loved Africa or merely covered it.

"This Mwami's some potentate," Mark said. "Colonial authorities exiled him twice. First time for twenty-three years. Set up a puppet in his place." Eric recognized the Consul's briefing. "Then when he returned, he had the puppet Mwami and two retainers beheaded. Right?"

Eric shrugged. The Consul relished stories that made him seem to be holding the line against barbarism. During the summer he had cabled Washington to report that the Mwami had forbidden Kabare women to carry wood into Bukavu, cutting off a commodity important to the town. According to the Consul, the Mwami had confiscated trucks from coffee and tea plantations. Occasionally he boasted that he would descend into Bukavu with hundreds of warriors to force his claim against Europeans who had taken Kabare land without ever compensating him for it.

Mark asked, "You hear anything about the Mwami ordering two tribesmen to be buried alive last week?"

Eric watched the road. He was thinking that "potentate" and "tribesmen" were journalist's words. Had he ever seen those words outside news reports?

When Eric did not reply, Mark examined him. He hadn't been in Africa long enough to reply as Africans did, inspecting questions from every vantage before responding. So why was he studying his answer? The guy seemed bright enough. But at the Consul's dinner Mark had noticed that he neither drank nor smoked. Probably not getting much either. He seemed to have seen some of the world, but would not take a bite of it. Mark wondered what brought the guy to Africa.

Mark finally asked, "You didn't hear about those guys?"

"Lot of stories fly around," Eric said.

"You don't think they're true?"

"What is truth? Didn't somebody ask that?"

"Is it factual?" Mark asked, a little pissed. This was preparation for an interview, not a metaphysical discussion.

"Yeah, I guess it's factual," Eric said. "In Africa it's *why* that's so puzzling."

Mark shook his head. The guy was a jerk.

Eric thought, As if facts alone meant anything. But he didn't say it. Why say it? He mostly liked Mark. Why cast doubts on the Consul's careful briefing?

"Does this sound factual?" Mark asked. "Last week an excited tribesman rushes to police officials to report that the Mwami of Kabare has ordered villagers to bury two men alive. The officials rush up to Kabare. They find two guys buried up to their necks and manage to rescue them."

"Yeah," Eric said. "But, you know, I sometimes wonder if the Mwami and his counselors don't get bored up in the hills. So they say, 'Hey, let's see how long it takes them today.' They find someone who's been questioning the Mwami's authority and they give both him and the government of Kivu Central a scare."

Mark shrugged. Just the facts, please, he thought.

"Ought to be a great story," Eric assured Mark. "Your readers'll get some idea of what's at stake in bringing this country into the modern world." He said this because he supposed it was what the Consul would want him to say. He added, "I can see guys over coffee telling their wives, 'Hey, honey, you better read this.'"

Mark nodded. The USIS man was not supposed to fight him and, good, he wasn't going to. A tight, satisfied smile appeared on Mark's mouth.

The film van climbed past Bagira, one of the communes colonial authorities had built for workers lured away from the life of Kabare villages. Déo held film shows on the soccer field; he saluted it by honking the horn. The van left the paved road, ascending toward low-hanging overcast that lay on the mountain tops. The air was cool here. Children receiving lessons in a roadside school stood at the sight of the van. Déo leaned from the driver's window to wave. Children broke from their class; they ran beside the van yelling, *"Cinéma! Cinéma! États-Unis d'Amérique."*

"Your tax dollars at work," Eric said.

Mark craned his neck at the sight of a child picking lice from the braided hair of a woman. He took a pad from his jacket and made a note.

Déo tooted the horn, delighted at being a celebrity. Eric watched him. He had begun to understand that in Bukavu the film van was an aphrodisiac. It excited desire in the many young Congolese women who had never ridden in a vehicle of any kind. They would gladly offer Déo access to their bodies for a chance to ride in the van. Eric worried that Déo was exploiting their generosity.

"We're fantastically lucky to have Déo in Bukavu," USIS people in the capital said. Déo had served as a Lomani District delegate to the Congo's first constituent assembly, they told Eric, very impressed. However, no one seemed to know where Lomani was. "A self-starter," they said. "Knows everyone. Worked for the Kivu Information Ministry before we doubled his pay and hired him away."

Still Eric wondered about Déo's conduct. The Consul had seen the van parked outside night clubs and was concerned about appearances. The previous week Déo had sought an advance of 25,000 francs. When Eric asked the Consul's advice, he said, "'God-be-thanked' owes me 10,000 francs! Don't give him a penny!" Déo's landlord visited to complain that Déo had paid no rent in five months. A distressed African came by to report that Déo had his daughter with child.

Déo pulled himself inside the van. *"Tout le monde m'aime,"* he told Eric. In the rearview mirror he watched children chasing him. *"Tout le monde m'appelle Cinéma!"*

Eric nodded—and wondered, What do I do about this guy?

Outside the village of Kabare, oil drums blocked the road. A young guard wearing a brown beret with "Kabare" sewn on it in white thread sat on a stool. In his hands he played a *likembe,* a "thumb piano," plucking its metal strips fastened to a sound box. Reaching the roadblock, the van stopped. When he finished his tune, the guard moved to the van; he peered at its passengers. Déo gestured to Mark and explained in Swahili that the Mwami was awaiting this very important guest.

The guard nodded and pushed two oil drums out of the road.

"The Mwami has his own police?" Mark asked Déo.

"Bien entendu, Monsieur," Déo replied. "And his own tax-collectors. The government of Kivu Central, it's a joke up here."

Mark nodded and made half a page of notes in his pad.

The offices of the Kabare *chefferie* were open, but deserted. Eric noticed Mark's mouth tighten. Mark walked through the building, thinking, "Shit! That Consul better not have fucked up!" He was scheduled to catch a four o'clock plane to Usumbura; he would file the story there. When he returned outside, he shot a glance at the USIS man that said, "I thought you guys set this up."

Eric thought, "Easy, Pulitzer. Where do you think you are?"

An old man appeared. He wore frayed shorts, a threadbare overcoat, and a black policeman's cap green with age. No, the Mwami was not coming to the *chefferie* offices, he told Déo in Swahili. No, there was no appointment. No, the Mwami did not accept to receive American journalists. Eric thought, "Easy." The old man might not even know what a journalist was. But the muscles around Mark Stern's mouth pulled tighter. Yes, the old man agreed, he would conduct the three visitors to the Mwami's *palais*.

The "*palais*" proved to be a complex of buildings, dominated by a large house a European planter had abandoned three years earlier when the Congo acceded to independence. The old man left them to announce their arrival to the Mwami. In a small meadow fenced with chest-high bushes two horses grazed. "The guy keeps horses?" Mark muttered. He surveyed the surroundings and made notes in his pad.

Glancing around, Eric thought how heady it must be to live in mountains that scraped the clouds. The gods were supposed to live here. Well, he mused, why not? They had to live somewhere.

The Mwami sat on the porch of his palace in pajamas and slippers. He had finished the mid-morning ritual of receiving the tribal notables and clan heads. He watched the horses, thinking about a dispute between two clans which he must adjudicate.

A young man who attended him hurried onto the porch. He bowed low and waited to be recognized. The Mwami said, "Speak." The young man reported that two white men were on the lawn, accompanied by an African who was not one of the people. The Mwami nodded. The young man stood, apparently desiring to speak, but nervous. It tired the Mwami to see a young man in his service who became agitated at the mere approach of white men. Was he not, after all, the Mwami of Kabare, chief of all the lands hereabouts? And were the white men not mere supplicants? The Mwami flicked his hand tiredly. The young retainer bowed low and withdrew. The Mwami looked back at the horses. The whites could wait.

Déo watched the horses frolic in the meadow, cantering in large circles. To show the journalist that he was a man of the world, he enthused, *"Ah, j'aime les chez vous."*

Mark ignored him. Eric glanced around. "My *chez vous?"* he thought. "My apartment?" Somewhat puzzled, Eric said, *"Vous voulez dire mon appartement?"*

Déo frowned.

Ah! Eric thought. Déo was being *homme du monde.* The *"chez vous"* were the *"chevaux,"* the horses. As if he rode. Eric grunted, *"Ah, oui."*

When the old man did not reappear, the three men drifted toward the Mwami's house. They came upon a group of ancients clustered on the steps of a side porch. Many of these men smoked pipes; many wore what Eric thought of as goat beards, straggly collections of tightly coiled chin hair, some of the hairs whitening. Two of the men protected their old heads with monkey-skin caps. Dressed in patched jackets and shorts, in baggy, uncreased trousers turning purple with age, they beheld the newcomers suspiciously. *"Les notables,"* Déo whispered. "Tribal elders come every morning to greet the Mwami."

Mark nodded. He watched the old men as intently as they watched him.

Because the visitors were white men, the notables stood and stepped forward. They presented themselves with caution and a certain rigidity. They bowed slightly, folding forward stiffly, and offered their hands. The visitors shook them, bowing slightly with deference, then stepped back.

While the ancients examined the visitors, Déo explained to them in Swahili that Mark Stern, gesturing to him, was a very important visitor whom the Mwami had agreed to receive. The ancients gazed at Mark out of eyes so old that streaks of brown discolored them. They said nothing.

Déo sensed difficulties. The Mwami had forgotten the meeting. Or had never been told. The Americans must not know. Déo saw the notables glancing toward the front of the *palais*. Still praising Mark and his paper, Déo looked in that direction. He saw the figure in the chair; he recognized and broke toward it, exclaiming, *"Bonjour, Mwami!"*

Mark hurried forward. Eric grabbed his arm, held him back. Mark shot him a glare of fury. "Slow down," Eric whispered. "That's a king."

"Take your fucking hand off me," Mark muttered.

But Eric did not release his grip until Mark stood respectfully, waiting for the Mwami to signal to him.

The Mwami leaned his head back in the chair. His eyes started to close. Suddenly behind him footsteps sounded. Before he could look around, he saw a grinning face bending toward him. *"Bonjour, Mwami,"* the face said.

The Mwami sat up, thought, "Who is this man? How dare he approach without being announced?" Then he recognized the pushy fellow his people called *"Cinéma,"* the white man's toady who considered himself a great personage because he drove the white man's truck and wore his clothes and spoke his language. Cinéma of eager grins, a pudgy frame, and a smooth, fast tongue. He had dark skin, almost black, and was not one of the people. The Mwami recalled hearing that he came from the grasslands on the far side of the mountains. He might be a dignitary in Bukavu, but in Kabare he was a nuisance, an upstart.

Cinéma stepped back. He put his feet together and bowed, an overdue gesture of respect for the Mwami's power, for his being.

The Mwami nodded. He recalled now what was said of this

Cinéma. That he enticed maidens from among the people into his truck and played sex with them. That when he took his light machine to a secondary school, he demanded that the principal send him a maiden. That he frequented the bars of Bukavu, having more women even than a Mwami had, but without a Mwami's position and power.

Cinéma did not bow low, the Mwami noticed. A feigner of obsequiousness to the white man, he supposed a Mwami would not know true respect. He dared to stand in a Mwami's presence unannounced. As if a Mwami would not distinguish between true respect owed a man of power and the feigned deference shown to white men.

"I bring an American who desires to talk with the Mwami," this Cinéma said. He talked on, but the Mwami stopped listening, feeling cold now in his pajamas and old in the presence of this black-skinned outsider from the grasslands who knew no decorum. The Mwami looked off toward the clouds that shrouded the trees. What kind of white men were "Amay Ricans," he wondered. Belgians, he knew and hated. And the new rulers: toad-eaters, jackals in men's skins, former postal clerks to whom the people were said to have given power by dropping papers in a box. He was beginning to know them. But Amay Ricans, the Mwami did not know. He had heard that they came to steal the land. So he must beware of them.

"The Consul sent a letter, Mwami. The journalist wishes to ask you questions—"

The Mwami looked up sharply. Cinéma stopped his smooth tongue. Ask questions? Truly, this Cinéma knew no decorum. Visitors entreated. Visitors begged humbly. Or sought the Mwami's patronage. But questions? No! If there were questions, it was the Mwami who asked.

The upstart began speaking again, but the Mwami did not listen. He stood. Attendants appeared from inside the palace. The white men's menial burst into smiles, thinking his request had been granted. "An important man, you say?" the Mwami asked. He spoke Swahili because he would not use the white men's words.

"Very important, Mwami." The toady grinned like a hyena when it smells carrion. He extended an arm, gesturing toward the porch where his masters waited.

"I cannot receive an important white man dressed as I am now dressed," the Mwami said. "You see how I am dressed."

"They will be honored to see you just as you are, Mwami," this Cinéma said. Finally he bowed low.

"Because he is important," said the Mwami, "it is proper for me to show respect for that importance. Just as a Mwami might expect to receive the respect rightfully accorded a Mwami."

The hyena grin faded from the fawner's face.

"Tell him that the Mwami is not yet ready to receive important visitors. Have him wait."

As the Mwami moved toward the house, one of his young men opened the door. The Mwami entered and did not look back.

"Oooo la la!" thought Déogratias. "With this Mwami there are always difficulties. But the Americans must not know." He put a grin onto his face and stepped lightly across the grass. *"Bonnes nouvelles, Messieurs,"* he announced. "The Mwami is honored that you're here. He wants to receive you in a way that befits the occasion!"

Mark was accustomed to this sort of reception and felt encouraged. That USIS guy! When he'd held him back! Shithead.

But things were working out. He opened his notebook to the question list. A couple of controversial ones. Good!

Eric was relieved that Déo had come through. They were right in Léo. The guy did seem to know everyone. Eric wondered what a "potentate" made of the Western ceremony of the press interview.

A young man who said he was the Mwami's secretary appeared from inside the house. He carried himself with a dignity that merited attention from Mark. Was this the Kabare heir the Consul had mentioned, the young man of promise the Mwami had adopted as his son? The secretary invited the visitors to enter the house. He escorted them onto a small, enclosed porch where two other men also awaited the Mwami. He showed Eric and Mark to heavily upholstered chairs drawn up on opposite sides of a low table and then withdrew. Déo stood against a wall.

Minutes passed. No one spoke. Déo took a seat.

The secretary returned to apologize in French for the delay. And for the fact that *"effectivement"* he spoke no French. Eric wondered how much French he actually knew. Watching Mark examine the man, he knew that Mark wondered the same thing.

One of the waiting Africans turned out to be a *chefferie* tax collector. Mark zeroed in on him. He had heard, Mark said, that the Mwami collected taxes in cattle that the government had not authorized. Was this true? The tax collector glanced at the secretary. The secretary's expression did not change. The tax collector denied that the Mwami collected unauthorized taxes. He had heard, Mark said, that the Mwami set taxes according to his whim. Was this true? No, it was not true, said the tax collector. If farmers did not pay the taxes demanded, Mark asked, was it not true that the Mwami's police threw them off their land? The collector denied that this was true. The secretary spoke to the tax collector. Mark and Eric watched Déo. He shook his head very slightly, indicating that he could not follow what was being said. The secretary departed. For some moments no one spoke.

Mark jotted notes in his pad. After a time, the tax collector explained that the farmers did not own the land they farmed. The Mwami owned it—for the people. The farmers used it at the Mwami's pleasure. Mark nodded and made more notes.

Several notables entered. They bowed stiffly and extended their hands. Eric rose to shake them. When he resumed his seat, he watched Mark making notes. "The guy's never left New York!" he thought. Here they were in a place so remote that whites had not settled it until after the First World War. They were waiting for an audience with a Mwami who beheaded people when he felt like it or had them buried alive. Was it not obvious to Mark that he and the Mwami lived by different codes? Mark Stern's code gave Mark Stern the right, nay the obligation, to grill people he interviewed. He could interrogate the Mayor of New York, who accepted his code, on the way taxes were collected. But the Mwami of Kabare? Eric hoped the Mwami felt generous this morning. Then he might just let Mark and Déo and him walk out of Kabare alive.

Long minutes passed.

A young African joined the group. "You are Americans?" he asked in English. "I learned English in Kenya," he explained. Then he added, "I have come to petition the Mwami for money. To continue my studies. It would be well, don't you think, for the Mwami to have someone in his household who speaks English?"

"Tell me," Mark said watching him. "The Mwami's secretary. He was here a few minutes ago. Is he the Mwami's heir?"

The petitioner's face went blank. He studied the question.

Eric thought, "Mark must know what he's doing." But he himself would not have phrased the question so directly.

Mark thought, "Must be the right question. He's really looking it over."

At last the petitioner asked, "Air?" He waved his hand through the air. "So many words the same in English."

"That's true," said Mark. He made more notes in his pad.

While waiting for his attendants to lay out his clothes, the Mwami smoked a pipe. He remembered the first white man he had ever seen.

He was very young then, the adopted son and presumed heir of the Mwami who preceded him. That Mwami had received in a night vision a warning from the ancestors that beings from the dead would come to Kabare. Late that day after he received this vision, warriors raced into his court to tell of a being with white flesh and hair the color of sunset. The being had entered Kabare and was building a camp where the fingers of land extended into the Water of the Ancestors. Many women had left off tilling to watch him.

In the Mwami's court the vision and the warriors' report caused profound apprehension. A being with flesh of a hue seen only on the dead? What did this portend for Kabare? The young man who would become Mwami had returned with the warriors to watch. The being with white flesh bartered with beads and mirrors for food and drink. He ate with his mouth. He squatted to defecate and stood to make water. When the being washed in a stream, his whiteness stayed. So this whiteness was not made by ashes rubbed on his skin. All of his flesh was pink-white, and—except for its color—his body was in every way like the bodies of Kabare men. The being came from a people who did not circumcise. The Mwami reported all of these observations to his predecessor.

The being stayed at his camp many days, hunting gazelles with a stick that spat metal and roasting their flesh. He picked fruit without thought of compensating the person who had the use of the tree and its fruit. He plundered materials and constructed a shelter in a form different from any ever seen in Kabare. The being enticed a maiden into his shelter and lay with her. Although he mounted her in a manner little known in Kabare, the being seemed to have the same desire for a maiden's body that warriors felt. Warriors, however, controlled these desires and the white being did not.

The notables of Kabare held counsel with the Mwami. Some said that the being—since he ate, slept, relieved his body of waste, and desired maidens just as the men of Kabare did—was a man like other men. As lions and leopards were much the same except for the markings of their hides and some of their habits, so this white being was a man not unlike themselves.

The Mwami of that day concluded otherwise. He proclaimed that the being was a spirit of the dead. The present Mwami had always accepted that conclusion.

Mark placed an *x* at the end of the sentence. He read over what he had written. "Last week one of the few tribal despots left in this troubled country had two men buried alive. Fortunately for the men, civil authorities in Bukavu learned of the executions in progress. When they arrived here in the hills that form part of the backbone of Africa, they found the men buried to their necks and succeeded in rescuing them from the cruel rule of the Mwami of Kabare."

Mark did not want to use this lead. He still wanted to portray the Mwami as a rogue. But what if the interview proved a bust? He swore in his mind. His watch read 11:47. He glanced at the USIS man. "This gonna happen?" he asked.

"Head of the UN team in Bukavu waited two hours to see the Mwami," the USIS man said. "And he was offering more than his name in the paper." USIS grinned. Mark was not amused. "We've only been here— What?"

"One hundred and ten minutes," Mark said. "You don't wear a watch?"

"Gave it up," said the USIS man. "When in Rome."

Mark turned back to his notes. "Cruel rule" would not do. He crossed out "cruel" and printed "brutal" in small letters above it.

A jet black poodle gamboled onto the porch, dripping water as if it had just emerged from a swim. It moved to the center of the porch and vigorously shook itself. Sparkles of water flashed through the air. Déo raised his legs and shouted, *"Oooo la la!"* Mark thought, "Fucker!" He covered his pad and swatted the pooch.

Minutes evaporated like the fog that had lifted outside. Eric examined the curtains, mere lengths of cloth, hanging by metal loops from thick, wooden dowels.

Mark asked the notables questions, using Déo as an interpreter. They explained that they could do no work until their ritual of greeting the Mwami had been accomplished. Eric tried to remember college course work about Louis XIV. Hadn't his nobles appeared to watch him rise, bathe, and dress?

The secretary who spoke no French appeared. *"Entrez, Messieurs, s'il vous plâit,"* he offered, inviting the men into the living room. For a *"palais"* the room struck Eric as small. Three heavy couches of post-Victorian design diminished its size. An archway stood across from Eric. Lengths of thin, unhemmed material, one pink, one beige, curtained off the room beyond. As they settled in, Mark shot the USIS man a look. "I'm supposed to file this story this afternoon from Usumbura," he said.

"This is not a deadline culture," Eric remarked.

Mark raised an irritated eyebrow.

The men heard the Mwami moving around the other rooms. But he did not appear. Eric saw shoes visible below the pink and beige material. He caught Mark's eye and nodded toward the shoes. Mark noticed them, but said nothing. When the shoes disappeared, Mark said, *"Déo, mon ami. Ça marchera?"*

"Oui, ça marche, Monsieur," Déo told him. *"Bien sur! Le Mwami comprend que votre journal est très important!"*

Mark nodded, but the muscles of his mouth grew tight.

Eric watched the lengths of material. The shoes reappeared behind them.

As they prepared the Mwami to hear the dispute among the clans, his attendants set out the hat of colobus monkey skin that he would wear. They took from its box the leopard skin they would drape over his shoulders. Impatient, the Mwami would turn away and enter the room where he could look through the closed curtains at the white men. He would watch his notables detain the men as he had directed them to do. He would appraise the visitors and then return to his dressing room. Then he would decide to appraise them once again as he was doing now.

He studied the man writing in the pad. This business of asking questions, he thought. It was a game of mischief and trickery the white men played. Why they played it, he did not understand.

Long ago it had been possible to humor white men who asked questions. Such men would be brought into court. While the Mwami stood in the rear, watching the visitor, a notable would greet the men. He would listen to their questions; perhaps he would offer replies. While this happened, the Mwami would examine the visitors. But this was no longer possible, for Cinéma, the white men's toady, knew who the Mwami was. Now a Mwami must study visitors by watching behind a curtain. The Mwami returned to his dressing room. He told his attendants to offer the white men beer.

Mark reworked the lead he would use if the interview did not happen. Could he describe the Mwami as "a thoroughly unreformed tribal despot." Was that too much? After all, the methodology of reform was exile, prison.

Eric noticed the Africans pick copies of *Perspectives Américaines* off the coffee table and glance through them. *Perspectives* was a newspaper published by USIS. Should he, Eric wondered, compose an Evidence-of-Effectiveness report on this discovery? Or perhaps he should do a reader survey, "Excuse me, Mr. Notable. Which articles in that newspaper do you find most interesting?"

A servant arrived with two glasses of beer. He set one before Mark, the other before Eric. The Americans exchanged a glance. Eight men, two beers? The Americans would not drink if the others were not served. They ignored the beers. Eric noticed that Déo looked thirstily at the untouched beers. He saw that the shoes that kept watch behind the curtains had returned. He signaled Mark.

Mark nodded. So the Mwami was watching them. Mark felt an almost undeniable urge to rush the curtains, grab the Mwami and say, *"Votre excellence, je voudrais vous poser quelques questions."* What would the Mwami do? The fact that Mark did not know kept him sitting at the table.

The Mwami watched the white man with the notepad. So he came to ask questions about taxes! What insolence! Who sent him? What did he really want?

The Mwami perceived behind the open, smiling face the self-importance that most white men possessed. If he permitted the man to enter his presence, he would ask if the Mwami buried people alive. Or if he beheaded them. The whites were always curious about death. Because they were beings from the dead.

A Mwami embodied his people. Did the white man not know this? A Mwami sought to rule by consensus. Did the notables not greet him every morning to inform him of problems demanding his attention? In this way a Mwami strengthened the people. But if some man challenged a Mwami outside the established system, if he blocked consensus, if he sought to excite the people to rebellion and imperil unity. . . . Well, he must be warned. If he persisted, he must be punished. Sometimes it was enough to bury such a man up to his head. After a day or two he saw that the Mwami's authority must be maintained. But if he continued to think that his own will was more important than the people's unity, then he was beheaded. Because a Mwami's power wasted away if he did not use it. Because the people must know that survival depended on submission to the Mwami. The Mwami alone protected their future.

Watching the white men, the Mwami understood that if he granted them an audience he would jeopardize the health of his people. When these white men left, they would do their small something—whatever it was—to hasten the death of Kabare.

The Mwami stepped back from the curtains and called for his car.

Eric studied the room's adornments: the elephant tusk, the small Kivu drums, the animal horn carved to resemble a fish, the two ignored beers going flat.

"I wouldn't wait this long to interview President Kennedy," Mark said.

"You can wait," Eric told him. "Or you can blow it."

Mark swore under his breath. Then he whimpered, "I want my Mwami!"

Eric bit his tongue so as not to laugh. The notables regarded him curiously.

Mark said, "Mwark mwants his Mwami."

Eric looked at the floor, trying not to laugh.

Mark said, "Mwaiting for Mwami mwakes mwe mweary."

Suddenly the pink and beige curtains parted. Mark stood, ready to smile, ready to bow or offer his hand. A notable with a cane hobbled into the room. He announced, *"Le Mwami est parti."*

Gone? Mark looked at Eric, at Déo. Gone? They were standing now, perplexed looks on their faces. Gone? How? They heard a motor. They rushed onto the porch. A black Mercedes was parked outside the house, its engine idling. The Mwami sat inside it. He wore a leopard pelt over his shoulders and a hat of a colobus monkey skin. As soon as he saw the two white men, he signaled the driver. The car sped down the driveway and out of sight.

Mark was furious. He turned to complain. But the notables had disappeared. The secretary who spoke no French was still on the porch. "Does the Mwami always act this way?" Mark asked the secretary curtly in French.

"Easy, Pulitzer," Eric soothed.

"I'm not Foreign Service," Mark replied. "Fuck it! Fuck them!" He swore in French at the secretary who spoke no French.

"Don't mess it up for us," Eric said.

Déo appeared, wiping his hand across his mouth, having dispatched the beers. Mark swore at him. The secretary disappeared. "I give a certain tolerance for African custom," Mark said, "but this is going too far." He started toward the house.

"Don't get moralistic," Eric advised. "That won't help."

"Fuck you!" Mark said. "Piss-ass USIS man. Fuck you!"

Returning to the van, Déo insisted that the Mwami had confirmed the interview. The Mwami was still inside the house, he contended; a stooge had left in the car.

When Mark asked why the Mwami would stay in the house, Déo said, *"Pour jouer au sex avec des jeunes femmes."*

"Déo, you're full of shit," Eric said in English. Then he added, *"C'est toi qui veux jouer au sex."*

Déo laughed richly. *"Mais oui, M'sieur,"* he said, *"c'est amusant, ça."* Then he added, *"Mais pas quand on travaille."*

"Not when you're working," Eric said. "Of course not."

The *chefferie* office was closed. Mark and Déo walked about the building, peering into windows. Once Eric was out of sight, Déo whispered, *"Monsieur, si tu as besoin d'un représentant à Bukavu . . . Ou si tu veux une fille . . ."*

"I get my own women," Mark said. He walked off. Déo shrugged.

Out of nowhere appeared an old man with two missing teeth and a narrow beard that dropped from his ears to follow the line of his chin. Veins stood out on his forehead. He demanded to know why the men were peering through the *chefferie* office windows. Not one to tolerate questions, Mark demanded to know if the man was a *chefferie* clerk. The old man refused to admit that he was. However, he wore an evident badge of rank: an old tuxedo jacket with black satin lapels.

Mark exploded at the man. If the Mwami did not want to be interviewed, why didn't he just say so?

The tuxedoed clerk exploded back. Everyone, he insisted, must arrange interviews with the Mwami—in advance, by writing.

"How many days in advance?" Mark asked.

The clerk answered in an approximation of French.

"Deux jours?" Mark repeated.

"Oui, deux jours!" the clerk snapped back.

"Ou est-ce dix jours?" asked Eric who had heard ten days.

"Mais oui!" exclaimed the clerk. *"Dix jours!"*

"Dix-deux jours," said Eric.

"Deux-dix jours," said Mark.

As they headed back down the mountain, Mark said, "This fucking Africa! Nothing works. The people are ignorant, primitive, stupid. What the fuck's gonna happen here?" He leaned his head against the seat and tried to devise a way to write up an interview that had not taken place. He'd do something. Relate the "wild and bloody saga" of the Mwami's beheadings, of his burying his tribesmen up to their ears. Call the old fraud "a tribal despot." That'd show him.

When they drove through Bagira, children again recognized the film van. They shouted, *"Cinéma! Cinéma!"* Déogratias leaned out of the window to wave.

Reaching Lake Kivu, they passed small beaches with huts crowding the shore. Pirogues cut slowly through the water. Trees bent toward the lake, their leaves drooping into the water. Across the lake blue-gray silhouettes of mountains rose tall and misty in the far distance. Islands seemed to float on the lake, not as distinct shapes, but as blue patterns. Above them cumulus clouds, blue-black, the elephants of the sky, marched along. Water stretched between the film van and the islands, some of it dark, reflecting the clouds, patches of it silvered by the sun.

"Fucking Africa?" Eric thought. "Oh, no!" It was so beautiful! He wondered what mysteries dwelt on those islands. What adventure beckoned from the mountains? Then he understood that the islands, the mountains, the clouds were not realities at all. They were dreams, yearnings that nature had given blue shapes. They were longings set across an uncrossable stretch of dark and silvered water. They were out of reach like the Mwami, like all dreams.

MADAGASCAR

WHEN GRAEME OWEN LEFT THE EMBASSY, he tried to appear offhand. "Say," he suggested to Tom Swayze, "could we do coffee?" They were in Antananarivo, the capital of the island nation of Madagascar, and Graeme had just interviewed the American Ambassador. As press attaché, Tom had set up the interview. "I'd like to check a few things."

Tom regarded Graeme through the dark glasses he had just put on, measuring him, suspicious perhaps of the "do coffee" phrase. Then he said, "Sure. There's a place nearby."

They walked to a milk-bar. As they approached it, a young woman—French, in her early twenties—left the place. Seeing Tom, color came to her cheeks. She smiled and offered her hand. Tom smiled back, expressing affection. He introduced her to Graeme simply as Vivienne and lingered with her a moment. Graeme went on inside the milk-bar. He understood that Tom and the woman were lovers.

He thought: How Gallic! How American! This was certainly

not Johannesburg where Graeme lived. Never on the super-conventional streets of that place would a man Tom's age—he must be thirty-eight—act in a way that notified the world that he and a young woman had sex. Yet Graeme also felt thrilled. A curious worldliness gripped—and agitated—him. This kind of freedom South Africans did not yet possess. In its presence Graeme felt both stimulated and nervous.

After Vivienne hurried off, the two men had coffee on a terrace. Graeme verified quotes and some spellings, then confessed, "My bosses want sexy copy out of Madagascar. I'm not sure I can provide it." Sexy: he figured that was something an American would understand. But Swayze only smiled.

"Actually it's a couple of kilometers short of astonishing that I got sent here," Graeme went on—even though "sent" was not precisely the word. Graeme had told his editors at the South African Press Service, where local news was the mainstay, that he and his wife were planning a vacation in Madagascar. He had asked SAPS to pick up a week's expenses for them in exchange for a series of situationers.

"Situationers, man?" his editors had asked. "About what? Nothing's going on there." Graeme had reminded them that within the past year Madagascar had experienced a change of government almost as revolutionary as the one South Africans had lived through. SAPS readers might want to know how change was working in one of their closest neighbors. Graeme stressed that he would pick up the travel costs; he had the time coming. Finally his editors agreed. But with stipulations. "When we get it, man," they warned, "that copy better sing!"

Once SAPS approved the plan, Graeme told Nella that he was being sent on assignment to the island nation. She did not want to join him—she was pregnant, after all—but he insisted. The trip, he stressed, was sure to lead to better things for him. For them. "You've never been outside the Republic," he reminded her. "Time you went." Nella agreed only at her father's urging. Andries De Kock was impressed that SAPS had sufficient confidence in Graeme to send him on an overseas assignment.

To win Tom's trust, Graeme joked about his own people. Tom smiled, aware of being courted. Finally Graeme said, "You wouldn't know how a bloke like me could get a job on an American paper, would you? I've got to get to the States."

"Why?" Tom asked. "It's out of control. Full of crime, pollution, violence."

"And opportunity. Which is one thing we don't have in South Africa."

Tom said, "You play your cards right, there's opportunity for you."

"South Africa will go the way all Africa has gone," Graeme predicted. "Crime. Corruption. Tribal slaughter." Tom shrugged. "Maybe that's opportunity for a journalist. But I've got a wife. She's expecting a baby."

Tom finally said, "My speaking frankly won't insult you, will it?"

Graeme managed a smile. "Is it going to be that bad?"

"I've visited South Africa," Tom said. "In so many ways you're thirty, forty years behind us. You're just beginning to do away with race. We in America are doing away with families. An outsider like you can't catch up with our pace of self-destruction, not in a cutting edge profession like journalism. The question, of course, is why you'd want to."

Graeme did not know what to say. Tom watched him as if he were an unfamiliar life form that might be worthy of study, perhaps from outer space.

"You said your wife's with you?" Tom asked. Graeme nodded.

"Why don't you stay with me?" Graeme's surprise was so obvious that Tom smiled. It struck Graeme that an American journalist would have masked his reaction. Perhaps he did have some catching up to do.

"I know how the hotels are," Tom said. Again Graeme felt himself being scrutinized. "I'm single, but I'm assigned a mansion. So I have plenty of room. I'm sure your wife would be more comfortable there."

Graeme made no effort to hide his delight. "I know Nella would be glad to be in a home," he said. Let Tom study him, he thought. He wanted to study Tom.

"We could go up to Antsirabe for the weekend," Tom suggested. "It's an old French watering-hole on the high plateau. You ought to see it. I could bring a friend along."

"I'd love that," Graeme said. Nella might refuse to go on a weekend with a couple who were not married, but he would persuade her. He felt sure she would like Vivienne. "Let me try it on my wife," he said. "I'm sure she'll agree."

Tom put the Owens into the guest wing of his house. It was like no set of rooms Graeme had ever seen. In the hall expensively framed photographs of Africans hung. One showed a tall, slender girl, naked except for a necklace. With a stately, sculptural grace, she stood before a river, oblivious of her nakedness. "Gracious!" exclaimed Nella. The corners of her mouth tightened. But the photographs awakened in Graeme an awareness of Africa's primitive beauty.

The guest bedroom contained the largest bed Graeme had ever seen. "A sandbox for the senses," he said, laughing. He immediately regretted the words, for Nella shuddered. He could see her wondering how many people had soiled the sandbox.

While Nella was in the bathroom, Graeme picked up several books from the bedside table. They were paperbacks, illustrated scenarios of artsy soft-porn films. Graeme recognized the titles. The films would not be shown in South Africa, at least not in cinemas that he was likely to patronize. He thumbed through the books. One contained a photo essay, stunningly designed, of a man and a woman having sex; it showed how their bodies joined. The man was black, the woman white.

Graeme studied the photos with rapt disbelief. His throat thickened; saliva flooded his mouth. He had seen photos of sex taken in Swaziland brothels, but in those the men were white and the women black. He had never seen anything like this. When Nella entered, she asked, "What's that?" Graeme blushed and closed the book. She pulled it from him and opened it. When she saw the photographs, she threw the book into a chair.

"What kind of place is this?" she asked. "Wait till you see the photos in the bathroom! I knew we shouldn't come."

In fact, when Graeme had broached the idea of staying with Tom Swayze, Nella had blurted out, "But we don't even know him!"

"I want to see how Americans live," he had replied. "This is our chance. Anyway, he seems a good sort."

Graeme had a theory that people developed long-term interests in those they helped. So he gave anyone who might possibly assist him the opportunity to do so. He intended that Tom would help him get to America.

"There's one of those bidet things in there," Nella said of the bathroom. She gathered up the books and handed them to Graeme. "I won't sleep in the same room with these."

In the bathroom Graeme found expensive, scented soap, recently used, lying in the bidet soap dish. Toys lay in a rack beside the bathtub: wind-up frogs, swans that floated, a water pistol. On a wall two photographs hung. One showed twin boys sitting naked on training potties. Tom himself smiled from the other photograph. He, too, was naked, perched spread-legged on a toilet; one of the twins, a year or two older, sat naked before him, now a master of the pot. The photograph made Graeme smile; it seemed an invitation to enjoy life.

"Well, what did you think?" Nella asked when he returned to the bedroom.

"I thought it was funny. You don't really see anything."

"What about the pictures in those books?"

Graeme shrugged. He shoved the books under the bed. Nella seemed relieved. She sat on the bed, tired and puzzled. "Do you think Tom's playing some kind of joke on us?" she asked.

"I think he just lives this way. Maybe Americans have this kind of stuff around their homes."

"Then why does he want us here?"

"He's hospitable." Graeme lifted Nella's suitcase onto the bed beside her. "Maybe he's lonely. Maybe he's interested in us."

"But why?"

"I asked him about emigrating to the States," Graeme said. "I think he'd like to help."

Tears began to stream down Nella's cheeks.

"It wouldn't be forever."

Nella said nothing.

"Just while I got some training, some American experience that I— Why don't you take a nap, Nell? You're tired."

"How long would it be?"

"Two years. Maybe three." He tried to smile. "That's not for-ever. Come on and take a nap."

She kicked off her shoes and lay down. "What are you going to do?"

"I should do a story. I made some notes this morning." He opened the suitcase, fished his wife's dressing gown out of it, and covered her with it. "You mustn't get overtired, Nell."

"I'm sorry to be this way," she said. He kissed her forehead and saw fresh tears in her eyes.

"What is it?"

"I can't sleep in the same room with those books."

"Sweet one!" Graeme embraced her, careful not to place his weight against the baby. He took the books from under the bed, got his laptop and found a room down the hall. Before starting to work, he thumbed again through the paperbacks. His throat thickened; he shook his head. It seemed astonishing to him that societies existed—even functioned successfully—where such books were not banned. Once he laid the books aside, he found it difficult to work.

Tom was going to a party and asked the Owens to accompany him. Nella begged off; she was too tired, she said. With her eyes she implored Graeme to stay with her. He knew she felt ungainly, but he would not forego the opportunity to socialize with diplomats as a friend of Tom's. And, indeed, Tom seemed to know everyone. At the party Graeme met Lucie and Joelle, both French, two Marie-Claires, both Malagasy, and several Chantals. One of these was the Liberian Ambassador's daughter.

"So you're Tom's friend," this Chantal said as they chatted in English. "Tell me what you know about him. Has style, doesn't he?" She watched Graeme with an amused expression as the party's gossip drifted about them in French.

Graeme nodded. "He's very 'cool,' as Americans say."

"The most glamorous man in Antananarivo."

"That covers a lot of territory, I expect."

"But so does Tom." Chantal laughed slyly. "But maybe you do, too, eh? I think I like you."

"I rather like you," Graeme heard himself saying. The words surprised him.

"You have a funny accent."

"In my country only the best-educated people speak this way," he replied exaggeratedly, conscious of trying to charm her. He was not doing anything behind Nella's back, he told himself. He was merely performing a patriotic duty: proving that white South Africans were human beings. He noticed the light glowing in Chantal's Bantu eyes and the milk-chocolate fineness of her skin. "I'm one of those people," he said. "I went to our best university."

"Harvard?"

"Witswatersrand."

"Oh, bloody shit!" she said. "I assumed you were American."

"Do I say thanks?"

She cocked her eyebrow, a glint of irony flashing in her eyes. "Is South Africa different these days? Or is it the more things change the more they're the same?"

"A little of both," he said. "Does it bother you that I'm South African?"

She studied him, started to say something, then changed her mind.

"You can say it," Graeme told her. "I'm a consenting adult." She laughed. Graeme glowed at the success of his banter. He wondered what Nella would think of his flirting—and was annoyed with himself for wondering.

"Does it bother you that my mother's French and my father from West Africa?"

"You're beautiful," Graeme said. "They obviously do good work together." She smiled. He felt pleased with his compliment. At the same time he wondered at the words, at the way they tumbled out. What made me say that, he asked himself—and to a Bantu! He never talked that way to women at home.

Chantal gazed at him, glowing with his compliment. "Would you like to make love to me?" she asked. Graeme was dumbfounded. She smiled, enjoying his confusion. "There's a bedroom upstairs."

Graeme swallowed. Had he heard her correctly? She gazed at him—with a look of readiness. Graeme blushed.

"What a lovely color," she teased. "Let's go upstairs. We can lock the door."

Graeme felt flummoxed. He reached for his drink and took a long swallow.

"Have I embarrassed you?" Chantal asked, delighted. "Let me read your palm. Maybe we'll find the answer there." She took his hand. "My grandfather's a witchdoctor. He taught me." Graeme looked at her quizzically. She laughed. "He really did," she said. Her hands held his softly. Graeme finished off his drink.

"I see this trip," she said, studying his palm. "It's a landmark in your life." She paused. "Just a minute. What's this?" She looked deeper, turned his palm toward the light. "I see. . . . A girl. You will have a romance here."

"On Madagascar!" Graeme pulled his palm away, grinning. "That will surprise my wife!"

"Is she here?"

"She's at Tom's. She needs her sleep. She's seven months pregnant."

"Double bloody shit!" Chantal laughed, covering her mouth with her hand, her eyes shining. "Have I said the wrong thing!"

She moved closer to him, still giggling, her breast pushing against his arm. "In fact, I know nothing about palms," she confessed. "My grandfather was a diplomat like my father. All I know is that men in strange countries like that fortune. It's the only one I know."

They laughed together. Chantal took his arm and led him to a couch. They sat and talked quietly like friends. She told him of the places she had lived and what she thought of them. He knew that Nella would not have liked nor trusted their rapport. Neither would she have understood the sense of freedom he felt in talking openly with this dark-skinned woman. But he did not think of Nella; she was home asleep.

Later someone put Malagasy music on the CD player. It pulsed with surging, intoxicating rhythms. The guests began to dance. They determined to teach Graeme some of the island's folklore. "Come on, it's easy," Chantal said. "I'll show you."

Graeme smiled, but shook his head. It was one thing to talk with this woman, but something quite different to dance with her. For Nella's sake, he could not do that. "I really don't dance," he told Chantal. She grinned, standing before him, his hands in hers. Playfully she attempted to pull him to his feet.

"I'm dreadfully clumsy," he pleaded. "Really I am."

"Come along," Chantal urged. "I promise not to take you upstairs."

"Debout! Debout!" the Malagasy guests chanted.

"I can't!" Graeme called out over the music. He wanted to dance. But he could not break faith with Nella, not when she was pregnant. "Really, I can't."

Chantal tossed her shoulders invitingly, sexily. Graeme shook his head. He felt himself excited, his body responding to her. That made him afraid. He pulled his hands away. Chantal suddenly froze, offended, angry. "It has nothing to do with you," Graeme said quickly. He stood. "My wife wouldn't—"

Chantal turned from him. She picked her way across the crowded room. He followed, took her by the arm. "All right then. Let's dance."

"Let go of me!" she whispered furiously. She jerked free and ran upstairs. Graeme started after her, but stopped himself. No, he told himself, he mustn't be upstairs with her. He went outside. When he returned to the party, he watched Chantal, but he talked only with men, mainly Americans.

While packing for Antsirabe, Nella expressed reservations about the trip. "Maybe if I spoke French," she said. "I know this girl-friend of Tom's won't like me."

"I'm sure she will," Graeme replied. "Tom wouldn't bring someone you can't talk to." He assured her that when she saw Tom and Vivienne together, she would know that special feel-ings existed between them. Those feelings weren't the same as marriage, that was true, but the world was changing. Who knew that better than South Africans? Special feelings were enough for now. He promised that she and Vivienne would get along.

When the Owens went down to meet Vivienne, they were surprised to find Chantal in Tom's car. "Nice to see you again," Graeme said to her. Nella seemed disoriented. How did her husband know this Bantu woman? She regarded her with dis-trust and glared at him as if he had intentionally deceived her. He introduced them. "Chantal and I met at that party Tom took me to," he explained. Nella shook the woman's hand and laced her arm through Graeme's.

She was still holding onto him when Tom finished loading

the trunk. "Nella," he said, "why don't you sit in front with me?" Graeme felt Nella's grip on his arm tighten. She glanced at him; he saw the uncertainty in her eyes. "You'll be more comfortable up here," Tom explained.

"You won't feel the bumps so much there, Koekie," Graeme pointed out. He smiled and she agreed, thanking them all for their thoughtfulness.

As Graeme climbed into the rear seat, his arm brushed against Chantal. He settled into a corner, away from her, but his arm where he had touched her tingled. He thought of her standing before him, imploring him to dance. The car started off. As Tom chatted with Nella, driving through the suburbs of Antananarivo, past horse carts and rice fields and the plateau people's burial tombs, Graeme and Chantal did not once look at one another. But Graeme thought only of her: her skin so dark and lustrous, the scent she gave off, her laugh and teasing wit.

At lunch he talked sociably with his three companions, prattling actually, not always making sense, because in fact he was conscious only of Chantal. He rarely addressed her directly, yet never stopped watching her. Nella did not notice. She sat beside him like a mindless lump of matter, her hand resting on his forearm. Tom chatted with the maitre d', playing at being gourmet. When conversation lapsed, Graeme gazed at the hills, seeing nothing, aware only of Chantal's dark fingers, of the way they held the straw, of her dark lips taking the straw and drawing Coca-Cola into her mouth. Agitated, he patted Nella's hand. She gave him the bovine smile she had begun to wear in pregnancy. He returned the smile, not thinking of Nella, thinking: Chantal is so slender; she moves so lightly.

At the end of the meal Nella waddled off to the ladies' room. Tom left to compliment the chef. After a long moment Graeme said, "You're so beautiful, Chantal. If I were single and living here, I'd want to see you."

He asked himself: What's happening? Why am I saying just what I'm thinking? Even so, he had a feeling of release, of pleasurable danger, in saying such things to her. And yet he was afraid to look at her. She did not answer him.

"I do apologize for the other night," he said. "I told you I was clumsy." He managed to look at her at last.

She gazed at him. "I accept your apology."

"I really meant no offense."

"I wasn't offended."

An urge to touch her seized him. In order to control it he stood.

Later in the car he surrendered to the urge. Their knees touched as Tom swung the car around a curve. Graeme allowed his knee to rest against hers and a strange sensation of heat swept over him. He glanced at her legs, at the short skirt. Then at her eyes. She was watching him. Her expression was enigmatic, neither friendly nor hostile. He smiled slightly, without full control of his features, and removed his knee.

Later, as he tried to nap, the car's swaying sent his knee against the outside of her thigh. The drowsiness vanished immediately. He feigned sleep so as not to withdraw the knee. His mind threw up unbidden images from the books he had seen in Tom's house. His thoughts grew snarled: by the warmth of her African skin, by his own uncertainty about what he was doing, by the beating of his heart.

He pretended to wake. Withdrawing his knee, he rolled down his window, muttered, "Sorry," in Chantal's direction and held his breath. She smiled again, less enigmatically now. Graeme thrust his face into the airstream. He watched Madagascar's rice paddies flash past. Their new shoots made a green blur. After the breeze had cooled him, he glanced over at Nella. She sat in dreamy contentment—like a great overripe pear—musing about the baby. Graeme relaxed. He felt more absent from his wife than if he had left her at home.

A Malagasy bellboy, dark-skinned but slight, with straight black hair, led the two couples down a stuffy corridor of the Hotel Truchet. Nella moved beside Graeme, still wearing her smile of sublime contentment. "What a nice ride," she said. "I was thinking of names. I dreamt you let me call him Andries."

"We'll see," Graeme answered. He would not have his son called after his father-in-law, but he was not thinking of that now. As they followed Tom and Chantal, Graeme studied Chantal's dark, slim legs, watched the round, lustrous part of her left thigh just behind the place where his knee had rested.

"Father would be so pleased," Nella said. "That would make things easier."

"The baby may be a girl." Graeme watched Chantal's hips.

"We could call her Andrea then," Nella said.

"What if we later had a boy?"

The reception had assigned them corner rooms. They stood opposite each other at the end of a hall which looked through French doors onto a balcony.

"Do you like the name Andrea?"

Graeme watched Tom close the door behind Chantal and felt suddenly short-tempered. "Do we have to decide now?" The bellboy showed them into their room.

"Malagasies look so Oriental!" Nella exclaimed after the bellboy had gone.

"You like them better because of it?"

"No," she replied. "But it does explain the rice paddies and the rickshas." Then she looked at him defensively. "Are you mad at me?"

"I'm tired, I guess." Then more softly, "Of course, I'm not mad at you. Why don't you have a wash?"

There was no door to their bathroom, only plastic strips. Nella made a face. "I'm sorry it's so French," Graeme said. He went out onto the balcony.

The balcony spanned the entire end of the building. It contained a wicker table, some chairs and a chaise longue, and it overlooked a garden less well tended now, Graeme was sure, than in the days when Antsirabe had been the Deauville of the island. In the garden wrought-iron benches stood among beds of flowers. A group of people, dark Malagasies and pale Frenchmen and the children of their marriages, sat on them eating cakes. The benches had never borne labels—"Whites Only," "Non-Whites Only"—and the people seemed happy together. Graeme watched them. He felt a kind of joy, almost an envy, at the naturalness they expressed.

When he looked away, he saw Chantal standing at the opposite end of the balcony. Inspecting her face in a compact, she touched a lipstick to her mouth. As Graeme watched, agitation replaced his joy. Then Chantal looked up. Their eyes met. Graeme bowed with mock chivalry. She smiled, flirtatiously, Graeme thought. She seemed about to speak, then suddenly turned and went inside.

Going to Tom. Lucky Tom. Graeme felt annoyed.

He remained irritable most of the afternoon: throughout Nella's nap, during their ricksha ride and their walk through the open-air market. His testiness increased when he saw Tom and Chantal walking together. But he soon noticed that, although they were laughing, they did not exude the affectionate energy so remarkable when Tom was with Vivienne. Perhaps they had not yet slept together. Perhaps they were just pals. Graeme's irritability dissolved. He led Nella to the cathedral, chatting jovially. She took his hand, smiling, and said, "I'm glad you're feeling better."

That night in the hotel room, Graeme lay awake. Outside insects sang. Graeme listened to them. He stared into the darkness, uncomfortable on the sagging bed with the mosquito netting about it. Beside him Nella stirred and called his name. "Sweet Koekie," he answered. "Haven't you slept yet?" He reached over and touched her hair.

"What are you thinking?" she asked. Her voice was heavy with slumber. "You thinking of Tom and Chantal?"

"No," he said. But he had been thinking of them. She had, too, he knew.

"What do you think they're doing?"

He wanted to say, "Fucking, of course," but he did not use rough language with Nella. Especially now that she was pregnant, so very pregnant. He listened to the crickets—or cicadas or whatever the hell they were—and finally said, "On the balcony this afternoon, I watched families having tea and cakes in the garden. Mixed couple families."

"Whites and Bantus together?" she asked.

"Europeans and Malagasies," he corrected. He felt annoyed. They had left the Republic, but she had brought its apartheid-era racial classifications with them. "The Malagasies came from the east. They're Malays, not Bantus."

"I may never get used to that," she said. "They're being together."

"People do live that way," he said. "They've lived that way here for decades." And because her father always contended that mixed race children inherited the worst traits of both racial strains, he added, "And the children are beautiful."

"I'm glad," Nella said. "I've never thought the ones at home were. Shame."

Graeme smiled grimly to himself. Her father's daughter. Nella snuggled into his side. He lay still. The damn French with their beds, he thought. Damn mattress! Nella turned again, awkward in her seventh month. "You all right?" he asked. "The drive wasn't too bumpy, was it?"

"Un-un." Then, "You think Tom and Chantal are 'doing it'?"

"Of course," Graeme said, hating her school-girl expression. "They're enjoying unspeakable perversions."

"Do you wish we were?"

"I'm not sure we'd know one, even if we did it."

Nella laughed and curled against him, feeling safe.

He listened to the damn cicadas and their buzz. And acknowledged to himself that there was a buzz inside him. Was he annoyed with her because she was pregnant? He hoped not.

"You're incredibly beautiful the way you are now," he said to reassure her. "But once the baby comes, I'll be glad to get back to 'having parties.'" The words sounded pompous to him, but Nella would not care. She wouldn't even know.

"Tom's really awfully nice," she said at last. "For an American. Isn't he?" A short silence. "She's even rather nice. So cultured. Is Chantal a French name?"

"Her mother's French. From Martinique or someplace. She studied at the Sorbonne."

"She's the Liberian Ambassador's daughter?"

"Something like that."

"Liberia— Isn't that where the Americans sent their slaves? Don't they speak English?"

"I think so," Graeme said.

"A kind of English," she said with a laugh. "Just like me. The vowels and consonants of English with the music of Afrikaans." She yawned. Then she asked, "Isn't Liberia where they've had that dreadful civil war?" Before he could answer, she went on, "Or is that Sierra Leone? Or Rwanda? Hard to keep it all straight."

She was teasing him. But instead of smiling and touching her, he thought, That's what you get for marrying an Afrikaner. He wondered if he would ever escape the self-justifying Afrikaner banter. Probably not. Afrikaners were a righteous crowd, especially when they were wrong. He would have to endure the we-were-right jesting all his life. Unless they left South Africa. Or unless he left Nella. Would that happen? Would he prove her father right? Or would the baby keep them together?

Nella settled into sleep, murmuring endearments in Afrikaans. And now Graeme's other nocturnal companion settled heavily upon him, like a weight on his chest. That companion was a near-desperation about the course of his life. He felt imprisoned. He had to leave South Africa; he had to get free. He would offer Madagascar pieces to the American newspapers for which he had done some Joburg stringing. That might lead to a reporter's job on one of them. And that might lead to freedom.

Later Nella stirred, waking out of slumber. Once she sensed that Graeme was awake, she said, "Tom's been divorced three times. That little boy in the bathroom photograph is his son. Funny, I . . ." Her voice trailed off.

"Marriage is not for everyone, sweet. He has tried."

"I keep being surprised that he's so thoughtful. He really is." Then, "We never meet people like this at home." She cuddled against him. "It's good for us. Are you glad you brought me along?"

"I haven't decided yet," he said and kissed her shoulder.

"Do you always work this hard on trips?"

"Harder," he said. "This is vacation, remember."

"Ha! You've filed every day." Then she asked, "Do you think Tom and Chantal had been together before we saw them at the market? They seemed shy with each other. Did you notice?" He said nothing. After a moment she asked, "Do you think Chantal's pretty?"

"I suppose." It was a trick question and must be handled carefully. So he elaborated in the language of apartheid. "For a Bantu," he said.

"You think Tom's fond of her?"

"Can't you guess what Tom's fond of?"

"It must be awful for you," Nella said. "I know you miss it. It has been a long time." Graeme said nothing. "You poor thing, lying here, thinking about them—"

"I'm not thinking about them. Go to sleep."

"I'll make it up to you."

Graeme smiled in the darkness. Make it up? Nella would never surprise him with unspeakable perversions. "All right, silly," he said. "Go to sleep."

She curled beside him, trying now to fall asleep like an obedient six-year-old. He wondered, Was she learning anything? She seemed not to understand that he had brought her here for her education, that he wanted her capable of moving into the wider world beyond her homeland. She spent so much time sleeping! And seemed content merely to be amused.

But even if she had refused to come here, he would not have let her stay alone. Now that blacks moved about unchallenged anywhere in the country the threat of crime was too great. And he would not let her go to her parents. Whenever she stayed with them, the Afrikaner mind-set reasserted its claims. It was bad enough that she was affected. Graeme did not want her father's ideas seeping into her womb, and he did not want her parents to think the child was theirs.

Nella's breathing grew regular: up and down, up and down. If he did land a job overseas, Graeme wondered, would Nella come with him? Would he dare go without her? Yes, he would. He wondered what Andries De Kock would think of Tom and Chantal. He would certainly take Graeme to task for exposing his daughter to mixed-race lovers. Old Andries hunkered down in his mental redoubt. Plagued with pigmentation obsession. The Madagascar trip would confirm his conviction that Graeme was subversive to his daughter's morals. Graeme grinned in the darkness and saw himself escaping. He ripped through the mosquito net, leapt over the balcony and soared into the night.

But in fairness to Old Andries, Graeme had to admit that he was not certain what he himself thought of Tom and Chantal. True, they were different from people he and Nella met at home— and were stimulating for that reason. But, despite Tom's hospitality, Graeme felt off balance with him. More like a specimen than a person. And he was even more unsure of himself with Chantal.

Chantal. Thinking of her, Graeme grew restless, caught inside the mosquito net. He crawled outside it and looked at his watch. He took a blanket and, wrapping himself in it, listened to Nella. She breathed with heavy regularity. He opened the door and stepped onto the balcony.

The night air was cold. It smelled of pines. Graeme leaned against the railing, trying to clear his mind. He thought of nothing. After a while he glanced toward Tom's and Chantal's room. The windows were dark. They would be asleep, wound about each other. He pulled the blanket close about him.

"Hello," a voice said softly.

Graeme did not move.

"Hello," it said again.

Graeme felt a pang of nervousness. He peered into the darkness. Chantal was sitting on the chaise longue. He nerved himself and tiptoed to it. "Have you been there all this time?" he asked.

"Hmm-mmm."

"You must be freezing." He took the blanket off and gave it to her. "Why have you been sitting there?"

"I've been waiting for you."

Had she spoken those words? Graeme could not believe it. He said nothing, hardly breathing.

"I've been waiting for you," she said again. "Tom and I had an argument." Then, "I arranged for us to have it."

Graeme tightened his hold on the balcony railing.

"I felt you calling me."

Graeme held his breath. He felt almost too nervous now to think.

"I've been calling you."

Graeme rubbed his arms. "Is this like the exotic fortune?" he tried to ask lightly. "Something you tell all men?"

"I'm very good at fortunes," Chantal said. She laughed in a way Graeme thought of as Bantu; he felt her pulling him closer as if by witchcraft. He took a step backwards.

"Don't be frightened," she said. "Let's see. I'll tell you something less scary." She hesitated, pondering. "I know. Eventually Tom, even Tom, gets tired. We didn't argue. He fell asleep. So I came out for a smoke. Is that better?"

He stood, his hands on the railing, for what seemed a very long time.

"Don't hold back, Graeme. You're not at home."

For the first time she spoke his name. He felt himself pulled toward her. He gripped the railing tighter, fearful that if he moved, he would leap across a brink.

"Don't you want this?"

He closed his eyes. For a moment he held his breath. Then he reached out to touch her.

"Hello," she said.

He fumbled in the darkness. "Where are you?" He laughed stealthily, nervously. She took his hand. "Thanks." She pulled him beside her. His confidence returned. It's going to be all right, he told himself.

Groping about, he wrapped the blanket around them. They kissed. She laughed welcomingly and bit his neck. At last his mind stopped working. Sensation filled him, like music. He moved with it, holding the African girl, and their bodies flowed together. He felt himself leap, truly over the brink now, and Chantal clung to him as Nella never had.

Finally he leaned away from her and laughed with relief. "God," he said. He felt more satisfied physically than he ever had. His body ached lightly, pleasurably.

Somewhat later he thought of Nella, trustful, pregnant Nella. He suddenly felt overcome with guilt. What had he done? He withdrew his hand from Chantal's skin, as if he were touching a whore. "Do you do this with anyone?" he asked.

"Don't spoil it."

"Do you?"

"I do it with men I like. Isn't that natural?"

For a while Graeme said nothing, thinking of what Chantal had said, but also thinking of Nella. Sweet Nella, he said to himself; she'll never suspect this. He felt safe and caressed the

African girl again. He said, "You like me, do you?"

"Poor Graeme," Chantal said. "You're looking out at the world through a plate glass window. You want to come join us and you're trying. I like that." She paused. "You can't know how flattering it's been to watch you discover me as a person and as a woman. Tom could never pay me such a compliment!" She took his hand and Graeme watched her press his white fingers against her dark cheek.

Later he woke from the cold. Chantal had gone. He lay on the chaise for a long time and at last tiptoed into the warm room. In the bed Nella was still lightly snoring. He regarded her fondly—his Nella—and did not feel as if he had betrayed her. He told himself that most South African men—probably even her father—had at one time or another had a Bantu girl. It was not a betrayal; it was a safety valve. It meant nothing.

He and Nella slept until eight thirty. At breakfast Tom asked if they had spent a good night. Smiling vacantly, Nella said they had. Tom left to conduct some business. Chantal did not appear.

Nella napped most of the morning, a contented smile on her face. Graeme left her sleeping. He quietly closed the door and tiptoed across the hall. With blood pounding in his head he knocked at the door. Chantal's voice called, *"Entrez."* Graeme did not move. When she called a second time, he opened the door and stepped inside. "Good morning," he said.

"Hello, Graeme." She was sitting in bed in a dressing gown eating a *petit dejeuner* from a tray. She smiled at him. "Come in. I saved you a croissant." She buttered the pastry and handed it to him. Graeme took it, thrilled, but nervous. "Do sit down."

He took a chair. Not knowing what to say, he bit into the croissant. Chantal poured herself coffee. "Want some?" she asked, already pouring him a cup. Graeme took the cup, chewing on the croissant and feeling amazed at himself. Finally he said, "I hope your bed is better than ours. Ours sags in the middle." It seemed almost traitorous for him to speak to this woman, his Bantu lover, of "our bed," his and Nella's, and yet he was doing this.

"This coffee smells of Paris," she said, sniffing it.

"It tastes awful."

"Yes, but it smells of Paris." She smiled at him and he felt comfortable.

"Tell me about Paris," he said. He kicked off his shoes and put his feet on the bottom of the bed.

She told him about Paris and West Africa and Martinique. As they talked, she left the bed, slipped through the plastic strips hanging at the bathroom entrance and ran water for a bath. Graeme put on his shoes. "Don't go," Chantal said. "Come talk." Graeme hesitated, uncertain what to do. "I love to talk in the bath," she said. She took his hand and led him into the bathroom. As he watched, she slipped out of her dressing gown. With the same unconsciousness of her nakedness as the woman in the hallway photo in Tom's house, she stepped into the tub.

Graeme thought he must be inside some dream. Was this happening? Had he and Chantal really been together the night before? He sat on the floor beside the tub, talking to Chantal and thinking that at any moment he might wake up to find Nella sleeping beside him.

"There's room enough for you," Chantal finally said. "Want to come in?"

He shed his clothes, very conscious of his nakedness and the obviousness of his excitement. "Hmmm," she said with a grin. He returned the smile, slipped into the water beside her and held her, clung to her. Later they washed each other, Chantal bathing him like a mother, soaping and rinsing every inch of him. When they left the bath, he toweled her dry and kissed her when they finished. "I'm going back to bed," she said, putting on a nightie. "Come tuck me in."

In fact, he joined her in bed. He lay holding her for a long while, thinking with his skin, not with his mind. He felt strangely content merely to hold her.

When he went back across the hall, Nella was still asleep. He smiled at her tenderly. Above her mountainous body her face wore an expression of contentment. Graeme felt released and full of joy; he regarded his wife with profound affection. He loved her, he thought, almost more than he ever had.

Chantal did not appear at lunch. Graeme and Nella and Tom ate alone. After they finished, Chantal strolled onto the dining terrace, a bag slung *à la Parisienne* over her shoulder. She shook hands with all of them and, hardly speaking, drank some coffee.

Tom insisted on a siesta after lunch. He and Chantal arrived at the car twenty minutes later than the two couples had agreed to meet. Tom complained of a headache, so severe, he said, that he could not drive. He asked Graeme to chauffeur them back to Antananarivo. Nella smiled knowingly at Graeme as Tom and Chantal slid into the rear of the car. They had hardly left Antsirabe before Tom fell asleep, his white palm resting on Chantal's brown thigh.

Back in the capital Graeme bade Chantal a warm goodbye. She gave him what seemed an encouraging smile and his heart leaped. He hoped to see her again.

But he found it impossible to contact her. It turned out that the Liberian Embassy had closed. Instead of returning to Monrovia, the ambassador had bought a trading company in Antananarivo. Graeme could think of no plausible way to trace Chantal through the company. He was a married man, after all.

Naturally, he lacked the courage to ask Tom for Chantal's phone number. He did not want Tom to know what he was thinking. Nor Nella either. When they were together at his house, Graeme felt Tom watching him—as if waiting for him to make some move. He sometimes wondered if Tom had put Chantal up to widening his experience of life. As it worked out, he did not see her again.

Back in Johannesburg, Graeme wrote about Madagascar nonstop for several days. For SAPS he cranked out pieces about trade possibilities and about the island's ethnic tensions. For overseas editors he carefully crafted travel pieces, reports about development in isolation, and think-pieces on environmental devastation in a seeming paradise. Then he got swept up in covering developments in the new South Africa. Very soon Madagascar seemed a dream. Chantal became a figure who was never quite real. Memory transformed Antsirabe into a virtual reality interlude that never truly occurred.

When Nella went to hospital for the baby, Andries De Kock paid Graeme a visit. "Look, lad," he said. "Fatherhood's upon you. Time to give up this notion about America. Its racial problem is more entrenched than ours and there's no will there to solve it. Here we're coming to grips with the problem. There's more opportunity here than you know."

"I need overseas experience," Graeme told him.

"They think highly of you at the Press Service," De Kock assured Graeme. "You know the managing director's an old friend of mine. Shall I speak to him?"

"Please, don't! I've got to know if I can get ahead on my own."

Once the baby arrived, Graeme felt a strange erosion of ambition. He became more content with his life. He chose to regard this condition as evidence of new maturity. Parenthood made him feel less constrained in his homeland, less hungry for freedom and experience.

Now and then something would remind him of Chantal. Yes, he would think, he had slept with an African woman. He felt more of a man for that and recognized that Chantal had contributed to his improved view of himself. Because of her he felt himself a better reporter, too. He always regarded the Madagascar pieces as some of his best writing, the most colorful and atmospheric.

His stories from the island produced appreciative letters from editors overseas. He followed up with inquiries about positions on their newspapers—although, because of the baby, less quickly than he intended. He received an offer of a paid internship in Philadelphia and accepted it, but lost time sorting out the immigration procedures. Learning that he was serious about America, the Press Service offered Graeme an editorship.

Shortly afterwards Nella informed him that she was pregnant again. They had a long talk about their lives. Graeme agreed to accept the editorship. He knew Nella was right: it was time to settle down.

DR. KLECKNER

EMILY STOPPED LISTENING TO THE CONVERSATION. She wondered if she should check again with Mamadou the cook. But what would she tell him? She had no idea when their final guest would arrive. She glanced at John. He smiled at her, gave a small shrug about Dr. Kleckner's tardiness, and made a little face about their other guests' tendency toward competitiveness. He seemed relaxed. So Emily remained where she was.

Although she would not have admitted the fact, Emily was a little afraid of her husband: of his ambition and relentless pursuit of achievement, of his intellect, of the ease with which he conversed with almost anyone, and of his tendency to be a tiny bit impatient with her and their two boys. In Washington, where they were last stationed, Emily had been heavily involved at their sons' school; she had also worked in a travel business. But John had asked that for their first year in Ouagadougou she devote herself entirely to helping him become a successful Ambassador. She had agreed and she was often lonely. The two boys were at boarding school in Switzerland. They were in their mid-teens and Emily feared that they had left the nest forever. With them gone, she did not know for certain what her role was. Or for that matter what it would be for the rest of her life.

Now Emily often thought of her husband not as John, but as The Ambassador. She wanted to stay attractive for him and representative of his position. Since she had a tiny tendency to put on weight, she did a video workout every morning after he left for the office. She was relieved—immensely relieved!—that he had been appointed Ambassador even if it was to an unimportant country like Burkina Faso with a capital called Wa-ga. Finally they could relax. Worries that John's ambitions would always be thwarted gnawed less ferociously at them now. Emily no longer feared that her every act might impact his chances for success. Of course, they hoped for a more prestigious post next time. But even in Ougadougou she wanted everything to be right for him, including a dinner *en famille* for three American academics, especially for the Adams couple, John's longtime mentors, who gossiped across the room. She could see that their admiration was good for his ego.

The mentors came from the college in Maine where John had done his undergraduate work. Horton Converse Adams III, called Tripp, was a sociologist who specialized in the training of elites. His wife Sarah was an historian. Newly retired, designated as "emeriti," they were venturing around the world. They had come to Ouagadougou expressly to visit John, to bask in the success that had come to him upon being named Ambassador. While there, they hoped to catch sight of their faculty colleague Charlotte Kleckner.

But Dr. Kleckner was late. She had come in the night before from Bobo-Dioulasso. Emily had talked with her by phone, inviting her for seven. The clock hands were now moving toward eight.

Adams announced, "I'm getting a little worried."

"So am I," said Sarah. "Is Kleckie safe?"

"I wouldn't worry yet," replied the Ambassador. "One gets casual about time in West Africa. That's the tradition."

"I'm sure you're right, John," said Adams. "But Kleckie's not African."

"She's hopelessly punctual," agreed his historian wife. "It comes from working with statistics."

The professors looked at one another as if something ought to be done.

"Should I call her hotel?" Emily asked her husband.

"Let's give her a bit longer," suggested the Ambassador.

"But just a bit," said Sarah.

As they waited, Adams silently beat his winter-bleached thumbs together. Then he chuckled and observed, "Charlotte Kleckner in Africa!" He shook his head. "I can hardly imagine it!" He and his wife smiled at one another.

"Have you met her?" asked Sarah. John and Emily indicated they had not. The historian sighed. "She's delicate. Pale-skinned."

"Sexless, she means," her husband declared. Since they were with John, whom they had known so long, it was permissible to gossip. Sarah laughed and lightly slapped her husband's arm.

"She has hollow cheeks and long hair—" Adams continued.

"Unfailingly dressed in a bun," added the wife.

"Lives entirely in her head," said Adams.

Dr. Kleckner walked across Emily's mind in a gray tweed suit and sensible shoes: a parched, stereotypical maiden academic.

"How did she happen to come here?" the Ambassador asked.

"Funding for her sabbatical study didn't come through," Adams explained. "She was determined to get away and this came up. So she agreed. Need I say . . . Impulsively."

"In a fit of madness," his wife added.

The sociologist looked at his watch and tapped his finger against it. "Do you know if she's going to finish out the year?" he asked.

The Ambassador did not know. But he reassuringly said, "I should think so," because those were the words ambassadors used on such occasions. Emily said nothing. But when she had spoken with Dr. Kleckner by phone the night before, she had sounded quite capable of dealing with Africa.

"I suppose she's glad to get out of Bobo to come see us," Adams remarked.

"Probably lonely," opined his wife. "Homesick for shop talk."

"For talk about ideas."

The professors nodded to one another. Great talkers, the emeriti, Emily thought, but she noticed that their concern was real. As their words flowed out, they crossed and recrossed their legs. They drummed their chair arms with long, thin fingers. Watching them, Emily wondered how they would fare on their trip when they were no longer fortunate enough to be the guests of an ambassador. She also felt herself growing a bit upset with this woman academic. After all, she was delaying an occasion provided for her by the American Ambassador. Didn't Dr. Kleckner realize that an American Ambassador was a busy man?

"I suppose we should reassure Kleckie that her career won't be damaged if she decides not to finish her study," Adams mused.

"You needn't bother," his wife interjected. "You know she'll tell us everything's wonderful. That's what you'd tell her if she dropped out of nowhere to visit you."

"I think we should reassure her no one at the college will blame her if she comes back early," Adams persisted. "Face it, this entire continent's a basket case."

At last they heard a car enter the drive. A moment later Dr. Kleckner appeared. "Kleckie!" exclaimed the professors.

"Hello!" she said. "Nice to see you!" She took Tripp and Sarah by the hands and kissed their cheeks in the French style. Emily and the Ambassador introduced themselves. Dr. Kleckner kissed their cheeks, too. Then she enthused to all of them, "Don't you love this country!"

From the professors' description Emily had expected to receive some dried-up maiden aunt. But Dr. Kleckner was tanned and vibrant. She wore sandals and a dress made of mammy cloth. It was quite becoming: bold red- and yellow-petaled flowers on a field of blue. A cloth tied about her head in the manner of Burkina women matched the blue of her dress and accented the color of her eyes.

"Kleckie, it's really you!" said Adams as the party sat down.

"Yes." She leaned back comfortably. "Really me."

The emeriti examined their colleague intently.

"I'm sorry I'm so late," Dr. Kleckner continued. "I was walking around the Ziniare market and completely lost track of time."

"Around Ziniare?" asked Adams. He turned to the Ambassador. "Isn't that where we drove today?"

"Yes," said the Ambassador.

"You weren't there alone, I hope!" commented Sarah lightly.

"Of course I was!" Dr. Kleckner laughed. "It's not a bandits' hideout, you know. People live there."

"Really?" Adams joshed. He grinned at his sociologist colleague as if to let her know they saw through her pose.

"It's rather like where I live in Koumi outside Bobo," said Dr. Kleckner.

The emeriti exchanged a glance. "Really?" said Adams again.

"I love Koumi!" she said. "It vibrates with vitality, kids playing, trucks honking. I love to watch women gossiping in the market while they carry pots on their heads and babies on their backs. And hear their laughter. And all the while they're wearing huge gold earrings and gigantic headcloths. They pick out red peppers and oranges and those stubby, sweet, yellow bananas. They inspect papayas in woven baskets and fish in bright enamel pans. I love the way their eyes shine when they laugh. I love their skin, that chocolatey luster. Don't you?"

The Adamses tried to stare without being impolite.

"Don't you feel sometimes that white skin is awfully washed out?"

The emeriti raised eyebrows at one another and did not bother to hide their surprise.

"I bought myself a couple of kola nuts," Dr. Kleckner rattled on. "They're really so refreshing! And where did the time go? I had a little trouble hitching a ride."

"You hitched a ride?" asked Adams. "Well, well. How prole!"

"With a passing truck." Dr. Kleckner smiled. "The driver took me right to the hotel. The desk clerk brought me out here."

A silence. Then Sarah commented rather formally, "I thought the housing in Ziniare rather poor."

"The government is trying to improve it," Dr. Kleckner replied. "These things take time. Did you get out into the countryside?"

"No, we didn't."

"Oh, what you missed!" she exclaimed. "That's how Africa really lives. I go out there whenever I can. A village family has sort of adopted me." Dr. Kleckner dug into her bag of woven fiber and withdrew an envelope of photos. "This is the concession," she said, displaying a snapshot of a large compound surrounded by a mud wall. "The extended family lives here."

"As do sheep and goats!" exclaimed Sarah when Dr. Kleckner produced the next photo.

"Yes, chickens roam everywhere," she said. "Fodder for the animals is stored here." She offered other photos. "This is the patriarch's house at the entrance to the living compound. Rather grand, don't you think?"

"Is this him?" asked John, taking a photo from the sociologist.

"Yes. Moussa. He's about fifty, I think, though it's impossible to tell."

John glanced at the photo and passed it to Emily. She saw a lean-faced, very dark-skinned man with eyes so penetrating that their gaze seemed to peer inside her. He seemed the essence of Africa. Emily stopped looking at the other photos, without quite realizing that she had.

"He has four wives," said Dr. Kleckner. "They're Muslims, of course. Plus two women he inherited when a brother died." Emily gave a hurried glance at snapshots of the women and children and found her eyes drawn back to the photo of Moussa the patriarch. "The wives live in their own quarters with their children. Each one has her hut."

"Quite a busy place," observed Adams who was collecting the photos.

"Oh, yes!" said Dr. Kleckner, taking them from him. "Children everywhere. Some have the same names because the first boy always seems to be called after his father. Very confusing. I've finally got it sorted out. And they've got me straight. The patriarch calls me Nana, which is a common first name for women."

"Where do you stay when you go there?" Emily asked.

"They built me my own hut," said Dr. Kleckner. "Even my own private loo."

"And you eat— What?" ventured Sarah.

"What everyone else eats. Not a very interesting diet. Usually millet of some kind with a sauce. Peanuts or something."

"These inherited women," Sarah said. "The widows of the dead brother. What happens to them?"

"Moussa takes care of them." An unasked question hung in the air. "In Africa, of course, that means he sleeps with them," Dr. Kleckner explained in an academic way. Then her eyes twinkled. She said, "Why should a good woman go to waste? That's how they look at it."

"Have you gone to waste, Kleckie?" teased Adams. "You're a good woman."

Dr. Kleckner blushed. Quite becomingly, Emily thought.

"Why are you blushing, Kleckie?" Adams bantered. "We demand to know." He began to watch her with real interest. His wife was not quite so amused.

"Life is so different here," Dr. Kleckner said. She shrugged. "Here a man will watch you in a market or at a bus stop. Then he'll come and say, 'Marry me. I think we should get married.'"

"By marriage," Adams said, wishing to be precise, "he presumably means something different than what we mean. Is that right?"

"Do you think American men talk marriage only when they mean it?" asked Dr. Kleckner. "Usually these proposals aren't rude or insistent, just admiring. Peace Corps girls visiting Bobo get half a dozen of them in a single day."

"All these proposals," Adams joshed. "Have you been tempted, Kleckie?"

"Well, I'm relieved you're here with us safe and sound,"

interjected his historian wife, seeking to change the subject.

"Have you been tempted, Kleckie?" persisted Adams.

At that moment Mamadou announced dinner.

Watching Dr. Kleckner as they went into the dining room, Emily did not find it difficult to believe that African men found her attractive. She noticed Tripp Adams observing her as if for the first time. She smiled privately at that. Then she heard his wife whisper to him, "She's conning you. Don't encourage her." Emily smiled privately at that, too.

Then, moving past a mirror, she glanced at the reflection of a slender, rather pretty woman and tried to appraise her as if she had never seen her before. Occasionally the Ambassador's chauffeur drove her to the market. He waited in the car while she walked among the stalls, doing more looking than buying. She was younger than Dr. Kleckner. And more attractive. Why, she wondered, had no man ever approached her in the market to suggest that they get married?

After dinner Emily took Dr. Kleckner outside onto the terrace. The night was balmy. Mamadou had set out half a dozen mosquito-repellent candles so that the Ambassador and his guests would be free of the annoyance of insects. Through the iron bars of the safety fence the Department had insisted John erect, the fire of the house guard glowed and crackled.

"Please excuse my husband, Dr. Kleckner," Emily said. The Ambassador and the Adamses had remained in the dining room.

"Call me Charlotte, please. Or Kleckie. Or Nana."

"In his first Foreign Service post," Emily explained, "at the first diplomatic dinner party he ever attended, the men remained in the dining room for brandy and cigars."

"While the little women went off to chatter?"

"I suppose. That ceremony has always been for him the quintessence of diplomatic life. Now that he's Ambassador, he always offers brandy and cigars. And women are free to stay. You saw that Sarah did."

"I'm quite happy here," said Charlotte Kleckner. "Rather nice to have 'girl-talk' with another American woman."

"You're teasing me."

"Not at all." Charlotte Kleckner gazed at her. "Are you happy here?"

"You certainly seem to be."

"Yes, I love it. And you?" she asked again.

Emily glanced toward the house, wondering where Mamadou was. When she turned back, Charlotte Kleckner was watching her, a compassionate smile on her face. "We'll have coffee in just a moment," said Emily, resenting the smile. She would not acknowledge to this woman she did not know if she were happy or unhappy. Or even that she was at loose ends, merely getting through till the boys came home for Christmas. So she was a little surprised to hear herself say, "I confess I've wondered why no African has ever asked me to marry him. I don't suppose it's because I wear a wedding band."

Mamadou brought the coffee. Instead of waiting as Emily knew that the Ambassador preferred her to do, she poured her guest a demitasse. Charlotte Kleckner studied her face and Emily, feeling the other woman's eyes on her, wondered what secrets her guest could read in the lines around her eyes, in the tightness of her mouth.

"Milk?" Emily asked as she set the small cup before her guest. "Sugar?"

"I prefer it straight," Charlotte Kleckner said. Then in a way that seemed merely conversational, but, Emily thought, might not be, the professor commented, almost musing, "I was desperately unhappy when I first came out here. Of course, I knew things would be different. Knew it intellectually. I was aware that Africa had lost ground since the days of independence. While the rest of the world grew ever more prosperous, in Africa the money economy was giving way to subsistence. Arable land was being eaten up by the Sahara. We hoped Africans would catapult themselves out of the tribal-colonial mix—which was foolish of us; we really are hopeless optimists—and they just couldn't manage it." Dr. Kleckner sighed aloud at the frustration she had first felt in Bobo.

"Africa struck me as hopelessly primitive," she went on. "The people seemed content with mediocrity, ignorance, poverty. I had come here to teach. And to do some research. But the university looked like something out of Beau Geste and the students were all blockheads. I suppose it's no surprise that I had trouble connecting with them. I've done a lot of teaching, but still I thought it was their fault. Furthermore, I was sure my colleagues at home would never believe any serious research could be done in a place called Bobo. I was ready to throw it all in and go home."

"A bad case of WAWA."

Charlotte Kleckner laughed. "West Africa Wins Again! That difficult malady."

"I've had terrible bouts of WAWA," Emily confessed.

"I struggle with it every day," Dr. Kleckner admitted. "I knew it would be different here. But—"

"But not this different?" Emily suggested.

The women smiled at one another.

"I love the balminess of these nights," Dr. Kleckner said. "Do you know what the temperature is right now in Boston?" She held her arms out as if to embrace the air.

"When I had all but decided to leave," she went on, "something happened. Or rather nothing happened—except that it did. I can only think of the nothing-that-happened as magical, but in a kind of WAWA way. I was walking along a street one hot afternoon. Ahead of me I noticed a large, tall, amply rounded Bobo woman. She wore a pink, diaphanous headcloth of some faux silk material, tied in a manner that was all the mode in town just then. The pink was perfect against the lustrous dark-chocolate of her skin and inside an over-garment of the same material she floated along. She was barefoot in sandals and she really did float, her hands waving delicately a little out from her sides. As I drew parallel to her, I caught a sweet, womanly scent—not at all what I would have expected when I noticed beads of perspiration catching the light on her brow. She glanced at me and smiled. Smiled in a way that was like a shining in her face. She was a large, sweating woman, walking in the afternoon sun. But she moved with absolute grace. She was serene; she was beautiful. She knew who she was and was happy to be that person. Her smile made me smile."

Dr. Kleckner took a sip of her coffee and smiled herself, smiled at Emily. Emily was not sure why, but she smiled back.

"What about that moment could possibly have been magical?" Charlotte Kleckner asked. "I've wondered that so often. Maybe it was the fact that I stopped hurrying to my appointment. I turned back and smiled again at the woman. Then as if she had spoken to me, I heard a voice say, 'Let them teach you.'"

"I wish I'd seen her," Emily said.

"Women like her are all over the streets. Once I started looking, there they were." She sipped her coffee again, then leaned forward, not asking Emily's permission, and refilled her cup.

"Until that moment it seemed preposterous that—I mean . . . I was the one who had come to teach, right? I was the one with the doctorate from Harvard. We think so little of Africans. But they are so— Gentle. And joyful. So sweet-tempered. So beautiful."

The two women sat silently for a moment. "Seeing that woman changed me," Charlotte Kleckner said. "I did let them teach me."

Again they sat without speaking.

Finally the visitor added, "I had hired a house man to cook for me and I had let him do the marketing. I began going to market with him. I didn't want to bargain. I thought it was un-dignified. He taught me how."

"I'm not very good at it," Emily admitted. "Are you?"

"I insist on a fair price."

The two woman laughed.

"I began to have relationships with market women. We greet each other as friends now. I speak a bit of their language and I even know a little something of their lives."

"I wonder if that's something I could do," Emily mused.

"Probably," said Charlotte Kleckner. "I started wearing san-dals. Then looser dresses, African prints. I put away those suits I used to teach in. Then a market woman said I should wear a headcloth and as a lark I tried one."

They sat again without speaking. The professor's mouth wore the curve of a smile and Emily wondered what memory pro-voked it. "As I began to learn from them," Charlotte Kleckner said, "I discovered that they were beginning to learn from me. I found that the work I was doing with women's groups became more productive."

"Could I come visit you in Bobo, Nana?" Emily asked. Then, as if to retreat from the question's presumption, she quickly added, "You really don't mind my calling you that?"

"No, no. I like it."

"I would love to see the work you're doing," Emily said. She was surprised to hear the urgency in those words and realized how much the visit might mean to her.

"How about coming next week?"

"Tuesday?"

"Fine."

"I'll have Mamadou pack us a lunch."

"Good."

For a moment the two women were silent. They listened to the watchman talking with a friend as they crouched beside the fire.

"The patriarch's naming you," Emily said. "It seems such an intimate thing."

"Does it?" Nana Kleckner cocked her head to consider the statement. "It's quite a complex relationship we have," she said. "I mean, for really having no relationship at all. Sometimes for village ceremonies I sit with the men, accepted by them. Sometimes with the women. Moussa would like to know me in a way he will never be able to. I would like to know him in a way I won't be able to."

She gazed off across the yard. "One evening I was sitting with him outside his house. He had a copy of People Magazine— God forbid!—and the ads fascinated him. He asked me to explain some of the pictures. I did what I could and then he said to me, 'Let us talk all night. We will watch the moon rise and you will tell me about the places you have seen that I will never visit.'" Nana's voice drifted off and Emily thought of her sitting in the darkness with Moussa's penetrating gaze reaching out to her.

Nana Kleckner seemed for a moment to have lost all awareness that Emily was with her. Then, glancing at Emily, she said, "I couldn't stay with him, even if we never went inside that house. Which eventually he would have expected us to do. Across the compound his wives were watching us. The wife whose turn it was to be with him kept calling her children, quite loudly, even though the children were already in her hut. We both knew that I was—and must always be—one of those places he would never visit."

Nana watched her a long moment. She asked, "Would you like to come to the concession sometime and meet the people there?"

Emily sat back in her chair. Heavens! she thought. What ever made Dr. Kleckner think that? She poured them more coffee and thought perhaps she would like to go.

When the Ambassador led the Adamses onto the terrace, he glanced at Emily, a little surprised that she had already served coffee. "Welcome to civilization," Emily said. "We wondered if we would ever see you again." These were the words she always said when the Ambassador returned with guests from brandy and cigars.

Then she did something she had never done during all the dinner parties she had presided over as her husband's hostess. "I'm going to let you serve yourselves," she told the newcomers. John looked astonished. "And, darling, while you're up," she went on, "would you mind telling Mamadou we'd love more coffee?" He threw her a who-me? expression that made her smile at him with love. He obediently went off to speak to Mamadou while the professors helped themselves to coffee.

Later when the Ambassador himself was serving his guests liqueurs, Adams gazed a long moment at his colleague. In a lightly teasing tone he commented, "I think Burkina Faso becomes you, Kleckie."

"You've gained a bit of weight," noted his historian wife.

"Indeed you have," said the sociologist. "You're positively curvaceous."

"Nothing like peanut oil to round a girl out," Dr. Kleckner acknowledged in the darkness. "I've gotten some new clothes, too. I threw away all those gray suits."

"Really?" asked Sarah. "You'll need them when you get back."

Dr. Kleckner said nothing and there followed a spate of shop talk: about the college in Maine and its sociology department, about new research, colleagues, and mutual friends. Emily and John listened, pleased at the animation of the voices.

To Emily's surprise, the Ambassador reached over and took her hand. When she looked at him, he gave her a smile.

Eventually Adams said with a chuckle, "You know, Kleckie, I think people in the department will hardly recognize you when you get back." Emily watched him looking at Dr. Kleckner, seeing her not merely as a colleague but as a woman. Emily noticed that his wife was watching him, too. "When are you returning?" he asked.

"I'm not," Dr. Kleckner replied.

A stunned silence. The emeriti shot glances back and forth at one another.

"The study is more involved than I thought."

"But you will return at the end of the sabbatical," Adams said.

"No," Nana Kleckner replied, "I'm not returning at all."

"Kleckie!" blurted the sociologist.

"Your career is at the college!" exclaimed his wife. "Surely, it is."

They both stared at her. But the historian began very faintly to smile.

"Kleckie, dear," implored Adams, "be serious. Where's your perspective?"

"You don't miss the college? Or Boston?" asked his wife.

"Now and then I do hunger for a night at Symphony Hall."

"Don't you miss *us?*" asked Adams.

"Of course," Nana Kleckner said with real warmth in her voice. "I think of you often"—teasing them gently—"slogging about in snow under gray skies or tramping sidewalks in wan sunlight with newspapers blowing about your feet."

After a moment she said more seriously, "And I've thought of myself: thin and lonely, walking for winter exercise down the streets of a college town, wearing old maid's shoes and gray tweeds. Hungering for color without knowing it."

"I believe you really *want* to stay here, Kleckie," said Adams.

"Yes, I do," she said. "I'm happy here. I'm rounded and tan. I work with people, not statistics. I've found color. I live in it and it's lovely."

Later, saying goodbye, the professors stood apart, their thin, white arms folded across their chests. Emily and Dr. Kleckner had gone to the kitchen to thank Mamadou and to fix the time of Emily's arrival the following Tuesday in Bobo-Dioulasso.

As he heard Nana Kleckner chatting with Mamadou in an African tongue, Adams whispered to his wife, "She'll be back. Mark my words."

"You think so?" asked his wife. "At home she was plain. Here she's beautiful. Why should she give that up?"

"Well, we'll see," said the sociologist. "She is certainly beautiful," he acknowledged. "Extraordinary, isn't it?"

As they lay together waiting for sleep, John told Emily about this exchange between the Adamses. They laughed quietly about it. And although this rarely happened when guests were in the house, they made love. As they held each other afterwards, John said to Emily, "Missus, you are so lovely. Marry me. I think we should be married."

NIGHT VIGIL

IT WAS THREE THIRTY IN THE MORNING. The night had grown cold. Derek had been reading, but now the cold distracted him, that and the crying from across the hall. The waiting room was small and close and poorly lit. Derek thought it smelled of Africa which meant, although he did not know it, that he felt far from home. He looked up from his book to find that the missionary sitting opposite him had stopped reading his Bible. They listened to a baby yowling.

"Life begins with a cry," the missionary said.

In the early afternoon he had brought a Kamba woman to the hospital; she had taken the third place in the four-bed "labor ward" in which Derek and his wife spent most of the day. This birth would be the Kamba woman's eighth. She was the wife of a catechist who worked for the missionary. During their sharing of the waiting room the missionary had explained that to Derek. Because the couple had so many children, the husband had not come in from his catechizing safari.

Derek's wife was having their first baby. She was at this moment in the delivery room at the end of the hall. Because Derek had heard his wife crying out in pain, the wailing of the babies unnerved him. He half-envied the absent catechist and yet he could not imagine being away from his wife at this time. Seeing that the missionary wanted to talk, he looked quickly back at his book. Derek's profession required him to be interested in all kinds of people. But just now he was not inclined to chat with a person he would never see again, especially not this missionary. The man possessed the happy, morbid blandness that came, so Derek thought, to one certain that Providence had chosen him, but not necessarily others.

"Life begins with pain," the missionary said. "And often ends with it."

"Cold tonight," Derek said. He did not want the missionary to declare, not just now, that at least the process of making children brought couples joy.

Suddenly the crying ceased; the last flutterings of breath muted into silence. The two men looked at one another, almost startled. A half-smile tilted on the missionary's mouth. They listened to the nearby soundlessness. But the consciousness of the other crying he had heard made Derek cold. He stood. He wondered what was happening at the end of the long corridor behind them.

"Not worried, are you?" asked the missionary. "Once the little ones arrive, women forget the pain." He added, "And the child starts to feel it. That's 'cause we put our fingerprints all over the poor kid." He grinned, shrugged.

"I'm not worried," Derek said. "I'm freezing."

Derek checked the window that he had closed an hour earlier, shortly after they had heard the doctor, her heels clicking competently on the tiling, pass the waiting room, turn and proceed down the hall.

One of the babies started yowling again. The others quickly joined in.

Derek left the waiting room. He stood in the hall he had paced with Dee again and again in the late afternoon and early evening. He peered down its length, through the tunnel of darkness to the brightly-lit white doors at its end. Dee was behind those doors.

He moved forward uncertainly, passing through that darkness. He entered the labor ward, seeking the sweater left on the chair beside Dee's bed. He heard the Kamba woman sleeping fitfully behind flower-patterned curtains in the bed beside his wife's. Across the room stood the bed of a young Asian woman; Dee had made friends with her. They had paced together along the terrace while Derek was at dinner. The Asian woman's husband was with her now, sitting in the darkness behind drawn curtains. Derek saw his feet below the bed. He took Dee's sweater.

In the hall Derek put Dee's sweater around his neck and shoulders like a muffler. He went to the white-lit end of the corridor and stood outside the door. "Relax your legs now," he heard the doctor counsel. "Relax your legs." Behind it he heard his wife weeping against the pain, her voice like a cry to him. "Push now!" the doctor instructed. "Push!" Derek heard his wife's voice whimpering in exertion, emitting a sound of hurt that he had never heard from her before.

The sound immobilized him. He stood, feeling powerless, irrelevant. He wished he could help her: bear her pain or share it. Suddenly his head swam. He felt faint. He recognized the beginnings of fear. In fact, his wife had a very low tolerance for pain. Now and then, inadvertently, he would kick or elbow her and she would wince, sometimes even writhe, with discomfort. When these things happened, Derek was often impatient with her. Now he felt only sympathy. What could he do to make the pain go away?

But there was nothing he could do.

Earlier, around 1:00 AM, when Dee was suffering with every contraction, the nurse had told her not to push against them, not till the doctor arrived. Derek had felt something should be done. He had spoken sharply to the nurse, a young Kikuyu woman who struck him as being busy, not doing her job, but playing a role: Miss East African Efficiency. He had told her, "Could you do something here? My wife's getting ready to deliver." The nurse had taken offense.

In fact, she had complained to a supervisor, claiming that Dee was rude to her. This charge infuriated Derek. Dee was a saint. She was never rude. By contrast, he practically always was. Nursie should put the blame where it belonged. He had started to tell her, "Hey! We've never done this before. You do it every day. Give us some help here!" But he realized they needed the nurse as an ally. So he smiled at her in tacit apology and held his tongue.

Nurses came and went through the delivery room door. He wanted to ask if everything were all right, but the earlier exchange had chastised him. Now he knew he must do nothing but express confidence in the hospital and its staff.

Derek had prayed earlier in the day. Now as he moved back along the hall through the tunnel of darkness, past the roses and carnations and chrysanthemums which the old Kikuyu women took each evening from the rooms of the new mothers, he prayed again. He invited God not to forget them. Once again he heard a nurse leave the room where Dee was. He turned. He saw into the delivery room, heard the doctor encouraging with distant crispness, "That's it. Now harder!" Then the delivery room door closed and he heard only the crying of the newborns.

He went back to the waiting room. The missionary was standing, doing deep knee-bends. He stopped when Derek appeared. "Any news?" he asked.

Derek shook his head. Then supposing he should say something, he heard words he hardly recognized emerging from his mouth. "My mother claims," he said, "that if men and women both had babies, the men would insist the women go first. Masculine politeness. And no family would have more than three kids."

The missionary nodded. "The night our first one was born," he observed, "I spent a long time wondering why in human life pain has to accompany birth."

"Yeah?"

"I decided that only in this way could nature purify human love. It takes selflessness to raise a kid."

Derek nodded.

"Maybe to a journalist that sounds pretty namby-pamby."

Derek shrugged. He acknowledged to himself that, although there were plenty of bad parents, this notion might be true. Still, it was not the sort of thing he would ever admit to another person, not even to Dee.

"I guess you see the worst of the world," the missionary said. "Even go looking for it."

"I'm just looking to keep warm right now," Derek said. "Guess I'll walk."

He paced to the farthest end of the hospital corridors. He

stood looking out the window, seeing nothing, thinking of how the day had started: in darkness, strange sounds penetrating his sleep. Waking he had stumbled into the bathroom. There he had found Dee emitting mystified squeals. She gave him a look that was full of joy—and full of apprehension. "My water broke," she said. They stared at one another, knowing they were crossing into territory where neither one of them had ever been.

Derek wondered how the day would end. Returning to the hospital after midnight he saw something that he had never seen before in Nairobi: army trucks in the streets. What were they doing? Was a coup about to be sprung? Out of superstition, out of fear of spreading alarm, he had told no one about the trucks. Except God. The trucks were one of the reasons he prayed.

The wife of a friend of Derek's had gone to the hospital to have her first baby the afternoon the Luo politician Tom Mboya was assassinated. There had been riots in Nairobi and she had called her husband, instructing him, "Bring the dogs and get me home." That baby had waited another full week to arrive. But that could not happen to Dee. Her water had already broken.

After a while Derek left the window. He returned the way he had come, past the closed pharmacy, through the darkened lobby, past the waiting room where the missionary was reading his Bible again. Derek walked until he could see the white doors. They were still closed.

He wondered if his wife wanted her mother. Probably. But he was glad that his parents-in-law were not with them. They had spent years overseas in the Foreign Service. Because of that his mother-in-law held strong views about the importance of birth control. Even now, if she were with them, she might be holding forth on the matter. Derek sometimes thought he had

had to bring his wife thousands of miles from her mother's influence in order for her to conceive. In any case, if her mother were with them, this process of starting a family would have turned into an affair strictly for women, just as their wedding had. Early in their marriage while they were still living in the States, whenever Dee visited her parents, she returned to Derek as a kind of child. "Infantilized by her parents" was how he expressed the idea, but only to himself. He did not express it to anyone else. Usually several weeks had to pass before Dee was restored to him as a woman.

Returning through the hospital this time Derek wandered out under the covered walkway leading to the nurses' quarters. The sky was overcast, the air cold and smelling of rain. Faintly he heard a vehicle slowing for the roundabout at the corner. He listened. Was it a car or an army truck?

There had been rain on and off all day. Derek and Dee watched it as they waited in the labor ward, wondering if the baby were merely teasing them or truly intended to come. All afternoon they studied clouds, monitored birds hunting insects on the fragrant, new-mown lawn, observed black and white heavy-bodied kites soaring from the tops of flame trees that blossomed orange-red. At nightfall a pair of aardvarks came to graze with their long, extensible tongues and the rain fell on with steady timelessness. Derek had gotten dinner at an Indian place where he and Dee often went. He had returned home at 9:30 and made a bed on the living room couch, only an arm's reach from the telephone. Dee had called at midnight.

Derek started back into the building, walking slowly. He wondered if it had rained the day he was born. What kind of sky had stretched over his grandparents' apartment on Mariposa Avenue in Los Angeles? He wondered if his father had gazed at that sky, uncertain then, as Derek was now, of what was happening and what the outcome would be. What kind of smells wafted through that apartment? It was the day before Thanksgiving. Was someone making cranberry sauce or stuffing in the kitchen? He wondered what his parents were like then; he felt close to them in a way he never previously had. A whole set of indistinctions about them began to clothe themselves in definition.

Derek thought of his father. Certainly his first encounter with childbirth had come as a surprise. He went to church the morning following the event and at an appropriate time in the service stood to tell the entire congregation that he had received early that Thanksgiving morning the blessing of twin sons. Derek smiled at a mental picture of his father, more than ten years younger than Derek himself was now, standing in that church service. And receiving congratulations afterward as Derek, the unexpected second to arrive, slept soundly in a laundry basket hastily converted into a bassinet.

Derek realized that he had not thought about his own birth since his childhood. Musing about it connected him to his own family so far away. Especially to his father. For the first time, Derek realized, he would be related to his father, not only as a son, but as one father to another.

In the waiting room the missionary had fallen asleep. Derek did not go into the room, but waited outside. He remembered that when he was small, he had had frequent dreams about fleeing from something across a dark, barren plain. Those dreams made him cry. He would wake up in bed, and his father would tiptoe into the room. He would hold and comfort Derek and chase the dream away. He remembered, too, that at one point his Dad had a daughter in boarding school and two sons away at college. His father, who was an excellent ballroom dancer, had paid tuition bills with the same grace he brought to a waltz.

When he was in college, Derek had supposed that one act was as effortless as the other. He was not much of a dancer. But he hoped his children would think the same sort of thing.

Derek thought now of his brother, his identical twin, his best friend, the first-born who had been given his father's name. Derek and his brother wrote long letters to one another two or three times a month. The brother had opinions about everything and he would have had one about what the baby should be named. "Just don't name him Scott! It's too trendy." That was the advice this brother had given their sister—without knowing that she had already chosen that name for her son.

But the brother had died. He had succumbed to an illness that Derek had felt certain he would overcome. Derek and Dee had agreed that she would name the baby if it were a girl; he would name it if it were a boy. If the naming fell to him, he would give the child the name of his father and his brother.

At the end of the corridor the white doors of the delivery room opened. A Kikuyu nurse hurried along the hall, grinning. "You have a son," she announced. Very soon the nurse Derek had offended came along, walking efficiently from the delivery room. She was carrying the baby lightly on her arm and she and Derek exchanged a smile. The baby wore a plastic identity bracelet on his ankle and his head was sticking out of coarse white swaddling. His eyes were open. He looked at his father and Derek found him to be clear-featured, finely formed, and alert.

The nurse warned Derek not to follow her and disappeared through a door. She flicked on the light in the nursery and left Derek trying to peek through a window and around the edge of the drawn curtain. Finally she placed the baby, wrapped and very small, in a waist-high crib. She pulled back the curtain and wheeled the crib beside the window.

Derek and his son regarded one another, making their introductions. The baby was small and sober, uncrying, and coolly observant of the world. He was not at all wrinkled, not at all red or prune-faced. He gazed at Derek with dark blue-gray eyes and a detached seriousness, and Derek thought of old snapshots he had seen of his father, a sober little boy in Redlands, California. Although Derek would not have acknowledged what he felt to any of his colleagues—he would soon be swapping stories about how the baby yowled at night—he perceived his son as terribly, terribly sweet.

Gazing at him, Derek understood that the child was not, as the missionary had said, a blank page on which his parents would leave their fingerprints. This child seemed complete, already himself, already aware of his identity. In his time he would show himself to Derek; he would make visible to his parents the identity which existed within him even now. Derek, of course, would never breathe any of this to his colleagues.

He heard the doctor's footsteps coming along the corridor. When he turned to her, she smiled at him. "Thanks for all you've done," he said. "How is she?"

"Fine. She worked hard, you know. She was splendid, though."

"Can I see her?"

"Of course."

As the doctor started down the hall, Derek called after her, "Be careful, Doctor." She turned and looked at him quizzically. "There are army trucks in the streets," he warned her. "I don't know why." He shrugged, aware that his apprehensions showed. "Will they be all right if there's trouble?"

"It's Madaraka Day," the doctor said. "Did you forget?"

"I don't even know what that is."

"A national holiday. There's a military parade. She'll be all right." The doctor smiled reassuringly and continued down the hall.

Derek gazed back at his son. Am I turning into a worrier? he asked the child without speaking. Or just a family man? The child was examining the side of his crib. Derek smiled at his intentness. He stepped back from the window, parted from his son for the first time, and hurried down the hall to see his wife.

In the delivery room he bent beside the table and embraced her as best he could. "He's beautiful," Derek said. He leaned down and gave his wife a kiss.

"What does he look like?" she asked. "I hardly saw him."

"He's perfect," he told his wife. "And terrific. And so are you."

Derek did not go directly home. He drove past the main post office and the Parliament Building and out toward the President's house just to satisfy himself that the army trucks really had left their motor pools for a parade.

At home Derek stood at the living room window in the first light of dawn. He thought about becoming a father. He and his journalist colleagues sometimes jokingly referred to themselves as The World Press. They reported, dissected, and analyzed the events of a continent. That gave those events significance, bestowed importance on them. Now Derek knew a secret. Those events meant nothing compared to the birth of his son.

LABAN AND MURUGI

H E WAS A THIN, YOUNG KIKUYU with a well-modeled face and dark, alert eyes. When Derek said that he and his wife had come to look at the house, the young man returned to the servant's quarters behind it and came back holding the keys on a piece of bent wire. He led them to the entry porch and unlocked the door.

"Do you live here?" Dee asked.

"Yes," he replied, pushing the door open and stepping back from the threshold, obliging and respectful.

"Is it a good house?" Derek asked.

"It is a good house," he answered, his face open and so honest that it told both all and nothing about him. "It is all right."

The Turners had not been long in Nairobi then and were looking for a place to live, a place with sufficient space for Derek to set up a journalist's office. The house stood on a five-acre plot of ground at the end of a lane of jacarandas in rolling country planted with coffee. An orange-brown anthill stretched, taller than Derek, beside the front walk. There was room enough for them to live well and for Derek's office, and the rent was controlled. Those were the advantages of the house, important ones for people who wanted to save money, but had also secretly dreamed of living on a plantation in Africa.

But there were disadvantages: an egregiously primitive kitchen, a location seven miles from town, rather farther out than they wanted to be, and an owner, a widow living in British Columbia, who was trying desperately to sell the house and get her money out of Kenya. The house had been on the market for several years. It seemed unlikely to sell. But if it did, the tenants would have to move.

While the Turners went from room to room, the young Kikuyu sat on the porch in the sun. Derek liked the house. Looking out across the lawn to the coffee, he knew he wanted to live in it. "I think we should take it," he told his wife. Dee nodded in agreement. Then Derek's eyes fell again on the young African and he wondered if his life was going to become involved with theirs.

Interviewing a prospective servant in Africa, Derek had heard, you looked him squarely in the face, trying to see what was there and not there. You took from him worn references withdrawn from a plastic bag or a wallet or a leather pouch, carefully unfolded them and read the statements of employers whose firms had transferred them elsewhere. You asked yourself questions, Is this man honest? Trustworthy? Of pleasant disposition? Will he steal sugar? Clothes? The checkbook? If I am fair to him, will he be fair to me?

A servant-search was not without its ironies. The Turners knew that the prospective servant was not someone they would know well enough to invite to dinner. And yet if they employed him, they were inviting him to share their lives. It would be at least a matter of weeks before they learned to know him as a servant. As a human being they might never know him at all.

When the Turners took possession of the house on Rosslyn Lone Tree Estate, the young Kikuyu caretaker was still living on the place. They asked his name and heard him answer, "It is Robin." When they inquired about his references and examined them, they discovered that the name, in fact, was Laban Waithaka Muturi. The Turners looked carefully at him and he bore their scrutiny. They asked if he would like to work for them, mainly caring for the grounds as he had already been doing. He said, "It is all right," which meant that he would. Derek suggested that they try the arrangement for a week to see how it went.

It went well. At the end of the week Derek typed out a letter of agreement between himself and the young Kikuyu. The Turners would pay Laban twice a month at the same rate he was being paid by the absent owner. He would (1) care for the garden, (2) clean inside the house on request, (3) wash the car, (4) act as watchman when the Turners were gone, (5) burn the garbage, and (6) do other chores as requested. His hours of work would be 8:00 AM to noon, 2:00 to 4:30 PM, Monday through Friday. He could remain in his quarters and friends could visit him, but "there will be no drinking of alcoholic beverages on the premises." The Turners agreed to pay for two shirts and one pair of trousers immediately and to finance two other garments when a probationary period was concluded at the end of the first month. They would also provide a bag of charcoal. Grounds for dismissal were enumerated: failure to perform duties, incompatibility, drunkenness, rowdiness.

Derek doubted that so specific a contract was necessary. But colleagues assured him it was a must. The worst possible nightmare that could befall an expatriate was to have a servant make an official charge that he had been cheated. Such charges were usually leveled just before the expat left on a transfer. Without a contract both parties had signed, the expat got caught in the con game. He paid exorbitantly just to get out of the country.

The Turners settled into the house. Dee made curtains out of burlap and struggled valiantly with the kitchen and the ancient "cooker." Derek established his office, did his research, and went into town to do reporting. The Turners found it difficult to make friends on Lone Tree Estate; the houses were too separated, and longtime white residents seemed uninterested in meeting transients. But a social life was available to them in town, even though late at night it often seemed a nuisance to make the long drive home on the unlighted highway.

They did not really share their lives with Laban. He spent much of his time tending the long, broad lawn that stretched down from the front of the house. There was no mower and Derek did not think of investing in one. Laban cut the grass with a long-bladed implement having a curved and sharpened end. He stood upright, swinging the implement back and forth, slowly cutting the grass.

Sometimes Derek interrupted his writing to watch Laban using the implement. He wondered how he himself would like to be doing that work. Laban had some education, at least enough to speak English. Didn't this mowing crush him? Didn't he find Lone Tree Estate rather isolated? What did he do for a social life? For friends? And yet, Derek would remind himself, Laban had a place to live and a job on the money economy. At least theoretically he was no longer tied to the land. Sometimes watching the man, he would wonder, Who is Laban anyway?

They really could not answer that question. That fact was borne out when the Turners made their first trip. They were going to Arusha where Derek would pick up stories about the East African Community and add to work he had been doing about poaching problems in game parks. They would be away a week and would leave Laban in charge of the house and property.

But the day before the trip was to start—a Saturday—Derek was overcome by reservations. "Do you think this is really a good idea?" he asked Dee. "Leaving the house this way. We really don't know the guy."

"I think he's honest," said Dee. "Anyway, what's there to take?"

"Clothes. Furniture. What if we come back and the house is empty? We'd have no idea where to find him."

So Derek spent Saturday afternoon lining up a guard from Securicor who would come and watch the house. He felt badly, distrusting Laban who seemed so honest, but he wanted to be sure.

The next morning when he and Dee were about to drive away, Laban waved and wished them well. "Hoping to see you again," he said.

Then the unexpected happened. The house was sold.

Instead of spending more time trying to find a place to live, Derek suggested to his editors that he do a tour of the territory he covered; it included all of sub-Saharan Africa. He proposed that he leave Nairobi for six, maybe eight, months. He would spend most of his time in South Africa where first-hand witnessing of the evils of apartheid always made good copy. The editors agreed to the plan and to paying Dee's travel expenses. The Turners would put their household goods and belongings into storage and live out of suitcases.

But what would happen to Laban? By then Dee and Derek

had come to feel affection for him. They knew now that he had a mother and a sister on a *shamba* in the environs of Limuru a bit north of Nairobi. Laban sometimes visited them on weekends. When he returned, he would bring greetings from his mother; sometimes Dee sent the woman return greetings and even small presents.

Derek hoped their departure would not mean that Laban was pushed out of the money economy back into the subsistence one. But that seemed likely. He gave Laban a letter of recommendation and assured him that the Turners would employ him again once they returned to Nairobi and got settled. They parted from Laban, feeling a little as if they were leaving a friend.

The Turners were not again settled into a house in Nairobi until eighteen months later. During those months they traveled through southern Africa, vacationed with Dee's parents in Europe, spent half a year in short-term "lets" around Nairobi while waiting for a promised house to become available. Finally they went to the States for two months home leave. Meanwhile, though they did not know it, Laban returned to his mother's *shamba* to live as a peasant in the subsistence economy.

Good to his word, Derek wrote to Laban at the address he had given the Turners in Kiroe Township. "If you do not have a job," the letter said, "would you like to come and work for us?" The letter sent the Turners' regards to Laban's mother and sister and closed with words Dee and Derek often repeated to one another, the words that Laban had used in sending them off on their first trip, "Hoping to see you again."

Derek had doubts that the letter would ever reach its destination. But only a few evenings later whom should he see pedaling down Riverside Paddocks toward the small bungalow at the end of the road? None other than Laban Waithaka Muturi. He had ridden in from Limuru, the bicycle his Pegasus, flying high in his triumphant return to the money economy. A grin spread the entire width of his face. "Hello!" he called to Derek.

"Habari!" Derek answered, ushering him into the drive. "Nice to see you again!"

"My mother sends her greetings," Laban told Dee when she came out of the house.

"Please give her our greetings," Dee replied. "I am going to be a mother myself."

Laban grinned and exclaimed, *"Nzuri sana!"*

Laban rejoined the household. He occupied more spacious quarters than those at Rosslyn, received a fifteen percent raise and two new sets of work clothes and was living now in a neighborhood where he could strike up friendships with other workers.

When the Turners brought the baby home from the hospital, he would not stop crying. Getting out of the car, Derek laughed with embarrassment. What bad manners his son had! There were, after all, people waiting to greet him. Dee felt distressed; so much about parenting was a mystery to both these parents! Laban admired the baby and approved of the Turners' following Kikuyu tradition by naming Paulie for his paternal grandfather. Standing quietly to one side was a woman. Laban told Dee, "This is the woman you asked me to find."

The woman stepped forward and said, *"Jambo, Memsah'b."*

"Jambo," Dee replied. The woman reached out to shield the baby's eyes from the sun and Dee thought, "This is the right person."

The woman was Murugi. She became a part-time member of the household and came three mornings a week to the bungalow on Riverside Paddocks. There she washed and ironed the laundry and, more importantly, Paulie's diapers. She also served as the *ayah*, the baby-sitter. She was frequently in the house at night and, as *ayah*, even in daytime. Derek might be working in his office while Dee was out doing errands or at her Swahili lesson. With her gone, Derek did not want to be bothered with the tasks of parenting. These were left to Murugi.

Derek's job required him to observe people, how they lived and how they thought, and Murugi was a puzzle to him. He would sometimes ask himself, Who is she anyway?

He recognized that many people, especially expatriates, share their lives with others they do not know. He had learned this with Laban. And he acknowledged that not knowing such people was not necessarily a bad thing. After all, every individual had a right to privacy. He sensed that the matter of privacy between servants and their employers required delicate handling.

In terms of their own privacy Dee and Derek hoped that Laban and Murugi did not spend much time thinking about them. About their being different, white. About how rich they were. Because they were not rich—although in the servants' eyes they might appear to have everything.

As for their own attitudes the Turners felt they should be interested in Murugi and Laban because, surely, indifference to servants—treating them like objects—was unpardonable. But they, too, deserved their privacy. When Laban became involved with Mary, a young *ayah* who lived in the neighborhood, and she began to sleep in his quarters, Dee and Derek agreed that this was not a matter they could inquire about to Laban—although Derek was glad he had a woman to sleep with. And neither could Derek say, "Hey, Murugi. Come have a cup of coffee with me and tell me all about yourself." That was not proper. And, in any case, it was not even feasible.

Murugi did not speak English.

"Do you think Murugi's married?" Derek occasionally asked Dee. They might be sitting in the back yard under the pepper tree having tea. The nightly broadcast of the BBC's Africa Service would have concluded without reporting any information that Derek had to act upon.

"I don't know," Dee would say. "But I think she has three children."

"Is she a widow?"

"Could be. Maybe she was the second or third wife of a man much older. Something her father arranged. Maybe her husband's dead now. And she has to earn money to take care of herself."

"Or maybe she— I wonder how Kikuyus divorce."

"There's a story idea for you," Dee would suggest. "Divorce among the Kikuyu."

"Front page. Banner headlines."

Or they would be in bed waiting for sleep and Derek would inquire, "Do you think Murugi's got hair under that headcloth she wears?" Kikuyu widows shaved their heads—or at least they had in traditional Kikuyu society. Neither Derek nor Dee had ever seen Murugi without a headcloth. The curiosity some men apply to wondering how a woman would look if she were not wearing a blouse, Derek applied to the question of how Murugi might look without her headcloth.

"I think maybe she left her husband," Dee would say. "And why not? Susie says all Kikuyu men beat their wives." Susie was a twelve-year-old Kikuyu friend of Dee's who had spent a night once when Derek was off on a reporting trip.

Then Dee might ask, "Where do you think she lives?"

"Wish I knew," Derek would reply.

In the evenings when Murugi babysat Paulie, Derek would drive her most of the way home. One night as they rode together, neither of them speaking, Derek thought of the route. He drove the length of Riverside Drive which was largely, though not exclusively, a European residential area. He crossed Uhuru Highway into Parklands which was largely, though not exclusively, an Asian quarter. He passed the Mayfair Hotel and the Ghelani house, where he and Dee had lived for three months in their "short lets" period. He turned into the unpaved alley-driveway beside what Murugi called the *petroli,* the gasoline station. He stopped at the usual place where the alley tapered into a footpath too narrow for a car.

Murugi opened the door and softly said, *"Kwa heri, Bwana,"* which meant "Goodbye, sir." Derek repeated what he had already said, *"Asante sana,"* which meant "Thank you very much," and watched her start down the footpath in the light of the car's high beams.

She moved quickly, as always, minding her own business if other Africans were about. That hurry always caused Derek to wonder if Murugi were anxious about her personal security or about the safety of the money he had given her. As her figure grew smaller, obscured by shadows and vegetation and by the downward slope of the path, she raised her arms for balance. Derek wondered how steep the path was, how rocky or covered with vines, and he mused once again about what kind of house she lived in and who her neighbors were. And he asked himself again as he always did, "Who is Murugi?"

He knew practically nothing about her. She was perhaps forty years of age, maybe a bit younger, not an age when life begins for a woman in Africa. She was trim and tallish, dignified and attractive in a modest way with a smile that lit up her face. Her children, maybe three, were grown. Although she did not speak English, she understood a good deal of it, more certainly than Derek knew of her Kikuyu and Swahili. She had not learned to read. So far as Derek could tell, she was able to write only her name, which she did every time she was paid, a task involving effort and concentration.

Derek knew only that about Murugi. But he admired her very much. And he was fascinated by the way the new Africa was grafting itself upon her.

No, Derek thought as he watched her disappear, he knew more than that about the woman. He knew that she was honest and a willing and careful worker. The mending had never been done with such exactness. (In fact, it had rarely been done at all.) Small changes—such as the manner of folding Bwana's socks— needed only to be mentioned once. Paulie was tended with affection and diligence and his diapers came to him ironed. Even Bwana got his undershorts ironed; such things can spoil a man.

But Derek had difficulty forging a relationship with Murugi. While her smiles to Paulie and *"Memsah'b"* were both beautiful and eloquent, Derek was never sure what Murugi thought of him. (This was important because Derek, being an American, wanted to feel liked.)

Murugi always seemed impassive when she and Derek were alone. The only exception was in the early mornings when she laughed at him, an unconscious clown, sleepy-eyed in bathrobe and slippers, putting out the laundry and diaper pail and unable to remember the proper sequence of *"Jambo-habari-nzuri,"* which meant, "Hello, how are you, I'm fine."

What fascinated Derek about Murugi was her chic. She had a quiet, understated sense of style. It was not obtrusive; one hardly noticed it at first. Derek always thought about her style as he watched her head down the homeward path in the darkness. It seemed amazing to him—and delightful—to discover that his Kikuyu *ayah*/washerwoman had clothes sense. Derek had little fashion awareness himself. So he was always surprised to find it, not in jet-set Africans for whom it was an important preoccupation, but in ordinary people like Murugi, people who had grown up as land-tending peasants, who earned so little and seemed to have such infrequent contact with fashionable worlds.

That evening as she left the car, Derek happened to glance at her wrist. On it she wore a small woman's watch with a leopard-skin band, perhaps an inch wide, simulating the wrist-watch fashions lately in vogue. It was a small symbol of the emerging Africa buckled to Murugi's wrist.

Derek thought about unexpected chic as he sat in the car at the place where the alley became a footpath. Murugi moved into the beam of the headlamps, her clean, well-pressed white dress brightly reflecting the light. Derek watched her lavender headcloth and lavender sweater and lavender tennis shoes enter the darkness. And as he backed the car down the alley, past the massive, sawn tree stump, he asked himself again, "Who is Murugi anyway? Who gives her fashion tips? Where did she get her style?"

But he would never ask such questions of her. She had a right to privacy.

Murugi came to Derek's house three times a week as a washerwoman; once, maybe twice, as an *ayah*. The Turners shared their clothes and their son and their lives with her. They trusted, but hardly knew each other. And that, Derek supposed, was the way it would probably remain.

Except that it didn't.

The night finally came when Derek, too, went down the hill. It was rainy and late and Derek held Murugi's elbow, hoping that neither of them would slip in the mud. He left her at what seemed a large house, but was indistinct in the rain, and climbed back up the path, slipping once or twice.

The next time Murugi was at the house, she said, with the help of Laban acting as translator, that she would prefer not to baby-sit at night. Or that if she did, she would like Bwana to drive her all the way home, not merely to leave her at the *petroli* where the downward path began.

Derek was more than happy to drive her home, especially after escorting her in the rain. He was sorry that she had not asked earlier or that he had not thought to offer. And so they now drove through the European area of Riverside Drive, then through the Asian quarter of Parklands and into an area Derek had not entered before. Murugi directed him to a house, built long ago by Europeans, but now very rundown. It had been transformed into a kind of boarding house or hostel.

On the road approaching the house on Sunday evenings a barber would be working in the last light of day. An impromptu religious service would be in progress nearby. Dogs hung about the boarding house, lean and inquisitive, sniffing around for food. Trash littered the yard. Children played among the bits of metal, the once components of now-cannibalized appliances. A stump peeked through tall grass. Cars that would never run again were pedestaled on wooden blocks. A faucet supplied water to the neighborhood; nearby women washed both children and laundry in buckets. Murugi's house seemed full of women. Another house, farther up the hill and more dilapidated, appeared occupied mainly by men.

The first time Derek left Murugi at the house, he was conscious that her neighbors watched him. This was Africa; most men taking women places in cars were assumed to enjoy access to their bodies. He hoped that such an assumption gave Murugi status—if that was what she wanted. But it occurred to him, too, that some of those neighbors would be asking her, "Who is that white man? He must be rich. Is he giving you money? If he isn't, you know, you can play him for some."

When Derek would return from taking Murugi home, he would tell his wife, "We must really look rich to Africans. And we think we're just getting by."

Then at a dinner party at the home of the regional director of Oxfam, Derek and Dee discovered that they were paying their servants less than all the other guests at the party, less than what the Oxfam people said was the going rate. The Turners were appalled. Since Derek had written articles from South Africa about whites exploiting African workers—"Slavery is not dead" had been the lead of a think-piece he wrote—he vowed to Dee that they must make amends.

The following day they called in Murugi and Laban. They apologized for knowing too little about local pay scales. They got out the paybooks, told them they were raising their wages and gave each of the Kikuyus a sum representing the difference between what they had earned since they started their employment and what would have earned at the higher rate.

Laban and Murugi seemed uncertain about what was going on. Europeans were strange, but they never acted this way. They did not give away money; they did not ask to be pardoned for oversights. However, when they understood that the back pay was really theirs, they signed for it and left the room grinning.

The day eventually came that Derek had always known must someday come. The Turners had completely adjusted to Nairobi. They had established a circle of friends. Derek enjoyed his work and, because the house was not big enough for both a baby and a working journalist, he had rented a one-room office downtown. Paulie was almost eleven months. He was just beginning to walk and the Kikuyu that Murugi spoke to him had become his first language. Sometimes on Sundays while having tea on the back lawn, Paulie in the playpen, the Turners would say, "Isn't it heaven when the servants are gone!" They would laugh at this notion because it was so contrary to what they actually felt. They knew they lived well thanks in part to what Laban and Murugi contributed to the household.

Then Derek's editors informed him that he was being transferred back to the States. The paper had closed one of its bureaus. Without their knowing it, the staff of correspondents had been placed in a game of musical chairs—several were being reassigned—and Derek was the man who was left standing, the man without a post. The experienced man replacing him knew nothing about Africa. This was not unusual in journalism. In fact, some editors felt that "new eyes" offered valuable insights. But Derek was distressed. He had been hired to do the Africa job. He knew a great deal about the continent, especially after four years on the job, and felt he offered the paper and its readers in-depth coverage of a kind a newcomer to the territory could not provide. Moreover, he had come to see himself as an advocate for the continent. The new man's lack of familiarity with Africa and its peoples and their ways of living might mean that his cultural baggage would color his reporting. That seemed bad for the paper and its readers, bad for Africa.

But there was no appeal to the decision. Derek and his colleagues had occasionally talked about transfers. The strong consensus was that a correspondent must be seen as a team player. Wherever the paper wanted to send him, that was the place he wanted to go.

So the Turners made preparations to leave. They informed friends and associates and landlords of their imminent departure, looked into shipping their household effects back to the States, began the process of filling out forms: for their income tax payments and for Laban's and Murugi's, for Paulie's citizenship papers and birth certificate, for the release and shipment of their household goods. They had a meeting with Murugi and Laban and told them the news. They assured the pair that they would write recommendations and, if possible, try to place them in new jobs. They would also give them a bit of money to tide them over.

Laban came back a day or two later to say that he wanted to try a different line of work: automobile repair. He knew a man in the industrial area who could train him in what was called "panel-beating" (which seemed to involve removing dents). The instruction would cost the equivalent of about five months' wages. Derek agreed to finance this instruction, which would take place after the Turners left East Africa. He very much hoped that Laban's contact was honest.

Dee's women friends quickly asked to have Paulie's crib, playpen, and other paraphernalia. Dee told them about Murugi and her good qualities. Since a steady flow of young expatriates was entering the country, it seemed likely that Murugi would find a place in another American household.

Then one Saturday night, five weeks before the Turners were to leave the country, they returned from seeing a play to find Murugi sitting uncomfortably on a chair outside the baby's room, wincing against pain and hardly able to move. She pointed to her ankle. She indicated that she had injured it, apparently while stepping off the small porch outside the kitchen.

"I better take her to the hospital," Derek told Dee.

The Turners stood on either side of Murugi, their arms under hers, and lifted her onto one foot. They carried her to the Turners' car and settled her inside.

Derek took her to Nairobi Hospital. During a consultation in Kikuyu, nurses examined her ankle and informed Murugi that they could do little for her then, in the middle of the night. She must come back in the morning. When this was relayed to Derek, he agreed to bring her first thing. He signed for a pair of crutches which the nurses gave to Murugi.

Although he had often left Murugi outside the hostel where she lived, Derek had never entered the building. Now he guided her up the porch stairway. Because she seemed uncertain about the crutches, Derek held her arm just under her armpit so that she would not fall. Residents idling on the porch watched the pair, a few of them standing in the presence of a white man, but none of them speaking or offering help.

As he took Murugi inside, Derek discovered that the main room, once a parlor, was a maze of curtains hung on wires. He helped Murugi down a hallway of cloth and shortly arrived at a cubicle. She pulled the fabric aside. Derek helped her into a curtained enclosure, large enough only for a bed, a chair, a small dresser, and a rod on which to hang clothes. He took the crutches and helped Murugi onto the bed. She kept repeating, *"Asante sana, Bwana. Asante sana."*

Returning outside, Derek found the porch filled with men and women. The news had spread of a white man in the building and the Africans stared at Derek as if he were responsible for Murugi's pain. He nodded and hurried to the car.

When Derek got back to the house, he found Dee in the nursery. She was sitting in the dim illumination of a night light, holding the baby, moving back and forth in a rocker. "How is she?"

"They couldn't do anything for her tonight," Derek said. "I take her back at 9:00 AM." He told his wife about the quarters in which Murugi lived.

The next day Derek fetched Murugi early and took her to the hospital. She had fractured her ankle. After it was set in a cast, Derek took her home.

He did not see her again until a few days later when on the last day of the month he went to her house with the wages owed her for the previous two weeks. She refused to accept them. Derek returned home and told Dee, "This is not good. And I have to hit the road again." Derek's editor had cabled, instructing him to take a ten-day trip to Malawi, Mozambique, Angola, and Rhodesia. "Why," he complained, "did this accident happen now?"

Dee told him, "Because it's a metaphor."

"Oh, yeah? Well, it's one that requires a cast." Dee smiled indulgently. Finally Derek relaxed and smiled, too. "Okay. How's it a metaphor?"

"It says, 'Your leaving does me injury. You leave and I break.'"

"Isn't that a little far-fetch—"

"But I reject that," said Dee, interrupting him. "For a year now we've had the Kikuyus here with us and they've enriched our lives. We're better people because Laban and Murugi have been in the house."

Derek nodded, but he was not completely convinced.

"And they're better off, too. Laban has a much stronger sense of himself," Dee went on. "He's ready to try a new line of work and he has a girlfriend who spends nights with him. Murugi has benefited too. Our going doesn't injure her. It gives her a chance to gather up her talents and use them to enrich somebody else's life. Right?"

Finally Derek nodded again.

Dee studied him carefully. "Your going doesn't injure you, either, Dare. If you believe that, Murugi's ankle will heal faster."

Derek gave his wife the look of a skeptical newsman. "Just the facts, please," he said.

"Go on your trip," Dee told him, "and do the best job you can."

When Derek returned from his trip, he learned that Laban had told Dee, as soon as she returned from the airport, that Murugi intended to ask for compensation for breaking her ankle.

"Did you give it to her?" Derek asked.

"No," Dee said. "I talked to her. Laban acted as translator."

"What'd you say?"

"I assured her that our leaving could not injure her," Dee explained. "I said we'd take care of the hospital costs and would try to find her a new job. I told her that she'd enriched our lives and we hoped we'd done the same for hers. There couldn't be any injury out of that."

"And she knew what you were talking about?"

"Of course," said Dee. "They understand these things a lot better than we do."

She continued, "While you were gone, every time I thought of Murugi, I affirmed all the good things about her: her affection for Paulie, her diligence and cleanliness, her good humor, her style. Her virtue. She really is virtuous, you know."

Derek nodded.

"And we're virtuous, too," Dee said. "And fair. And we love Murugi."

"And how is she?" Derek asked.

Dee smiled. "It is all right," she said, using the phrase with Laban's special inflection. "She never asked for compensation. I'm sure she won't."

By the time they all parted, the cast was off Murugi's ankle and she was walking normally again. The Turners had written laudatory reference letters for both Laban and Murugi. They had given them presents of money. Murugi seemed almost certain to find a new job and the Turners had given Laban the money he needed to cover his panel-beating training.

As they said goodbye, both Laban and Murugi bent respectfully forward to shake Derek's hand. Laban held Derek's hand with both of his in that special gesture of African regard. When they turned to Dee, neither Kikuyu spoke. But their eyes were misty. Dee was not prepared to say farewell by shaking hands. These people were members of the family. She hugged them both.

THE BARKING DOG

WHEN OXFAM SENT TOBY GOOCH to Bobo-Dioulasso in Burkina Faso as its director for West Africa, his wife Jenny found a house which a Dutch family had just left. The house suited the Gooches perfectly. Jenny was delighted. It was only after they moved in that they discovered why the Dutch family had moved out. The neighbors' dog barked every night.

It barked all night long. If there was light in the sky, it growled at shadows. It yipped at stars and howled at the moon. If the night was as black as the earth itself, the dog whimpered like a creature afraid of the dark. If someone passed on the road, it raised a ruckus; it rarr-rarr-rarred at being disturbed. Along about morning when the night was silent and empty, the dog whined with loneliness.

Every night Jenny sat up in bed. Toby would moan, "I'm afraid to turn over, afraid the damn dog will hear and wail louder." Jenny said nothing. She listened for the sound of her daughters sleeping. But she heard only the ruckus next door.

Dogs barking at night: the Gooches had faced this problem in Nairobi and Addis Ababa. There the barking had been sporadic; they had shrugged it off. This Burkina dog was the worst case they'd ever encountered. And now they had two small children. The girls needed restful sleep. But the prospects for that seemed doubtful.

Jenny sought out the previous residents of the house she and Toby occupied. They were aid technicians from the Netherlands. "That dog is a real problem," commiserated the Dutch woman. On several occasions, she told Jenny, she had appealed to her African neighbor, a school teacher, just as she would have to any other woman. "I said to her, 'Please, stop the dog barking! My children cannot sleep.' But she did nothing. We moved away because of that dog."

And it was still barking.

Now Jenny and Toby and their children were having to put up with it, with the howling, yowling, yapping, yipping, and yelping all night long.

Jenny pondered the Dutch woman's approach. There must be some reason why it failed. She appealed to the elderly servant who helped her run the house. "Achille," she said, "you are wise. I have no idea what to do about the barking dog. Your wisdom must guide me."

"Take a present to your neighbor," Achille advised. "She's intelligent. She will wonder why you've come."

"What kind of present?" Jenny asked.

"Perhaps something you have here," Achille suggested. "You keep hens."

"Should I take her some eggs?" Jenny asked.

"Precisely," Achille said. Then he counseled, "And please, Madame, you must say exactly the words I tell you to say."

Jenny selected the best eggs from the hens she and Toby kept. She placed them in a basket and called on her neighbor. The Burkina teacher received her pleasantly and Jenny offered her the eggs. "I am concerned about you," she told the neighbor, using exactly the words Achille told her to say. "Is there trouble at your house? We hear the dog all night. Can I help?"

The neighbor smiled and took the eggs. She thanked Jenny for her visit and said there was no trouble at her house.

"The visit went well, did it, Madame?" Achille asked when Jenny returned.

She assured him that it had gone well.

"Good," he said.

And that was that. The Gooches's relations remained cordial with the Burkina family next door. They saw the dog outside. It wagged its tail and sometimes barked a bit during the day. But never again did it bark at night.

A NEWSMAN SCRATCHES AN ITCH

GABRIEL GERRITY MADE HIS FIRST TRIP to South Africa to cover the election. He also went there to write a novel. Well before he arrived, he knew what both his dispatches and his novel would say. He figured that out on the train down from Rhodesia.

It was a boring and bumpy ride, a day and a half of high dry veld, first in western Rhodesia, then in eastern Botswana, lastly in the northern Transvaal. Gerrity kept busy, though. He read the papers he bought in Salisbury and the papers he bought in Bulawayo and did a wrap-up of his Rhodesia coverage. He took his meals in his compartment.

By the time he stopped for afternoon tea, he realized the train was passing through Botswana. He drank his tea looking at the high dry veld. When the train stopped at a siding, Gerrity got off and stood beside the track. He listened carefully and smelled the air for sense-impressions he would use in his novel. He stamped the ground and kicked together a pile of earth.

Then he bent down, scooped the earth into his hands, smelled it and let it filter through his fingers.

By this time Africans had appeared—apparently from no-where—to hawk carvings and trinkets, woven baskets and hats. When Gerrity reached into his pocket, the Africans clustered about him. He took out a notebook and said nothing. He jotted notes about the scent of the earth, the imploring faces, the ragged clothes, and the arrogance of white South Africans who leaned out of the train windows and bargained down the price of the trinkets. Then Gerrity took a deep breath, assessing the odors of the people about him, put away the notebook, and got back on the train.

When he appeared in his compartment, the hawkers clam-ored outside it. They knocked on the window, crying, *"Baas, baas,* master, master." They hoisted carvings about their heads, chanting the only English they knew, "Lovely souvenirs! Very cheap, too! Make me an offer, *baas."*

Gerrity turned away from the window and got out his typewriter. By dinnertime he had finished two pieces on Botswana: one a new-eyes-impressioner that catalogued the smell of the earth, the look of the people and the emptiness of the veld, the other a general situationer in which he discussed Botswana's development prospects. After dinner he wrote a story describing a first-time visitor's sense of moral outrage upon entering South Africa and realizing what apartheid really meant. Gerrity himself had not yet entered the country. He had not yet looked apartheid in the face. That was not a problem. That was the advantage of knowing the kind of reportage his editor expected.

The outrage piece completed, he opened his compartment door, stuck his head into the corridor and yelled to the African steward at the other end of it. "Hey, boy! C'mere!" When the steward arrived, Gerrity ordered early morning tea.

Late that evening at Mafeking the train actually crossed into South Africa. By then Gerrity was working on his novel.

Gerrity's novel was going to be about a journalist who went to South Africa to cover the election.

Gerrity saw South Africa—without ever having seen it—as so full of contradictions and tensions, conflicts, and submerged anxieties that all by itself his novel would explode into action. The country's cruelty would provide its own elements of drama. The journalist wandering through those elements would serve as the Catalyst; he would make the elements flame and flare and shatter. The journalist would be a kind of Graham Greene character: rootless and urbane, a world-weary Actor-Observer. Someone like himself, Gerrity thought.

Gerrity had a Theory about the creation of a novel. The main thing was truth—Truth. There was nothing complicated about capturing Truth. All you did was write everything down just the way it happened. Get it down, that was the basic thing.

Then you went through and tightened it, compressed it, eliminated all but the bare essentials. The fact that you scratched out the dross meant that what remained had Tension and Solidity. Tension and Solidity were parts of the iceberg that didn't show. They were there all the same, the sub-structure of what did show. And what did show was Art.

Of course, you had to have a story to tell. Gerrity had Theories about that, too. First, you had to have a Stress-Locale where contradictions and tensions, conflicts and submerged anxieties were present.

Second, you needed a Catalyst, an Actor-Observer, the novel's potential hero. (Gerrity knew that he himself possessed Actor-Observer potential. He was not merely one of those people who said, "There are several novels in my life." He had proved it. He had already written the first of them.) Once you identified the Actor-Observer, you introduced the character into the Stress-Locale.

Third, you required a Foil, a contrasting character. Gerrity's instincts told him that you could no longer do a novel where sex existed only for the reader who saw between the lines. Readers went to novels, in fact, to have non-physical sex experiences. And so for Gerrity the Foil was a device for SEX. The Foil became the Actor-Observer's lover. Gerrity planned to be obvious. His novel would describe coitus every twenty pages: in half a dozen different settings, using at least as many positions, at five different times of day, in three different states of passion: raw, refined, and relaxed.

It was more than Gerrity's instincts which produced these Theories. It was experience. He had learned from writing his first novel, from its failure. Writing that novel had taken him five years. He had started it the summer he returned from a year as a Fulbright scholar in Luxembourg. (Few scholars applied for Fulbrights to Luxembourg and so Gerrity was able to secure one.) At the time of writing he had considered Luxembourg, where he set the novel's action, to be a Stress-Locale. This was because Charles De Gaulle had said no to British entry into the Common Market the winter he was there. That had seemed (incorrectly, as it turned out) to change the course of Europe. A figure very much like Gerrity himself had been the Actor-Observer. There had been a Foil, too, a Luxembourger girl.

Unfortunately, Greta refused to have sex. That refusal caused Gerrity literary as well as physical frustrations. She came often to his room and lay with him on his bed in the darkness. She allowed him to kiss her and touch her a little, but that was all.

When he begged her to be more adventurous, she refused. When he demanded the reason, she would say, "I am a Catholic." He would answer, "But for God's sake you're not a nun!" She would push his hands away and turn her back.

Unable to undress her, Gerrity would undress himself. He would pace naked about the room, cursing the Pope and her convent education. He would beg her to join his nakedness. He would kiss her and caress her, but still she refused him. Finally he asked her to marry him. She refused him that, too.

To achieve Truth he had written it all down just as it happened. Then he had chipped and chipped away to get Tension and Solidity. Still, even after five years, it didn't quite gel. At least not for publishers. At first Gerrity thought himself ahead of his time, a stylistic pacesetter. Then he realized what he had vaguely suspected all along. The trouble was the absence of SEX. Damn Greta! With this new novel there would be purple passages of SEX every twenty pages.

Gerrity regarded South Africa as the ideal Stress-Locale. There a Foil would appear like a Femme Fatale emerging out of mist. However she reacted to the Actor-Observer (that is to say, to Gerrity himself), her response would pulsate with political implication. If she seethed with a passion so fierce as to devour him (which was what he hoped), that would demonstrate that apartheid civilization was a time-bomb on which the Foil must dance until the explosion came. If she reacted with inhibition, that would dramatize apartheid's blockage of normal human relations. Hesitation, vacillation: these would indicate insoluble moral dilemmas.

Whatever her response, there would be SEX. Amid a rising crescendo of coital descriptions, the Stress-Locale would frustrate the lovers. And Theme would emerge.

Just how it would do this, Gerrity did not know. But it did not matter. Once things were started right, the end would take care of itself. The muses or the graces would appropriate The Work and finish it for him.

The most important thing was to find the right Foil.

Notes on the novel so absorbed Gerrity's thoughts that he did not even realize the train had stopped. Then the door of his private compartment opened. A young woman, blonde, in a jersey and very short skirt entered the compartment, carrying a small plastic suitcase. Gerrity looked up. The girl glanced at him with wide and frightened eyes, then looked away. She sat as far from him as possible. She held the suitcase on her lap and bit her lips as if to control turbulent emotions.

Gerrity peered out the window and saw the station lights. "Have we stopped?" he asked. "What place is this?"

"Mafeking," the girl whispered.

Gerrity heard the awkward music of Afrikaans in her voice. He looked back at her and examined her carefully. She was tall, rather pretty, eighteen, maybe twenty. She looked straight ahead as he studied her, absenting herself from his scrutiny. She seemed very vulnerable as she rested the plastic suitcase on knees she held rigidly clamped together. She had long splendid legs that narrowed to bare ankles and feet that were encased in shoes so worn the leather had begun to split at the heels. Gerrity was a legs man. It was not easy for him to lift his eyes from the girl's tapered cylinders of temptation.

When he managed to do so, the girl looked at him. She said, "Sir, I know this is a private compartment. But, if you please, could I ride here for twenty minutes? Just till we get well away from Mafeking."

"Of course," said Gerrity. He wondered if she were a terrorist.

That was all there was. The writing simply stopped.

Tyler shook his head and studied the notebook. It was gray, of a convenient size to stick in your jacket pocket—just right for a journalist—and on its cover within a red shape that looked like an ink blot were the words CROXLEY NOTES a John Dickinson Product. Up in the top left-hand corner was the word GERRITY. It was printed by a hand that Tyler recognized as his own.

Inside the front cover were stapled notes about how the whatever-it-was-to-be about Gerrity writing his novel might evolve. They made little sense to Tyler. He could not remember writing them, but knew that he must have. And when would that have been? He had not been in South Africa in twenty-five years.

In the back of the notebook several pages lay covered with cramped scribblings, overlaid with interlineations, squiggly arrows, and marginal scratchings: the beginnings of another whatever-it-might-be. The scratchings read:

"Two extraordinary things happened to Ernest Dace that winter quarter. First, he fell in love with a student in one of the classes he taught. Not really in love, of course—although his dry throat did croak the words 'I love you' that late afternoon in his office as he flung himself upon the thigh-booted but otherwise naked body of the girl. Not really in love, of course, because Dace believed that no man could love, truly love, more than one woman at a time and Dace, of course, loved his wife.

"The second thing that happened to the professor that winter quarter was a threat against his life."

There was more about Dace, but not much more. There were also notes about a Cape Province town called Franschhoek, originally settled by French Huguenots. Tyler and his wife had holed up there for a week while he wrote dispatches, reporting on interviews with government leaders in Cape Town.

The notes said, "The valley was almost always windy. Sometimes the wind was gentle, sometimes harsh, heralding the approach of winter. Sometimes the sky was patched with clouds and sometimes it was a clear, uninterrupted curtain of blue with banks of clouds hovering behind the mountains, now and then caught in the spiked peaks that circled the valley, occasionally shrouding the peaks and flowing down from them—flowing, flowing but never actually reaching into the valley. Sometimes they hung there like a thick tablecloth edging over the headland."

There were too many uses of "sometimes" in the paragraph, Tyler thought, and the long sentence was much too long. But he recognized what the notes were: a newsman scratching an itch, working at being a writer. The scratcher was not satisfied with being merely a collector of facts, a rehearser of interviews. Something in him yearned to be more: a writer, an artist. He longed to create—in Dace and Gerrity and the girl who entered the compartment at Mafeking—characters who would have some semblance of life. He wondered if that long ago note-taker who was he had planned to place Gerrity in Franschhoek.

Would he seduce the Foil there? Or encounter some Catalytic Event? And what was the threat against Dace's life? He had no idea.

How cynical he had been! Gerrity and Dace, journalist and professor. Two purveyors of knowledge, both fools. Had he been writing about himself? Wasn't that what writers did? He had been a newsman then, one of those self-professed priests of Objectivity. Had a reporter's skepticism required him to view his characters—even himself—as fools? Had he regarded purveyors of knowledge as know-nothings? In any case, self-interested dunces did not make sympathetic Actor-Observers. Perhaps that was why he wrote about clouds over Franschhoek.

These scratchings of an itch that would not stop: they had punctuated Tyler's life as a journalist. The newsman knew more about the stories he reported than he could possibly tell, more about the people and how they looked and smelled, more about their probable motivations than space or the God of Objectivity or the Cult of Just-The-Facts would allow him to include. If the reporter were a writer, he sensed that fiction and the characters it would permit him to create could reveal a deeper, more complete truth than mere news reports. Moreover, his imagination needed freedom, room to run. It wanted to throw words about extravagantly, wantonly, not responsibly, but like a profligate.

But the paper demanded news: dispatches, situationers, brighteners, at least three pieces a week. News was like a train that never stopped. The reporter was on the train and if he were doing his job, he left his imagination in the baggage room at the station. He was always hustling. He was far too busy to spend time with characters like Gabriel Gerrity and Ernest Dace. He could allow them no more being than a shadow possessed flashing past the window of a train.

PEPPER

WHEN WE WERE SAYING GOODBYE outside the restaurant in the late afternoon light, I just could not help taking Jocelyn Maxwell's hands in mine and looking into those strangely guarded eyes of hers. "I do hope Pepper gets better," I said. "I hope she gets better soon."

She nodded, then managed a smile. "I do wish we could have entertained you at home," she replied. "But right now it's just not possible."

"But this was lovely!" I told her. She seemed so uncertain of herself that I gave her a hug. She held me tentatively, her body guarding itself the way her eyes guarded her soul. As if somehow we would criticize her or her husband. As if we would blame them for the condition of their child. When I released her, she turned to Bruce and offered him her hand. "Nice to see you again," she said. Bruce took the small hand and gave her one of his looks. "Journalist looks," I call them and I ask him please not to use them when we are being private people. It's as if his eyes are penetrating the very depths of your soul to see if you're lying. No wonder Jocelyn was feeling guarded; I hardly blamed her.

I turned to Hazen Maxwell and said goodbye to him and to the Forestas. I told them—really meaning it when I said it—that if they were ever in Johannesburg, we would like to take them to dinner. "I'm not sure we can manage a place quite as lovely as this," I said, "but we'll try."

We went off to our Land Cruiser—Bruce insists on renting Land Cruisers even though they're expensive—and the others went to their cars. When I glanced back at them, I was pleased to see that Hazen had his arm around Joss. She was looking at him with an intensity I would have called passionate in the days before Bruce made me conscious of my fondness for clichés. Even at the distance I was from them, the bond between them was palpable and I was glad. A relationship needs strong anchors if it's to survive the challenges of an emotionally disturbed child.

We were in Malawi, a small, pretty country stretched beside a long, narrow lake, and the Zomba plateau where we had met the Maxwells and the Forestas for Sunday lunch was truly a beautiful place. As we descended the plateau to Blantyre, the country's commercial capital, we passed through a region of tea plantations. The air was clear and fresh. In late afternoon light the bushes of tea, cut chest-high in benches so that workers could easily pluck off the leaves, shone with a splendid greenness. Light from the waning sun backlit the leaves and made them glow.

"I never thought I'd come to Malawi," I told Bruce. He grunted, staring at the road from behind the steering wheel. "Until I met you, I'm not sure I even knew Malawi existed." He smiled automatically, hearing my inflection more than my words. He had been preoccupied all afternoon. I wondered if he were working on a story. Or more precisely—I'm learning about precision of expression—I wondered what story he was working on. Stories are always at the back of a journalist's head.

We were on our way to Kenya. Officially Bruce's territory includes all of sub-Saharan Africa—although most of his stories deal, of course, with South Africa. Still, he likes to do pieces from other parts of the continent if only to remind readers that nations actually exist—like Malawi—that they've rarely, if ever, thought about. He enjoys the travel, too. He has a wanderlust. He tries to get to East Africa at least once a year. Readers want a wildlife situationer and he likes to stay on top of things going on in that area.

Now that we are married—we'd been married five months then—he lets me come along. My "new eyes," as he calls them, see things from a fresh perspective. "Why don't you do a piece about so-and-so?" I sometimes suggest. Usually he smiles indulgently, but now and then something actually comes of my ideas.

"Was Hazen Maxwell informative?" I asked.

"A very careful guy," Bruce said.

While the wives and I had walked around the gardens of the Zomba hotel, Bruce interviewed the two men. Maxwell was the American Embassy's Deputy Chief of Mission, and Foresta headed the Political Section. Since the Ambassador was away, Maxwell pointed out that he was actually Chargé d'Affaires.

"How about Jim Foresta?" I asked.

"More forthcoming. He wanted to talk about how the country's progressing now that it's finally gotten out from under the yoke of old Kamuzu Banda. But readers don't care. I'm not sure the State Department cares." Banda was the medical doctor who took Malawi to independence, consolidated his power with the usual excesses and impeded what Bruce's reporting would have called "the march toward full nationhood."

"Did they have theories about the murders?" I asked.

During the couple of days we'd been in Malawi Bruce had investigated a curious series of murders in Blantyre: someone dispatching enemies and trying to make it look like the work of leopards. The murders bore a witchcraft angle and possessed a resonance locally that we, who do not believe in witchcraft, cannot comprehend. Such things fascinate readers. They'll follow a story about bizarre murders to the final paragraph. But they'll hardly scan past the lead of a substantial story—like Malawi's progress toward nationhood. Bruce didn't want to talk; that was obvious. He shrugged. Staring meditatively at the road, he drove on. We really didn't talk again until dinner.

By then we were in the dining room of the Mount Soche Hotel in Blantyre, having soup and salad. The Mount Soche is an older hotel, built around the time of Independence. I liked its lack of pretension and its wonderful views over the countryside. "I'm glad the Maxwells liked Kenya," I told Bruce, hoping we might talk. There were few people in the dining room and the waiters watched us, eager to serve. I thought we ought to look as if we liked each other—at least enough to converse. "Are we going to Kilaguni and Mzima Springs?" I asked. "I'd love to see hippos under water."

Bruce grunted, removing tomatoes from the salad.

"Did you remember Hazen Maxwell from when you'd met him before?"

"Yeah. He looked familiar."

Bruce met the Maxwells on a trip to West Africa. Hazen was serving as the Embassy's Political Officer in Bamako, Mali. As

Bruce glanced at me across the table, I sensed that he felt some reservation about Hazen. I started to ask another question, but caught myself. Bruce hates me to interview him, as he calls it. It's best if I wait till he's ready to tell me things.

I had no idea what Bruce's reservation might be. As for myself, I quite liked the Maxwells. They had style and Jocelyn dressed well, using items picked up in local markets as accessories. They also seemed very much in love. I don't mean that they acted like newlyweds. In fact, they seemed controlled and unemotional. But now and then you'd catch a glance between them. It gave you a hint of heat in their relationship. Sentimental of me to like them for that, I suppose, but that's an unusual quality to sense in a marriage that's gone on for a dozen years. A more customary reaction is that a couple makes a good team, is "in synch," and that they work together well. This last is a real advantage in the Foreign Service. There a spouse is part of the country team whether she or he—usually she—likes it or not.

I also felt a sympathy for the Maxwells because I knew they'd had a rough go. Foreign Service sounds exciting and romantic: traveling and living in exotic places, meeting interesting people, watching history unfold. But the truth is the Foreign Service is full of hot, buggy, and undeveloped posts where you would not want to spend two days, much less two years. And a lot of the posts are dangerous. Time was when diplomats enjoyed an immunity from danger, but in these days of terrorists, diplomats and even their families are victimized by politically aggrieved groups happy to harm unprotected people.

In that sense journalism is much preferable. Foreign correspondents live in decent places. Those places have to be sufficiently developed to access a journalist's equipment. When a correspondent—or even his wife, if she's lucky like me—lands in some of these wretched places where FSOs are living, he stays only a few days. He picks people's brains and then moves on. And if there are terrorist groups, they don't want to kill him; they want to exploit him to publicize their plight.

The Maxwells had an additional challenge: an eight-year-old daughter with severe emotional problems. When that happens in the Foreign Service, it's very tough. The Maxwells were thinking of sending Pepper back to the States to live with his parents. That would mean not only terrible financial outlays beyond what insurance would cover, but the real likelihood that they would lose their daughter—at least until they returned for a Washington assignment. Or that they might lose her forever.

As if those weren't enough troubles, Joss Maxwell was in some kind of highway accident in Mali. It caused her memory loss and she mentioned something about restorative surgery to her face, poor woman. She was forced to apologize to Bruce about the memory loss when they met earlier that day. Bruce had apparently gone to the Maxwell's home in Bamako for a meal. Joss had to admit that she had no recollection of the occasion at all.

I admired the fact that, in spite of these challenges, Joss and Hazen seemed so happy together. They had marshaled their forces, all right. Plastic surgery sometimes extinguishes a man's love. It was clear that they were still very attracted to one another. During lunch Hazen and Joss touched each other—just casual, stay-connected touches—almost as much as Bruce touched me, and we've been married less than a year.

After dinner while I started to pack our duffels for Kenya, Bruce made us nightcaps and paced the room. "Sweets," I finally said. "Why are you so preoccupied?"

"Am I getting on your nerves? Sorry."

"You aren't working on a story, are you?" I watched him wandering around the room. "This isn't the working-on-a-story kind of preoccupation. I can tell."

He went to the window and stared down at the lighted pool behind the hotel. Finally he turned and asked, "Did I ever tell you about that trip to Bamako? When I first met the Maxwells?"

I was pleased that at last he was ready to talk. "Is this a trick question?" I asked, flirting a bit.

Bruce smiled. "It was about two years ago," he said. "I was doing a swing through West Africa. I'd been in Nigeria, Ghana, Ivory Coast, Burkina Faso. Flying in to Bamako, I thought, 'Jesus, do I have a visa to this place?'

"I checked my passport. Come to find out I did not have one. I'd requested one, thought I'd gotten it, but it had never come through. The plane was going on to Paris and I didn't want Mali Immigration to deny me entrance and ship me off to France.

"Fortunately, it's a small airport. As I walked through to the Immigration Desk, I saw a woman who had that unmistakable American look: sparkling eyes, a ready smile. She also had lovely hands, long, tapering fingers."

"You gave her a very thorough check-out," I said.

"Professional habit," he replied.

I tossed him another flirtatious smile.

"I called to her and said, 'Do you know any American Embassy people? I've arrived here without a visa and I don't want to be deported.' She turned out to be Jocelyn Maxwell."

"Really?" I said, a bit surprised. At dinner her eyes had seemed more veiled than sparkling—except during those glances at her husband. But then she and Bruce had both been alone at the Bamako airport, and Bruce was probably exuding that magnetic readiness for experience so characteristic of him.

Here Bruce and Jocelyn, accompanied by their spouses, were being demure.

"An Embassy family was leaving for France on the plane I'd come in on," Bruce continued. "She was sure her husband could straighten out my visa problems. Which he did."

"You didn't say anything about that today," I said.

"I started to—" He shrugged, "I thanked Maxwell again for saving my ass from the wrath of editors." Bruce took a meditative sip of his drink.

"You went to their house?" I asked. I didn't want him to wander off, pacing again.

"I had lunch with them. Followed Maxwell out to the house from the Embassy in my car because I was driving on up to Ségou to get a look at rural Mali. Pepper, the little girl, was there, brought home from school for lunch by a servant."

"Was it obvious that she had problems?"

Bruce gazed at me rather strangely. "I'd say it was obvious there were problems in the household." I could sense him being precise with language. "I felt that Maxwell and Joss weren't getting along—"

"But they seem so close."

"Yes, don't they?'

"The change of posts must have been good for the marriage."

Bruce looked at me with a curious ambivalence, almost on the brink of saying something, but holding back. He started moving around the room again.

"Don't pace," I said. "What are you not telling me?"

"At the house," he finally went on, "I saw that the little girl was very sensitive to the undercurrents of tension between her parents. She and her mother seemed very close. That wasn't surprising. They hadn't been in Mali all that long."

"They probably had to sustain each other through all kinds of adjustments."

"The girl and I talked a few minutes," Bruce said. "Maxwell had disappeared in the house somewhere and Joss was supervising things in the kitchen."

"What did you talk about?"

"A photo. I saw a framed picture of Joss and another woman on a shelf. The other woman was Joss's sister. Heather? Fern? Botanical, I think."

"Rose, perhaps. Or Petunia. Or Fleur. Don't you love Fleur?"

"*Ah, oui! Je l'aime*," said Bruce. We laughed. He relaxed. "The name was definitely English. Anyway, the photo made the two women look enough alike to be twins." He hesitated again. "Pepper said they 'hated' each other." He got a far-away look in his eyes, drifting off.

"Kids talk like that," I said, trying to keep him focused. "So— Did the lunch go all right?"

He nodded, coming back to me.

"Yeah. As we were having coffee—the servant had walked Pepper back to school by then—Max got a call from the Embassy. He was needed immediately. We left together. He got me headed toward Ségou and then went in the opposite direction toward town. I hadn't gone very far when I realized I'd left my coat. I could have picked it up later, but my notebook was in the pocket. So I went back."

We looked at each other across the room. And I suddenly understood why there was such hesitation in his relating the incident.

"And she was alone in the house," I said. "She'd sent the cook off on some errand."

"To market," Bruce said.

"So you slept with her," I said.

He shrugged.

"You dear tom cat," I said. "What had she done? Put your coat someplace where you wouldn't find it?"

He shrugged. Maybe. Maybe not.

I felt an irrational jealousy rising in me. Bruce is very attractive. He was single then and he liked new experiences. I knew there had been other women, probably more than I wanted to acknowledge, but as a gentleman he had never before told me about them. The jealousy was my problem, something I had to deal with. I did not want it to put strains in our relationship, especially when we were on a business trip. Still, I asked, "Why are you telling me this?"

After a long moment he said, "The woman I made love to that day is not the woman we had lunch with in Zomba."

I frowned.

"Did you notice that woman's hands?" he asked. "Very small. Short, stubby fingers."

He started pacing again. I watched him, wondering what he was talking about.

Finally he said, "Before I left the house that afternoon, I mentioned to Jocelyn that her daughter and I had talked about the photo of her and her sister. 'Are you twins?' I asked.

"'No,' she said. 'We're a year apart. People are always mistaking us for twins.'

"I said, 'Your daughter—'

"And before I could go on, Joss said, 'My sister's a bitch. She manipulates men.'

"I laughed at that," Bruce exclaimed. "In fact, I said, 'Haven't you just been manipulating me?'"

"I don't imagine she liked that," I remarked. "What did she say?"

"She said, 'She seduces my husband—to put it politely. He gets himself called back to Washington so he can fuck her.'"

"So she seduced you to get back at him."

Bruce laughed, one of those hearty, full-throated guffaws that I love. "And I thought it was because I was irresistible," he said. "Because correspondents are romantic. And well-known as boudoir athletes."

"Of course, they are," I twitted him. "I'm sure she wanted you as a trophy."

"I can't say I was flattered," Bruce admitted. "I asked her why she didn't divorce him and raise her child at home. She said she liked living overseas. God knows she may have even liked seducing itinerants like me. She was adamant that there'd be no divorce. She claimed she'd told her husband she'd ruin his Foreign Service career if he sued her for divorce." He finished off his drink. "Some of these FSOs are obsessed about promotion, you know. Maxwell struck me as being one of them."

I thought back over our afternoon together. Maxwell had seemed a little impressed with himself. He had mentioned several times that he was the Chargé d'Affaires.

Bruce refreshed our drinks and paced again. Finally he said, "The woman we had lunch with today is the woman in the photo, the almost twin."

"Heather," I said. "Or whoever."

He nodded.

"Wasn't something said at lunch about Jocelyn's sister having died?"

Bruce nodded again. "Give me the quote," he demanded. "Gotta memorize the quote. Sometimes you have to leave the interview mentally in order to fix the exact words."

I frowned. I wasn't sure what he meant.

"'It hurts too much to talk about it.' That's what she said. This Jocelyn we met at lunch said there was too much pain for her to talk about her sister. She put that subject off limits."

I remembered now that those were her words.

"Whenever we drifted close to anything personal, the Forestas jumped in to change the subject. You notice that?"

In fact, I had noticed that. Foresta, Maxwell's political officer, did exactly what he knew his superior wanted.

Bruce kept pacing. "I've been trying to figure out how they did it," he said.

"What's your hunch, trained observer?"

"I don't know," he replied. "Maxwell came down here on a direct transfer. Without home leave. They must have flown from Bamako to Paris. Maxwell would have needed to get Pepper out of the way. And to establish her as emotionally disturbed. Maybe he insisted that he and Jocelyn put her under psychiatric observation somewhere in Europe. For depression maybe. Then somewhere along the line—Paris, Athens, Nairobi, probably the earlier the easier—he and Heather killed Jocelyn and dumped her body."

Hearing the words made my stomach turn. At the same time my curiosity was aroused. "Dumped it how?" I asked.

"Tossed it along a roadside. Naked. Maybe there was semen in it. On it. Maybe they mutilated—"

"Oh, please! I don't even want to—"

"Another sex crime for local police to unravel."

He paced for a while, mulling it in his mind. I got the duffels ready for the flight the next morning. Finally he said, "Heather starts traveling on Jocelyn's passport. The resemblance is easily close enough for that. When they arrive here in Malawi, Maxwell introduces Heather to everyone as his wife. Heather becomes Jocelyn. He has her issued a new passport.

"The Foreign Service is a small community," Bruce went on, "but officers specializing in Francophone West Africa are not likely to be sent to English-speaking East Africa. And staff people without area expertise will probably be sent to other regions. People the Maxwells do run into, people like me, are told about the highway accident, the restorative surgery, and the memory loss. And the rules of etiquette, which still apply in the Foreign Service, prevent much probing. 'Oh, please! It hurts too much to talk about!'"

I tried to remember Jocelyn's expression when she said those words. I think she may have bitten her lower lip and glanced at her husband. And then Jim Foresta had changed the subject.

"As long as officers are competent," Bruce went on, "FSOs are very protective of the group. I'm sure Maxwell is competent. His ambassador is a political appointee so basically he runs things. He's Cardinal Wolsey and nobody in the Embassy challenges him. Why would they? I'm sure there's a sense here—the Forestas showed you what it is—that the Maxwells have made significant sacrifices for their country."

"Poor Pepper."

"Yes. She was a nice little kid."

We were quiet for a while. Eventually Bruce checked that all the documents we needed were in order. I watched him, trying not to think of the Maxwells. Finally he said, "Bedtime, lovely one. We've got an early flight."

After we turned out the lights and kissed goodnight, I stared for a long time at the darkness. I felt Bruce doing the same.

I could not help thinking of eight-year-old Pepper. Did Maxwell have her fly alone to South Africa, the cabin crew keeping an eye on her? Did he fetch her in Johannesburg?

When Pepper came to Malawi, to the new house, the new school, the only people she would have known were her father and her aunt who kept insisting that she was her mother. What did Pepper make of that? Did she begin to doubt herself? Did she come to believe, as everyone said, that things were wrong with her? Or was she strong enough to trust her knowledge that Heather was not her mother? If she was, in whom could she confide? And if she told someone what she must have suspected—that her father and aunt had killed her mother—would anyone believe her? Wouldn't Maxwell or Heather take the person aside and explain that Pepper was so disturbed—because of her mother's highway accident and surgery as well as her aunt's death—that she had everything mixed up in her head?

At last I whispered, "You still awake?"

Bruce murmured that he was.

"I wish you hadn't told me that story," I said.

"I thought maybe I shouldn't," he admitted. He took my hand under the covers. "But you don't like it when I get 'closed off,' as you say."

I moved beside him and he put his arms about me. I needed someone to hold me.

"I'm going to convince myself that you've slept with so many women you can't keep them straight," I whispered. "I mean, you are irresistible and it is romantic to sleep with a foreign correspondent and you are a world-class boudoir athlete."

"Of course, I am," Bruce said. He put his hand against my cheek and discovered that I was crying. "But I'm also a trained observer. And a reporter of unpleasant truths. And that woman is not the Jocelyn who was Maxwell's wife in Mali." He kissed me, but that didn't make it better.

The next morning we flew to Nairobi. We spent a week visiting game visiting game parks and observing animals. When we got back to town, Bruce interviewed wildlife people. I went to the library of the University of Nairobi. I checked back copies of the *East African Standard* and the *Daily Nation* during the period when Hazen Maxwell would have passed through Kenya. I found a report of a Land Cruiser full of tourists who had discovered hyenas and vultures on a kill about half a mile off the main Nairobi-Mombasa highway near the turn-off to Mzima Springs. Only it turned out not to be a kill. It was human body almost completely devoured, the body of a white woman.

I did not tell Bruce about the report, but I did make inquiries with the police. They mentioned a curiosity of the case: no women's garments had ever been found. The body had proved impossible to identify. They had buried the little of it that remained.

NORTH OF NAIROBI

AT EMBU THE ASPHALT PAVING ENDED. I did not go far along the murram road before I hit patches of standing water and mud. Once I traveled beyond the area where most people spoke some English, the car slid onto the shoulder and would not move. It was not badly mired, but I could not budge the car myself. I sounded the horn. No one came to help. I was stranded. I paced on the road and swore at everything in Africa that does not work.

After about half an hour a teenaged boy came riding along on a bicycle. He had two long planks of wood strapped to the carrying rack. I waved to him and called, "Could you help me?"

"It is all right," he answered, slowing and dismounting. "I have helped to push many people from mud. My father often gets himself stuck."

The teenager carefully laid down his bike so as not to damage the planks and came toward me. "Does your father have a car?" I asked. There would not be many car-owners in this district.

"He borrows a Toyota." The boy smiled behind his glasses, shyly, but with a knowing resignation. Then he added, "But he does not drive very well."

The boy examined the position of the car. He smiled and said, "I will look for some people to help us," and trudged off into the bush. I liked his openness and the curious feeling of confidence he gave me that he would shortly resolve my predicament. And he did. After about twenty minutes he reappeared with half a dozen Africans he had found somewhere. They pushed the car free of the shoulder on the first try. I thanked them all and offered the boy a ride.

We lashed his bicycle and the wooden planks to the rear of the car. As we started along the road, he asked, "Are you the American journalist?" It turned out that he knew my anthropologist friend Edgar and had heard from his father that a journalist was arriving for the weekend. "He is Edgar's great friend," said the boy.

I acknowledged that, indeed, I was a journalist. Wanting to be friendly—he had, after all, been friendly to me—and seeing a certain bafflement about me in his eyes, I explained that most overseas journalists reported only on events in places like Nairobi. Nonetheless, I had a hunch that the real life of Africa was in the countryside. So I had come to take a look.

"Will you write about us?" the boy asked.

I said that perhaps I might find something to interest American readers, but perhaps not.

"It is all right," he told me once again.

"I take it you can direct me to Edgar's house," I said. "I'm not sure I can find it from his directions."

The boy smiled as if with a knowledge that directions were not Edgar's strong point. Then he said, "I am sorry that it took me so long to get help. But when I speak their language, they hear my accent and they do not trust me."

I glanced at him. "You are not Mbere then?" I asked.

"I am from Nyanza." He spoke a sentence or two in a tribal language and watched my reaction. "That was Luo," he said. "Did you understand it?"

I shook my head. "What are you doing here?"

"I live here. My father is the government officer."

"You mean the district commissioner?"

The boy laughed. "He is really the agricultural assistant. But he calls himself the government officer to seem more important. The Mbere laugh at him for this."

"Do you think it's funny?"

"Yes," he said after a moment. Then he added, "But in Africa we do not laugh at our fathers."

"Do you like it here?"

"It is all right."

"But you'd rather be in Nyanza?"

"Yes, it is my home. My mother is there with my brothers and sisters." After a pause he added, "My father has taken an Mbere wife."

"I see."

"It is difficult," he said. I glanced across at him. He was look-ing straight ahead through the windshield and I wondered if he was glad to have someone to talk to about it. "She is no older than I am, and she does not really want me to live in the house." He fell silent. Then after pointing out a turning, he continued, "She does not speak Luo and she is not happy when my father and I use our own language. But if I speak Mbere, she laughs and calls me ignorant."

"Do you go to school here?" I asked. He nodded. "And

you have friends?"

"A few. But more and more it becomes complicated with them, too." He gazed pensively at the road. "Last summer all my Mbere friends were circumcised," he explained. "We Luos do not circumcise. Now my schoolmates think they have become men while I am still a child. And I do not think that Mbere men like it that an uncircumcised child-man like me lives in the same house with one of their women."

We reached the long, rutted drive to Edgar's house and I invited the boy to come in and say hello to my host. But he declined. He said that he might come by later in the afternoon. He untied the bicycle and the planks from their perch on the rear of the car and retied the planks to the carrying case. As he was about to ride off down the road, I asked, "Would you mind if I took your picture?"

The request surprised him. Why would I want his picture? Then he smiled shyly, "Will it appear in a magazine?"

"Maybe in a newspaper."

He seemed pleased at being connected to America in even so tangential a way and posed beside his bicycle. I withdrew the notebook from my jacket pocket and got his name—Stephen— and his age, which was sixteen. Then I asked, "Have you talked to your father about these problems with your schoolmates?"

Stephen nodded. "I asked him to let me go back to Nyanza. Edgar has told him that he should let me return. But my father says that we are all Kenyans now and it does not matter where we live or who is circumcised." Stephen said nothing for what seemed a long while. "The school fees he would have to pay in Nyanza are higher," he explained at last. I asked Stephen once again if he would like to come in and say hello to Edgar; perhaps we could have some lunch together. But he refused again very politely. "Perhaps I will come by later on," he said and rode off.

Edgar's house was large and stood on a rise of land. It was the former residence, so he'd told me, of the European foreman of the now-defunct British-American Tobacco Company processing plant. It was past two thirty. Hungry and quite thirsty, I was glad to arrive.

But the house was deserted. The doors were all locked. I walked around the house trying them. I hallooed, but no one was about, not even a servant. I was surprised to find the place deserted. Edgar had told me on the phone that he'd be there, drafting a report. But no matter. I took out reading I had brought and made myself comfortable on a porch overlooking the countryside.

In fact, I did not know Edgar well. The first time I met him, shortly after I'd been assigned overseas, he came to lunch with an historian specializing in pre-colonial Africa whom I'd called for a briefing. Edgar was then acting chair of the Anthropology Department at the University of California, Santa Barbara. As we ate together at the Faculty Club, a preoccupation intensified the school-masterish formality that he had picked up in some non-California life. He had grown up in English-speaking South Africa, I learned, and without evidence I attributed his fuss-budget quality to the schooling he'd received there. After attending university Edgar had joined the British Colonial Service during its last years and had served as a District Commissioner in what is now Tanzania. Later he received a PhD in Anthropology from Oxford; his dissertation detailed how life was lived and organized in a small town in the hinterlands behind Accra. During our lunch Edgar said quite frankly that he was fed up with California. Wistfully he mentioned more than once that he still owned land in the Ghanaian town and hoped to retire there.

While we waited for coffee, Edgar acknowledged that he'd become a center of controversy on campus. He had reprimanded a young social anthropologist; "dressed him down" was his term. This colleague was an iconoclast of romantic reputation who lectured barefoot wearing only khaki shorts and a tank top. Sometimes he did not appear for his classes at all. It was not surprising, Edgar said, given the nature of students, that many of them rallied to the instructor's defense. But I felt that it had surprised Edgar. I sensed that he still expected to be treated like a DC. Apparently students had picketed his classes; they had written angry letters to the student newspaper. Edgar merely said, "We soldier on."

After reading on the porch for about fifteen minutes I no longer felt alone. Looking up, I saw an African with a studiedly tweedy look staring at me through the glass of the porch doors. He wore glasses, a tie, a rumpled shirt, and suit trousers. He was smoking a pipe and a copy of the *Economist* hung from his hand. We stared at each other for a moment.

"Is Dr. Pettys around?" I finally asked, rising from the wooden chair.

"No, he's not," said the African through the door.

A pause. We continued to stare at each other. "This is his house, isn't it?"

"Yes, this is his house."

The African gazed at me without expression, and I noticed that he stood in stocking feet. "Dr. Pettys told me he'd be here."

"He's in hospital."

"Is he all right?" I tossed my reading aside. "Look, could you open this door? What's happened to Dr. Pettys?"

The African smiled, unlocked the door and opened it. "Perhaps I meant 'at' hospital," he said. I felt that he had taken some pleasure in needlessly arousing my concern. "Edgar's quite all right. The houseboy had an accident, and Edgar has run him to hospital."

I explained that I had come as a weekend guest and asked if I might come inside. "Yes, please come," the African said finally. "Have you had any lunch?"

"No, as a matter of fact, and I'm starving."

"Let's nip into the kitchen and see what's there." I brought my overnight case inside and found the kitchen myself. The stocking-footed African was there, getting beer for us. "There's tinned meat in the fridge," he said, "and bread there in the plastic. Make yourself a sandwich if you like."

I asked, "What happened to the servant?"

"He was putting my bicycle into a shed I use when I don't come by car. A large pane of glass fell on him. Nasty business."

"A pane of glass? How did that happen?"

"I've no idea. Curious kind of accident, isn't it?"

"Will the man be all right?"

"Oh, I expect so. These fellows are quite hearty. Here's to your health." He lifted his glass to me, drank some beer, and padded back into the main room of the house.

When I joined him there, he had settled onto the couch; he had apparently been napping there when I arrived. He was rattling his magazine and noisily sipping his beer. Standing over him I introduced myself, giving my name; I hoped to elicit a corresponding introduction from him. He offered his hand, but without otherwise stirring and then indicated a chair across from him.

"I'm afraid I haven't any idea who you are," I said, sitting down.

"Oh," he replied, "I'm Quentin Owino, the government officer here."

"Ah ha!" I said, taking fresh interest in the man. I wondered if Stephen had refused my invitations to come inside the house because he knew his father would be there. "Edgar has influential friends."

My flattery pleased him. He looked up from his paper and smiled. "I am the second most important man in Mbere," Owino said. "After Edgar." I smiled at this compliment to my host. "We are great chums," he added.

"Government officer?" I asked. "What does that mean: District Commissioner?" Owino would know that this was the position Edgar had held. I wondered if he saw himself in the same role, the civilizer's role.

"One does many jobs in a small place like this," he replied.

"I think it must have been your son who rescued me from some mud." I described the boy.

"That would be Stephen," Owino said. "A jolly good chap, if I may say so."

"Yes, I quite liked him. I suppose he must miss Nyanza."

"Did he say that?"

"He merely said his mother was living there."

"He gets there often enough," Owino said. "It is best for him to know more than one village." He smiled. "Travel broadens, as they say. Don't you agree?"

"I suppose it does. People here accept him, do they?"

"Of course. Why not? We're all Kenyans now." He smiled again. "Actually this is great experience for him. Look at the British. They sent their children off to school at the age of six. And they conquered the world." He laughed. "Stephen is happy here."

I drank some beer and looked about the room. Owino filled his pipe and continued to watch me. "It must be a great challenge," I said, wanting to draw him out, "being the government's officer in a place like this."

He shrugged this off. "Mbere is not much of a place," he said. "A small tribe, no political influence, clients of the Kikuyu. Most of the people are ignorant and want to stay that way."

"But it was chosen as a target area for rural development, wasn't it? Isn't that why Edgar's here?"

"Yes, but how much has been accomplished? Edgar can tell you about that." Then, perhaps recalling that I was a journalist, Owino fussed at the lighting of his pipe, watching me carefully, wondering if he would be quoted. "But, of course, government service is challenging anywhere," he commented for safety's sake.

"You're being too modest," I said, pushing him a little. "You are a Luo and that can't make you very popular here—even if you are all Kenyans."

He shrugged again and smiled half to himself. "Indeed, there is still some truth to that, regrettably," he acknowledged. "But I am perhaps unusual. I do not leave the division every weekend, for example, like most government officers. The people respect that. It means that I am less a stranger to them."

"You and Stephen live as bachelors, do you?"

"We Africans do not make good bachelors." Owino smiled and punctuated the smile with a shrug. Surely I understood. "I have taken an Mbere wife," he said. "A year ago. I needed a wife to cook my food and give me sons. Why should I have the expense of keeping a servant?" We laughed together. "You will say I am an exploiter," he giggled, "but it is not true."

The sweet scent of his pipe tobacco began to fill the room. Edgar's house was starting to seem more like the faculty club where I had met him than a living room in rural Africa. Owino smiled with a touch of bravado that masqueraded as pride. "She has already given me a son."

"You must be very proud of yourself," I said. "Congratulations."

He shrugged. "It is a way to show that we are all Kenyans." Then he added, "There are many sons left in me. It is good for the Mbere to understand that."

I sipped some beer. "Maybe I'll have a sandwich," I said. I went into the kitchen, found bread, peanut butter, and jam and proceeded to make us each a sandwich. I sensed that Owino would be happy to eat Edgar's food, especially if I prepared it.

He soon entered the kitchen and watched me. Then he challenged, "You perhaps do not think polygamy civilized."

"I have no views on the matter," I said. "However, I'm sure it's a lot more complicated to have two wives than to have only one."

"It is perhaps less civilized than monogamy," he said. "But the Mbere regard it as a sign of wealth and prestige. So it has done me no harm to have a local wife."

"Is it difficult for Stephen?"

"Why should it be?" he asked quickly. I answered with a shrug. "There are no difficulties." After a moment he added, "Some minor irritations, that's all. The woman wants to feel important and orders Stephen around. Of course, he does not like it. I tell him to be patient. She does it mainly because she is Mbere and knows she is ignorant. She feels inferior to us."

I cut the sandwiches in halves, put them onto coffee saucers that did not match and handed the larger sandwich to Owino. "Why not send him back to Nyanza?" I asked.

"A son is a joy to a father—especially a son who is so superior." I nodded. "You think me unreasonable," Owino charged.

"How could I? I know nothing about the matter."

"If I send him back to Nyanza," he explained, "his mother will put him to work. Ever since I married here, she complains that she has no money. I want Stephen here to make sure he does not neglect his education." Owino poured us each another beer, and we took them and the sandwiches back into the living room. "It is very probable that Stephen will pass his Higher School Certificate Examinations well enough so that the government pays his entire university education." Owino lowered his voice confidentially. "And I tell you his chances of getting a place at the University of Nairobi, which is entirely run by Kikuyus, are better if he passes from a school in Mbere than one in Nyanza."

"He should be very pleased with himself here then," I said.

"Well, yes." Owino shrugged. "Perhaps he does not like the living arrangements. He has his private room. I wanted to put an outside door in it for him, but it is a government house and this is against regulations. He wanted to build a small house for himself like some of his Mbere friends have done, but that, I think, is asking for trouble."

"Why is that?" I inquired. I remembered Stephen's wooden planks. Had he intended them for this purpose?

"Mbere boys build themselves small houses once they are circumcised. We Luos do not circumcise; manhood is more than the cutting off of a foreskin, although some people do not understand this. But if Stephen as an uncircumcised Luo builds himself a hut, there will be trouble. The Mbere do not yet regard him as a man. It is not the sort of trouble that cannot be straightened out. I am the government officer here, after all. Still trouble avoided is the best kind to have."

We now heard a car pull into the drive. "Must be Edgar," I said.

I started toward the door. Owino lagged behind, putting on his shoes.

Outside Edgar was standing before the Land Rover, peering into the garage where the glass had fallen. In a short-sleeved khaki shirt and work shorts that matched the sandy color of his hair, wearing desert boots and knee-socks, his arms akimbo, he seemed never to have stopped being a DC. We shook hands. I said I'd had no trouble finding the place and had had some lunch with the help of Owino.

"Still here, is he?" Edgar's voice carried an edge of irritation. "We've had a real balls-up," he said. "Owino tell you about it?" I said that he had. "No damn coincidence the glass fell."

"Foul play?"

"Bloody booby-trap. Meant to fall. Not sure who the intended victim was: me or Owino. I'm damned sure it wasn't Kamau."

Edgar wore the expression of fuss-budget impatience I remembered from our first meeting at UCSB. I was amused, but did not show my reaction; booby-traps were a serious matter. In fact, I was glad to see him—and not only because a working anthropologist makes an excellent contact for a journalist covering Africa.

When I first arrived in Nairobi, I often wished I had kept in closer contact with Edgar; I wondered if he were still at UCSB. Then on a reporting trip I saw him at Roberts Field in Liberia. We were waiting for the same plane. I re-introduced myself and we rode together to Freetown, Sierra Leone, where I left the flight.

He had just arrived from the States, he said, after what had been an almost intolerable year at UCSB. "I have never been so ready to leave anywhere," he said. "Faculty discipline totally collapsed. Faculty-student communication no longer exists." He had been forced to fire the young anthropologist who had been such a problem. The action had triggered a campus row. Students had demonstrated; some called him a "fascist pig" to his face. Colleagues had questioned his professional credentials, merely because he was born in South Africa. He shook his head as if still not quite able to conceive of what had gone wrong.

"I've never so longed for the order of Africa," he continued. "Yes, I said, the order. Life in the sophisticated world is too chaotic. That's why I've come back. I may give up teaching." He had arranged an early sabbatical and would spend the upcoming academic year in Kenya, evaluating an intensive development program in Mbere Division a couple of hours north of Nairobi. The program would be launched almost immediately. He was eager to get started.

Africa had given Edgar a giddy sense of renewal. When we said goodbye on the Freetown tarmac, his joyfulness amused—and also touched—me. "Look at that!" he said enthusiastically. He pointed across the airstrip to a trio of women carrying babies on their backs and clay pots on their heads. They were moving with a peasant grace beneath flowering trees; behind them lay crudely tilled fields and thatched huts. I saw them as elements in an overall picture of stunted personal development and cruel, needless poverty. Edgar saw them as beautiful.

"A classic scene!" Edgar commented, smiling. "Listen to their laughter!" And, indeed, a rich, throaty laughter floated from them through the morning heat and quietude. "They're in harmony with their environment," he said. "And their traditions." He grinned. "How glorious to be back home in Africa!" When my luggage arrived, we shook hands and agreed to meet in Nairobi.

Over the following months we did occasionally meet there. He always invited me to visit Mbere. But whenever I expressed interest in actually doing so, he suggested that I hold off. A few matters remained to be processed through the ministry. "Wait till the project really gets started," he would say. Behind this excuse I sensed that as a man might want to be alone with his bride, Edgar wanted to be alone with Africa. Since he was un-married—except to his work—I did not press the matter.

But ministerial delays dragged on. Eventually his invitations became more heartfelt. "You really ought to come," he would say in a tone of loneliness. "I'd love to talk with an American." He would add, "I live like a king in Mbere. Really, I've begun some ethnography. It's fascinating stuff."

By late April annoyance and frustration were sounding in his voice. The ministry had not acted. Misunderstandings, ineffi-ciency, and fear of decision-making had delayed the Mbere project by more than a year. His sabbatical was almost over; it had been wasted—at least in terms of his observing a micro-cosm of rural development and doing scholarly writing about it. Whether or not the ethnography would justify his remaining in Mbere seemed unclear. And so I had agreed to a visit.

"Will Kamau be all right?" I asked now.

"Oh, yes," he said. "In hospital for a week. I don't know what we'll do for *chak* while you're here. I cook worse than you do." He eyed me dryly. "My hunch is that as a chef you've given a few blokes the trots in your time." He looked back into the garage where the glass had fallen. "The question right now," he said, "is what do we do about this?"

A young man now emerged from so deep inside the garage that I had not seen him earlier. He was perhaps twenty, spare and loose-jointed, not tall so much as very slender. He wore a white long-sleeved shirt and dark trousers fastened by a belt so long that it seemed to loop beyond the buckle almost halfway around his body. He had a studious look, emphasized by glasses and a copy carried lightly in his hand of the tabloid-sized *Nairobi Daily Nation* which he used as a briefcase. He gazed at me without hostility, but I sensed that he was not prepared to accept me merely as a friend of Edgar's as both Stephen and Owino were ready to do. Instead he would watch to see who I turned out to be. "This is Barnabas," Edgar said. "The chief informant of my ethnographic study."

"Hello, Barnabas," I said, offering my hand which he shook. Since Edgar had not stated the information, I gave him my name and explained that I was an American from Nairobi.

"Journalist," Edgar said.

Barnabas nodded, but said nothing.

"Barnabas is a local celebrity," Edgar continued. "Passed his Higher School Certificate Examination. Which only about a dozen boys from Mbere have ever done."

"Congratulations," I said, wondering if this were not the exam Owino intended Stephen to pass. I wondered, too, if the time would ever come when Edgar would call a twenty-year-old a "young man" instead of a "boy."

"Barnabas goes to university next fall," Edgar went on. "And all the girls in the Division come out to watch him walk by."

Barnabas smiled and lowered his eyes.

"What would you like to study?" I asked.

"I would like to become a doctor," he told me. "The people here still practice traditional medicine. But they no longer believe strongly in its cures and so they are not so effective. I would like to bring modern medicine to Mbere."

"Good," I told him. "Can you study that in Nairobi?"

"Perhaps I must go to UK," he replied.

Inside the house Edgar made himself a sandwich in the kitchen while I talked with Barnabas and Owino. Before long Owino went to join Edgar. I could not help noticing the look of distrust that Barnabas cast at him as he left.

"I need a favor, old man," Owino said to Edgar in the kitchen. "You couldn't lend me five hundred *shillingi*, could you?" My conversation with Barnabas had not resumed and we both overheard Owino's request for what would have been about seventy dollars. I glanced at Barnabas.

"Jeremiah up to his old tricks?" we heard Edgar ask.

"I'm afraid so," Owino told him. I picked up a magazine and thumbed through it. Barnabas opened his copy of the *Daily Nation* and shuffled through papers. We both heard the conversation continue.

"You're going to have to stand up to him, you know," Edgar said.

"But how?" Owino asked. "If I refuse him money, he calls her home and I have no one to cook my meals."

"Just now I have no one to cook mine either," complained Edgar lightly.

"But I sleep with this cook," Owino reminded him. "So it is very hard."

"Send her and the baby up to Nyanza. Let her see how good you are to her. Let her see what it's like to be a second wife."

"She would never go to Nyanza."

"You're her husband. Make her go. In any case, I can't spare more *shillingi*."

I glanced again at Barnabas; he was studying me. Since it was obvious that we had both heard the conversation in the kitchen, I asked, "What's that all about?"

Barnabas paused a moment as if trying to decide if I merited an explanation.

"How about three hundred? Is that possible?"

"I'm sorry, Quentin. The bank is closed."

Barnabas and I were still looking at one another. He said quietly, "Owino's wife is the daughter of a local chief. He keeps changing the terms of the bridewealth arrangement because he wants money."

"I thought bridewealth was fixed at the time of the marriage."

Barnabas nodded. "But Owino is not Mbere. So when Jeremiah insists that he owes more money, his kinsmen support him. If Owino does not pay, they go to his place and bring his wife and the baby back to her father's *shamba*."

"Why does Jeremiah need money?" I asked.

"He buys cars," Barnabas said. "Toyotas. Used."

"He has more than one car?"

"It is not hard to drive a car into the ground here. Especially a used one, badly maintained. Jeremiah never gives care to his cars and when the local mechanics can no longer repair a car he has mistreated, he buys a new one. He bought his fifth Toyota this week. He's having a beer party for his kinsmen at his *shamba* today."

"The kind of money Owino's asking for in there: that can't buy a car."

"It buys the beer," said Barnabas.

"What buys the cars?"

"Jeremiah sells tribal land to Kikuyu land merchants. They pay him in used Toyotas."

"Is tribal land his to sell?"

"No. But he is the chief."

"Can't you get rid of him?" Barnabas said nothing. "There must be some process for that," I said.

"In the old days," he replied, "when a chief outlived his

wisdom, people killed him. We can't do that anymore."

I detected the slightest of twinkles in Barnabas's eyes.

Later that day outside Jeremiah's compound, young men sat drinking beer lolling on the fenders or sitting inside the rusting hulks of four Toyota sedans. Because my car was unknown to them, they stared when it pulled up and parked. When our party left the car and the young men saw who we were, they hailed Edgar in friendship, bidding him to have some beer. They sang out as well at Owino, in a manner that struck me as companionable, but also derisive. His status as government officer won him little respect with this gang. They hailed Barnabas, but he maintained a scholar's distance from the rowdies. As for Stephen, who had joined us, he too kept his distance. The young men seemed openly scornful of him.

We passed the newest Toyota, bright red and newly waxed. A once-dented front fender, now repaired, had paint of a different, more orange hue. I asked Barnabas about the young men's taunts. "They say Stephen cannot drink beer," he explained. "It is not for children. Beer can be drunk only by circumcised men."

The compound was no more than a collection of mud and wattle huts and granaries with a platform upon which grasses for thatching had been piled. There were also a small, roofed enclosure for calves and a larger cattle corral of thickly packed tree branches and stumps. Edgar led us through it with the measured, imperial pace that I supposed he had used during his tenure as a District Commissioner and had picked up from movie versions of "King Solomon's Mines." We moved forward to greet the patriarch—obviously Jeremiah—who sat on a contraption of bent tree branches shaped into a chair and covered with a cowhide. He had gray bristles for a beard and watched us through half-closed but intelligent and suspicious eyes. As Edgar reached him, he lurched to his feet. They bowed to one another and shook hands. Owino bowed as well, taking the old man's hand deferentially, holding it in both of his. I was introduced and bowed deeply.

Edgar congratulated the old man on his acquisition of yet another Toyota. He accepted beer and waited while Bentley, one of Jeremiah's sons, brought him a chair. He said to me in a low voice, "Have Owino give you a *shamba* tour. He's worked with Bentley. I'm going to give the old boy what-for about the glass in the garage."

I collected Owino who had gotten himself some beer and asked to see the *shamba*. He called to Bentley who ignored him until Edgar intervened and in his best DC manner instructed him to show me around. Barnabas and Stephen tagged along.

As we headed toward the fields, a figure flashed past. Stephen called out, "Anas!" and ran after him. A youth Stephen's age poked his head around the back of a hut. Barnabas called out to him, a friendly taunting in Mbere. The youth—Anastasio was his name—appeared. He was introduced to me and carefully wiped his hands against his shirt. He gazed at me as if beholding a ghost or some figure of wonder, then offered one of the still-wet hands for me to shake.

"He has never seen an American before," Barnabas said.

Stephen explained that we were old friends; he had rescued me from mud. "Anas" was impressed. Stephen grinned and asked, "Were you carrying water?"

Anas seemed uncertain what to say. But since his shoes and pants legs were splattered, the answer was clear.

"It is all right!" said Stephen with a laugh. "I won't tell. Barnabas doesn't care. And Bentley won't notice."

Anas looked up ahead where Owino was walking with Bentley. "It is so much easier for me to carry it than for her to," he said. "And anyway we are in higher school now and they are telling us things must change."

"I am going to build my house," Stephen told Anas. "Will you help me? Or do you have to stay and drink beer in those dead cars?"

"I can help you," Anas replied softly. "You helped me."

Barnabas looked concerned at hearing this declaration. He slowed his pace to separate himself from the others and since I was walking with him, I slowed as well. I asked about the *shamba*'s crops. He pointed out those in a five-acre plot: cow peas, finger millet, sorghum, and maize, subsistence crops all laid out in precisely straight rows. A three-acre section was devoted to cotton, Jeremiah's cash crop. "Owino has made quite a good *shamba* here for Jeremiah and Bentley," he said. He added, "It could do with a bit of weeding."

"What was all that about the water?" I asked. Barnabas glanced at me with a look of either confusion or defensiveness, I was not sure which. I persisted, "Is there something about Anas carrying water that is . . ." I let my voice trail off.

Barnabas said nothing for a moment, then decided to speak. "Anas is a man now. He has been circumcised."

"And carrying water: that's women's work?" On the drive up from Nairobi I had seen women struggling with large drums of water on their backs. They supported the drums, their necks straining, on tumplines that stretched across their foreheads. In Kikuyu villages I had seen women who had carried water this way for so long that tumplines had formed depressions across their foreheads.

"Traditionally carrying water is the work of women," Barnabas said. I made no reply. After a moment he continued, "Anas does not like to see his mother carrying water. He is much stronger than she is. But the other men here say that it is her job. So he does it when he hopes they will not see."

We walked on and I thought of the men drinking beer in the derelict Toyotas. After a moment I said lightly, "Sometimes my women readers ask me exactly what it is that African men do."

Barnabas smiled, but said nothing.

When we caught up with the others, Bentley was bending over a mesh trap he had built to cover a hole in the ground. Caught in the trap were hundreds of flying ants. They resembled large-bodied balls of fat the size of a little finger to the first joint; to these succulent blobs Nature had attached long, transparent wings. On these the fattened ants flew out of the ground, venturing forth to start a new colony. I had encountered such ants in my own yard. I had even felt terrorized by the fluttering of their wings for the entire experience was like an eco-horror movie come true. But I had learned not to step on the ants. Wherever I squished them, they left grease spots that lasted for months and I could not wear the shoes indoors.

Now Bentley stuck his hands beneath the mesh and extracted a handful of the ants. Some were motionless; the wings of others still fluttered. He closed the trap and transferred the ants into a woven basket he carried. He withdrew his hand with one of the insects held between his fingers. He closed the basket, ripped the wings from the specimen he held and plopped it into his mouth. He closed his eyes. He smiled as a child might with candy. The other Africans gathered around him, begging him to open the basket. When he did, they each reached in, withdrew insects, removed their wings, and ate them, chattering and laughing at the pleasure of the delicacy.

After a while Stephen came over to me, carrying several ants in a nest made of his hands. Barnabas and Anas tagged behind him. "Please," he said. "Would you like?"

I smiled. "No, thank you," I replied.

"They are delicious," Anas assured me.

"I'm sure they are."

"You will not have?" Stephen asked again.

When I declined, Stephen and Anas watched me with fascination, grinning, smacking and licking their lips as they plucked wings from the ants and tossed them into their mouths. Barnabas stood several paces away and watched me as well, eating ants as one might eat popcorn one kernel at a time.

"You think we are barbarians, don't you?" he challenged. "For eating ants."

"No," I said.

"Then why not have one?" he asked.

"Not my thing," I said. "I couldn't eat snails in France. Or greasy meat pies in England. I don't like tofu in Nigeria. Or in California."

Stephen and Anas watched me, grinning and eating. Barnabas studied me, unsure what to make of me. I realized that trotting out the places I'd been only exaggerated the differences between us.

Before I could think of a way to close the gap, we heard Owino and Bentley arguing. "But you must weed if you want good crops," Owino declared. Bentley shrugged off this advice, fiddling with the trap which he had now completely cleaned out. "If you don't weed, the worms will eat them, not your family." Bentley shook his head. He checked the trap again and moved off.

As we followed him back to the compound, Owino said, "He won't weed."

"It is women's work," said Anas.

"Well, where is his wife? Why doesn't she weed? They will lose their crops."

"She is eating right now at her father's *shamba*," said Anas.

"And he is surly to me because he's sleeping alone?" Owino dusted off his trousers and tightened the knot of his tie. "It is not my fault he's sleeping alone." We walked for a moment in silence. "Bentley has a good garden there, thanks to my advice," Owino said. "But he won't even do weeding for his own good. What ignorance!"

"It is not ignorance!" Anas said, obviously annoyed with Owino. "It is tradition."

I was surprised he spoke so forthrightly to a man so much older.

"Traditions are holding you back," replied Owino. "Time to abandon them."

"If we abandon our traditions," Anas replied, "we stop being Mbere."

"Is that a loss?" Owino asked. "What have the Mbere ever achieved?"

"Why do you say that?" Barnabas retorted. "You are not superior to us."

"No," Owino agreed, "I am not superior to you. But education is better than ignorance. Doing a little work is better than being lazy and drunk all the time."

"Let's not argue," Stephen said. "We are all friends."

"If education makes you superior to us," Barnabas asked, "why do you make yourself unclean with one of our women."

"I am not looking for an argument. We are all Kenyans now.

We must all work for a more productive Kenya. You know that's all I meant."

We walked the rest of the way back to the compound in silence. We found Edgar at the Land Rover, showing a rifle to Jeremiah and the drunken young men who watched in confused silence from the hulks of the abandoned Toyotas. I took it that Edgar had told Jeremiah about the glass positioned in his garage to do injury to someone. Now, by displaying the rifle, he was emphasizing that he would take action against anyone caught setting traps at his house. Perhaps this was the way a District Commissioner would handle matters in what, to me, was clearly a bygone era. Glancing at the sullen expressions of the men listening to Edgar, I wondered what their reactions would be to his treating them this way.

When we left, Owino stayed at Jeremiah's compound. He insisted that Stephen remain as well despite the taunts the drunken layabouts still directed toward him. No one urged the pair to remain, I noticed. I was not certain why Owino insisted. Perhaps it was the availability of free beer. Or perhaps he thought that he and Stephen should try to firm up relations with the locals.

Edgar wanted to give his two informants, Barnabas and Anas, new assignments and took the four of us to a village shop where he bought us *chai*, local tea brewed as dark and thick as a soup. As Edgar rattled on about the new material he wanted, the two young men studied me. The presence of an American seemed to make it impossible for them to concentrate on Edgar's instructions. Once we were alone I would apologize for spinning such webs of fascination.

After a time Barnabas asked me, "Will you write a story about us for your newspaper?"

"I've been wondering about that," I acknowledged. I asked what they considered newsworthy about Mbere. What in the Division might interest my readers? They seemed stumped at first, but finally settled on the fact that the situation of their lives was gradually improving. I did not tell them that such a report would baffle my editors, men who thought news should emphasize problems and prophesy crises. I told them I was glad to learn about improvements. But I admitted that some things mystified me. "For example," I said, "will Stephen ever be accepted in Mbere?"

The two young men looked at one another as if each hoped the other would deal with the question.

"Or is he accepted?" I went on. "His father keeps saying that all of you are Kenyans now. Is that true? Is the problem that I just don't see it?"

They shrugged. They glanced at one another and then at Edgar. He smiled encouragingly, interested to see how they would handle this test.

Barnabas offered, "Well, we are all Kenyans now. That's true."

"So it doesn't matter that Stephen is old enough to be a man and yet he is not circumcised?"

They were silent. Then Anas said, "Owino is not circumcised and everyone accepts that he is a man." He added, "Stephen is my friend. I accept him as a man."

I said I had the impression that the layabouts at Jeremiah's did not.

"What exactly is the problem?" asked Edgar. "Is it circumcision or tribalism?"

The young men seemed uneasy at the mention of tribalism. It was a subject that must be discussed very discreetly.

"Things are changing," Barnabas said. "But it takes time.

Twenty years ago when it came time for my oldest sister to be circumcised, my father announced that he would not allow this ritual to be performed on any of his daughters. And he had eight of them."

"Why was this?" I asked.

"Because it's painful. It hurts women. In male circumcision the body is not really damaged. The pain lasts only a few days. With women it is different."

"What happened?" I asked.

"Quite a famous story hereabouts," Edgar said.

"My father made his declaration and everyone opposed him. His parents. His brothers and their wives. My grandmother insisted that no Mbere girl achieved full womanhood unless she passed through this test. But my father held firm. When his parents and other villagers insisted it must be done, he moved away."

"And he's come back now?" I asked.

Barnabas nodded. "His mother lives with us now in the compound. Some of my uncles live there, too. My father has made things change. Maybe it is not so important about Stephen."

"What do you say?" I asked Anas.

He seemed unwilling at first to reply. When no one else spoke, he finally said, "My father is a chief. He upholds tradition."

"Owino claimed you should abandon tradition," I said.

"How can we do that?" Anas asked. "I think my father is right. If we abandon our traditions, we will stop being Mbere." He paused for a moment. Then he added, "But Stephen is my friend. I don't know what to say. I accept him as a man whether he has a foreskin or not."

Edgar and I found enough tins in the pantry to make ourselves some *chak*. While eating it, I asked how Jeremiah had reacted to receiving "what-for."

"His dignity is offended, of course," Edgar acknowledged. "But he'll get the word out. That's the important thing."

We talked about his informants and I tried out some of my impressions on Edgar. I said that Barnabas struck me as being one of the new men of Mbere, of Kenya. While Stephen and Anas were standing poised on the threshold of manhood, thrilled by the wider world opening before them, Barnabas had already crossed that threshold. He had taken a look at the world beyond it and had seen an alien culture with alien values, Western culture, white man's modernity. "Going to university," I said, "He's about to step out of the tribal culture into the modern one, right? Must be a scary prospect."

"Yes and no," Edgar replied. "Barnabas will spend much of his life traveling between the two cultures. He'll live with two sets of values, two styles of living."

"Will he study medicine?" I asked.

Edgar thought that unlikely. "The government will tell him what to study and what they need are people trained in agriculture. If Mbere Division is fortunate, Barnabas will practice what he's learned here. But most agriculture officials gravitate to the high-income areas. He may do that."

"Will he turn out to be Owino then?"

"I hope not," Edgar said. "Quentin's been shunted off to a backwater where he can do little good and little harm. Why, I'm not sure. Must have crossed someone. Or infuriated someone by trying to be a white man." Edgar assumed that upward mobility for Barnabas, who had an intellectual bent, would come through teaching and advanced degrees. "He might provide the brains for a successful agri-business—if he can partner himself with a man who has contacts. Probably a Kikuyu. Tough getting ahead when you're from a minor tribe."

"What about Anas? Always a peasant?"

"He'll finish school here. Maybe even manage a decent pass for his school certificate. Then he'll dash off to Nairobi. What happens then is anyone's guess."

"And Stephen?"

"A complicated question," Edgar said. "Barnabas is stuck being forever an Mbere. And there are times when that will seem a real prison. Stephen is going to be what his father has in mind when he says, 'We are Kenyans.' We won't know for a while whether that means he'll be nothing or a new kind of—"

There was a sharp knocking at the door. Then suddenly Barnabas was standing in the kitchen, panting hard, a look of terror on his face. "Could you come?" he asked Edgar. "Stephen's been hurt."

"What's happened?"

Barnabas looked at Edgar, then at me as if in my presence he could not speak. "You can tell us," Edgar said. "What's happened?"

Finally he managed to say, "They circumcised him."

Edgar and I did not understand. We frowned at one another.

"Please come," Barnabas pleaded. "They circumcised him. And the knife—"

"Where is he?" Edgar stood. He shoved his plate aside and nodded to me.

"He's at Jeremiah's," Barnabas said. "They slit the top of—"

"Can you drive?" Edgar asked me. "I'm low on petrol."

We hurried outside to the car. Edgar sat beside me in the passenger seat and Barnabas crawled into the back. I raced over unfamiliar roads in the dark. Edgar gave me directions and questioned Barnabas.

He reported that several hours after we left the compound Jeremiah and Owino argued about the bridewealth payment Jeremiah insisted Owino owed him. The young men drinking in the Toyotas had sided with Jeremiah. They had eventually gone to Owino's house to fetch his wife and bring her home, intending to keep her at Jeremiah's until the bridewealth debt was paid. At Owino's they discovered Stephen and Anas who had begun to build Stephen's house. The young men objected to this: Stephen was acting like a man, but he was not yet circumcised. They taunted and baited Stephen. A fight broke out. They seized both young men and took them back to the compound. There Jeremiah as chief would rule on whether or not Stephen could build the house. But Jeremiah wasn't there. The young men had more beer. Eventually they decided to settle the matter themselves. They stripped Stephen. When Anas tried to stop them, they tied him up. Five men held Stephen down, one on each of his arms and three on his legs. The man who wielded the knife sliced through most of the foreskin. Then his hand slipped. The knife had cut into the tip of Stephen's penis.

When we got to Jeremiah's place no one was around except the old man. He was dead drunk on too much beer—or pretending to be—sitting in his newest Toyota. Barnabas shouted repeatedly for Stephen. At last we heard whimpering and found him cowering in bushes in a fetal ball. He was holding a cloth to his groin and bleeding. He would not let us see the bleeding. I got a blanket I kept in the trunk of the car and cloaked him in it. When he would not stand, remaining coiled into himself, whimpering, Barnabas, Edgar, and I lifted him and carried him to the car. We placed him on the rear seat. We had to leave Barnabas behind; there was no room for him in the car. Edgar held

Stephen's hand. Once we hit the Nairobi road, he climbed into the rear seat. He held the boy like a father while I drove as fast as I dared through the black night.

When we got to Nairobi Hospital, nurses put Stephen on a gurney and rolled him into a surgery. Edgar in high DC dudgeon insisted on accompanying him. The head nurse telephoned a surgeon. When he arrived and saw me, he waved. He was an American I had met socially. I knew he would do the best he could.

The doctor insisted that Edgar leave the surgery. He joined me outside where the air was cool and the darkness peaceful. "Those infernal Africans," he said. "Drunken louts. How could they!"

I said nothing.

"I'm fed up with Kenya," Edgar went on. "This has been an intolerable year. I can't wait to get back to teaching people who want to learn."

I moved off and paced. Eventually I found another entrance to the hospital. I went inside and waited near the surgery.

Finally the doctor emerged. Stephen was going to be all right, he said. He had removed the foreskin and repaired the wound to the tip of the penis. "His equipment won't win any beauty contests," the surgeon said. "But he'll be able to father children."

"That's a relief," I replied.

"He may not have as much pleasure doing it as most men," he continued, "but he'll be able to do it."

I thanked the surgeon and went to find Edgar. I told him the news and we went to the car. As we drove to my house through the darkness, neither of us spoke.

EQUATEUR

ENTERING THE EQUATEUR. . . . Some have described it as traveling back to the beginnings of time.

Driving into the region you see little: only the track before you, the rutted, orange-colored road rising and falling, descending to a watercourse bridged by logs and rising again to the top of the next low ridge. Beside you flashes the jungle. It grows thick and dark and does not entice you. Above is the sky, brilliantly blue. It winds like a river through the leafy overhang of trees. And you go up and down, up and down on the orange laterite road.

When you fly into the Equateur, the land spreads below you with unrelieved flatness. It extends beyond the range of your eyes, beyond the haze lying across it in the dry season, beyond the reaches of binoculars during the rains when the air itself is as clear as a lens. It sweeps to the Atlantic; it stretches to the backbone of Africa: the Rift Valley Escarpment and the Mountains of the Moon.

Below lies the jungle, a green sponge of vegetation surging outward. It lies dense and endless over a space whose walls are the sky. Looking down you may spot a mud pond fringed by trampled grasses where elephants dance and bathe in the evenings. Or a river. Or an occasional plantation or mission, perhaps a cluster of huts. But as a rule you see only the greenness of vegetation.

Plantations untangle and order this verdure; they do not interrupt it. From the air you suddenly notice that the patternless intertwine of plant life has given way to textured design, to rubber trees or oil palms set out and tended in neat rows. A referee has stopped the struggle among the trees for space.

Along one edge of the textured design, plantation buildings hug the river's edge; corrugated roofs glint in the sun. The pattern of trees continues; then abruptly it ends. The chaos of jungle resumes.

Missions disappear even more quickly. A Protestant station is nothing more than a clearing and some buildings: a church, a school, a hospital, a home for the evangelist, and one for the doctor. A Catholic station usually has a cathedral in the Italian style and priests in white soutanes moving slowly across its lawns. But before you can think it incongruously ordered, the raw tangle of jungle has returned.

Villages line the roadways, eight or ten huts to a side. They stand at the regular intervals where colonial administrators resettled their residents to provide a maintenance force. They cluster close to plantations, too, and to missions and the old European trading towns. And they cling to the shorelines of rivers and swamps where the fishing is good.

Only rivers interrupt the jungle. From the air they have the appearance and much of the mystery of snakes. A jungle river is a silt-covered living force; it twists through primeval growth and sleeps in the sun.

In the Equateur the greatest of these river-serpents is the Congo. It is a broad flat boa with an island-dotted hide, curling out of Africa's heart. It travels north from the Katanga highlands, turns west sliding over the rapids at Kisangani, and at Mbandaka is moving south. Running broad and flecked with islands, its waters seep back into swamps. It swallows the Ruki; it absorbs the Ubangi and Kasai, sweeps past Kinshasa, plunges through a gorge and surges into the Atlantic. It meets the ocean with such force that it discolors the water for miles out into the sea.

For the Equateur the river is the central fact of life.

Sailing into the region you realize this. Going by sternwheeler the passage from Kinshasa takes four and a half days. During that time you are part of the river. Watching the shoreline you feel that nature has held itself unchanged for centuries. You pass fishing villages, some of them abandoned. Beached pirogues mark the inhabited ones. Men weaving nets wave to the boat.

You slip by short rises of ground where the trees thrust upward, yearning toward the sky. Profusions of lianas hang from their branches. You see the shoreless expanses of swamp: grass simply growing into the river.

Soon the variations lose significance. You realize that only the constants have meaning: the sky, the water, the land.

Your white sternwheeler is pushing several motored barges. You climb forward to observe them. The steerage passengers, having built squatter villages on them out of mats, are loving the breeze and the leisure, the change from daily routine. Gaiety enlivens their movements and cha-cha music fills the air. Nursing and bathing their infants, the women laugh and yak; their inflections are like a song. Men crowd the rails to bargain for food from fishermen who have pulled out to the paddlewheeler and lashed their pirogues alongside.

The hours pass. You return to the deck outside your cabin to read. But the sun is hot. It glares off the river and has already reddened your skin. You are reading Joseph Conrad: *Heart of Darkness*. The story is slow, the sentences as tangled as the jungle's vegetation. You put the book down. You watch the sky, the water, the land. You understand what is really here: space without time.

And silence. Silence. A great silence hangs over the river.

At night you hear it. You stand on the deck in darkness. The stars seem within reach. The air has at last turned cool. The water whispers below, sliding away from the boat. Do you see the shoreline or only imagine it? You cannot tell. Then you hear the silence. It is vast and heavy; it presses down on the Equateur.

The next day you try to read again. But again the sun is hot. You do not wait so long to close your book. You watch the sky, the water, the land, and now and then you doze. You begin to understand Africa's sense of time.

Time is like the river: vast and silent and ever onwardly flowing. You ride its currents. Time, like the river, is there: before you came, after you go. Like the river, time is bigger than you. And with or without you it flows.

CARD PLAYERS

IN THOSE DAYS SO MANY YEARS AGO we went to the Cercle Wallon almost every evening. The four of us arrived within minutes of each other. Promptly at 7:00 the bridge game began. And so on that particular night when Jamart did not come, we all grew worried.

"Where is he?" Moczar, the UN doctor, asked gruffly.

"Not to worry, Doctor," Pereira said, throwing in his game of solitaire. "Things do not always happen on time in this corner of the Congo. Not anymore."

This was true, but we were concerned. In those days there were only five white men left in Coquilhatville and one, a renegade, we rarely saw. Even so, we did not want our number reduced to four.

Ordinarily a little tardiness would not bother us. But the times were unusual. The Africa we knew was changing. Punctuality had become an obsession with us. Punctuality asserted our standard. It emphasized the differences between the old system and the new, between the passing European way of life and the coming African one. It helped us maintain our identity.

"Where the devil is Jamart?" Moczar asked again. In a half-hearted effort to improve his French he was thumbing through old copies of *La Libre Belgique*. He glanced at his watch. "It's already seven twenty."

I stood at the door, feeling the hush of the African night, feeling the humid air touch my skin. The darkness was liquid and quiet. Yet it contained a wildness to which I had never fully adjusted even after five years.

No one spoke. Eventually Moczar grumbled something in Polish. It sounded like cursing. As a distraction he actually began to read an article. But the delay irritated him; he was a man who expected things to move just so. "Dieudonné!" he called after a moment. *"Un thé glacé!"* The African steward, who was now all that remained of the Cercle staff, took him iced tea, serving it with a formality that already seemed out-of-date. I also ordered iced tea and took a chair. There were no sounds in the room except the drone of the ceiling fan and the crisp slap of Pereira's placing of cards. Often this sound delighted me: a little Portuguese baker's stylish handling of cards. Tonight it annoyed me.

"Jamart went to Bikoro today," Pereira said, looking over his cards.

"But he would certainly have returned by sundown," I replied.

"Perhaps he had trouble at a roadblock," Pereira suggested.

The last white man to have trouble at a roadblock was pulled from his car at eleven in the morning by soldiers who had been drinking for two days. They accused him of being a spy and beat him with rifle butts. He had left the Equateur, the Congo's remotest province, to us, the five who remained.

— 185 —

"But I doubt it," Pereira continued. "Jamart is too well known. He has interests these days along that road."

As Jamart's banker, I knew all about these interests. I was skeptical about the kind of future any European had in the independent Congo. Since shortly before independence I had advised the bank's European clients to liquidate their assets. I told them to salvage what they could and start again elsewhere.

Pereira and the other Portuguese had already sent their capital out of the country. Jamart was different. I had to call him to my office. I sent my Congolese assistant on an errand and turned up the air-conditioner so that its rattling obscured our voices. Then I explained the financial facts of life, even how to evade the foreign exchange regulations. Jamart rejected my advice. In helping to colonize the country he had become convinced of its future. He could not believe that it might collapse. That it was collapsing.

"This is a magnificent country," he told me.

"But not for your money."

"It's on the threshold of a great future."

"That future will not come in your lifetime."

He did not listen to me. "We only need vision, *mon cher ami*. Vision!" He stressed the word as if intoxicated by it. Certainly he had more of it—whatever its real name was—than any of the rest of us. As he looked out the window, he seemed to see already built the great river port the Belgians had never succeeded in constructing during the colonial era.

I myself had once believed that we would build it. When I first arrived three years before independence, ours had seemed a community of Europeans committed to making something of this remote, yet peaceful corner of the Congo. But that had been long before any of us considered that Belgium would one day relinquish its control.

As it turned out, we built little. Even now the town, provincial capital though it was, boasted no more than a few dozen buildings standing on a cleared space between the great river and the great jungle. And the white community had shrunk to five men. We had sent our women and children to safer places months before.

As the remnant of the whites, we five now knew each other well. To mitigate our loneliness we used the familiar *"tu"* form of address. In the old days Pereira, a baker who still spoke French with a heavy Portuguese accent, and Jamart, who owned a garage, employed the formal *"vous"* when speaking to me, a professional, a banker. Moczar, a United Nations doctor, the first of a promised team of experts who had failed to materialize, had joined us six months before.

The fifth one of us was Van Belle, the lawyer. He was Flemish, born in Africa, educated at Louvain in Belgium. Once independence and the violence came, once his family left for the safety of Europe, Van Belle took up with an African woman and "went native." He always seemed relaxed.

"I do not argue with nature," he told me. He fought no battles with the sky or the jungle or the immensity of time that overhung it. To Van Belle, Jamart was doing just that. He was arguing with nature, with the river and the sky, with the jungle, and the weight of time.

"Eventually things here will find their bottom," Jamart declared in my office. "They will start climbing again."

"It will take twenty years," I told him. "Thirty maybe."

"I can wait. I have faith in this country. In twenty years you will see I was right."

He believed what he said. At the time of independence he

owned only a house and the garage. When the *Force Publique* mutinied and the panic began, he did not flee as others did. He did not even get his capital out of the country. Instead, he bought properties from those who were fleeing. Now he owned two small plantations, a used car business, and the garage/service station in Bikoro. In addition, he was giving jobs to the Congolese he trusted. His foreman was now in charge of the operation in Bikoro.

At last I told the others, "I think we should find out what has happened."

Pereira said nothing, as if unconcerned. But he had not yet won a game that evening, a rare thing for a man who permits a little cheating in solitaire. He broke the silence by throwing in another hand.

"Dieudonné!" Moczar called after a moment. "Go *chez Monsieur Jamart*. Ask if he is coming."

"Oui, Monsieur," Dieudonné replied. He wheeled his bicycle out of the pantry where he kept it protected from thieves and rode out to find Jamart.

We waited in silence. Pereira threw in his cards and began to pace. Moczar tossed his newspaper aside. After a while we heard the motorcycles escorting the Congolese governor through town. My ears burned then as they always did when the motorcycles roared. In the Belgians' day there was efficient government—without motorcycles. Now there were motorcycles and sometimes sirens and the administration had almost ceased to function.

Dieudonné finally returned. "Monsieur comes," he said. Relief spread across the room. Moczar and I grinned. Pereira laid another game of solitaire and won it almost as quickly as he could turn over the cards. Dieudonné pushed his bicycle under the bar and stood with his back to us, fussing with bottles.

"He comes immediately?" Moczar asked.

"Oui, Monsieur." But the answer was hesitant and barely audible.

"Tell us the rest," Moczar growled.

"There was shouting, Monsieur," Dieudonné whispered.

"Chez Jamart?"

"Oui, Monsieur."

We glanced at each other, perplexed and apprehensive.

"Did you speak to Monsieur Jamart?" I asked.

"Oui, Monsieur. I knocked at the door and Monsieur opened. He said he was coming immediately."

"And it was Monsieur Jamart who was shouting?"

"Oui, Monsieur," Dieudonné replied, whispering again. He seemed deeply embarrassed to have interrupted Jamart in anger.

"It can't be too important if he's shouting," Moczar said. But it was not like Jamart to shout.

"Do you know why he was shouting?" I asked.

Dieudonné shook his head. "Non, Monsieur," he said and wheeled his bicycle into the pantry.

"Not to worry," Pereira said. "If he can both shout and answer his door, he cannot be in trouble."

Before Pereira had laid another hand of solitaire, Jamart arrived. He was a slight man of less than medium height. As usual at night he wore white shorts, a white short-sleeved shirt, and white knee socks. We looked at him carefully. His combination of nervous energy and unquestioning optimism ordinarily gave him a buoyancy. But this night he was subdued.

"I'm sorry to be late," he said. "Let's cut the cards."

This matter-of-fact casualness surprised us. So did his lack of explanations. But he avoided our eyes, spread a deck of cards across the table, drew one and turned it over. "Who's to be my partner tonight?" he asked.

Moczar and Pereira chose their cards and flipped them up. I drew mine, but before turning it over, I said, "Is anything the matter?"

"Nothing," he said.

"No trouble?"

"None." Still I did not turn the card.

"Tell us if something is wrong," I said. "We're your friends."

"But nothing is."

"Then why are you so late?" Moczar asked gruffly.

"A domestic affair," Jamart said. "A matter of no concern, I assure you."

It was on my lips to confront him about the shouting. But he looked in control of things and he had a right to privacy, after all, especially if we were to stick together.

During the first hand of bridge Jamart blundered badly. Moczar, his partner, a man who took bridge seriously, closed his eyes with icy disbelief; he cleared his throat. Jamart saw his mistake immediately. His face went ashen, showing us the act of will required to maintain his casualness.

"I'm afraid I wasn't concentrating," Jamart said at the end of the hand.

Moczar regarded him carefully, but only commented, "No matter."

Other blunders followed. Moczar almost scolded Jamart once or twice, but managed to choke the words back. I began to play poorly. I felt that nothing must rupture our solidarity, certainly not a game of cards.

Finally Moczar bid extravagantly and took the play. Jamart seemed relieved to be dummy. But he had not finished laying out his hand before the doctor began cursing angrily in Polish. "What have you done to me?" he asked Jamart. "How can I play this?" Jamart had misarranged his hand; he had bid it improperly. "A matter of no concern, indeed!" Moczar growled. He threw his cards onto the table. "Score it any way you like," he told Pereira. "I'm not going to play it." He glared across the table. Jamart said nothing.

"Tell us what happened that you cannot bid a decent game of bridge!" Moczar ordered.

Jamart glanced at me for support. "Perhaps we should know," I said quietly.

He examined his grease-stained hands, deciding what to do.

"Come on!" Moczar commanded. "Out with it!"

"When I returned from Bikoro this afternoon," Jamart said at length, "I took a bath. When I went to dress, I found my best suit, the one I wear to Léopoldville, on the floor of the armoire. I haven't worn that suit for months, and I always hang it very carefully. It would not have fallen by accident." He hesitated. A look of revulsion settled on his face. "I picked it up and I smelled it." He paused again. "Can you guess what it smelled of?"

No one answered.

"A thick, foul odor. Like the smell of a doused fire."

"Unwashed African," Pereira said.

"Exactly." Jamart shook his head as if the odor were again in his nostrils. "While I am out trying to make something of this country, my domestic is parading around in my clothes."

For a time none of us spoke. Pereira finally said, "You threw him out, of course."

"On the spot! Paid him off, threw him out of his quarters and told the *sentinelle* to hose them down. He's going to wash out the armoire, too. My suits are airing on the clothesline."

For several moments we all stared at the table. Then Moczar began to laugh. "And this is all that's bothering you?" he asked. "You are teasing us!"

Jamart stared at him with hostility.

"But this is not serious, my friend," Moczar insisted. "It's charming! Your domestic plays dress-up in your clothes. It's sweet, Jamart! You aren't using the suit so he does! What's the harm in that?"

Moczar laughed harder and, although I did not laugh, I too thought it more a joke than a catastrophe. Jamart looked away in disgust.

"Mais non!" Moczar insisted. "It is charming! We're all independent and equal now. So let's share our clothes." He continued to laugh. "See the joke, *mon vieux!* Haven't your children ever played dress-up in your clothes?"

"But they are clean," Jamart replied.

"And your domestic is not clean?"

"Not clean enough to wear my clothes."

"But clean enough to cook your food!" The doctor could not stop laughing.

"The man smells!" Jamart said, growing annoyed with Moczar. "How do I get that smell out of my best suit? For all I know he has lice."

"Impossible!" Moczar said. "They'd have jumped into your food!" He continued to laugh. Jamart turned his back on us and sat hunched over in his chair.

Pereira looked irritatedly at the doctor and leaned toward Jamart. "Do you think he's been wearing all your clothes?" he asked.

"I hadn't thought of that," Jamart said. "What if he has?"

"Maybe best to wash them in gasoline," Pereira suggested.

Moczar went on laughing. Finally Jamart turned in his chair and said, "Stop it!" The doctor looked up, surprised by the vehemence. For a moment his laughing subsided, then began again. "I'm sorry," he said, "but it's really very funny."

"Stop it!" Jamart repeated. He stood. "You are six months in this country and I am here twelve years. I will not be laughed at!"

"But, *mon vieux,*" Moczar pleaded, "we thought you might be dead someplace. And it was only this!" He laughed again and Jamart walked out of the Cercle. Pereira followed him.

"I am sorry," Moczar assured me. "But it's terribly funny." He went on laughing to himself.

Sometimes love flees at a look, a gesture, a small betrayal. So it was with Jamart's love of the Congo. That evening ended an era. Jamart never again played cards with the same zest. Soon he developed a light rash. Fearing witchcraft, he burned his clothes. Pereira suggested that he destroy them at night and in secret and he did so. Since all the Coquilhatville stores had closed, he had new clothes sent to him. He insisted that the new domestic scour his house completely. And now when he left the house, he always locked the armoire; the new servant would never wear his clothes. Despite these precautions, his skin condition did not improve.

Eventually Moczar recommended that he go to specialists in Léopoldville. Jamart seemed frightened by this suggestion, but eventually he agreed to go. Moczar and I took him to the airport. As we waited for the plane, Jamart tried to seem hopeful. But finally in a whisper he asked us, "What if I don't come back?" Tears of hopelessness and rage shone in his eyes.

"It's not a terminal illness," Moczar answered roughly. "You'll come back to this God-forsaken place—although why you should want to is beyond me."

I tried to joke as well. I had promised to make regular checks on Jamart's house and garage and asked, "Do you think I'd have agreed to that if it were going to be weeks?" He smiled, but the waiting dragged on. Moczar and I both felt relieved when his plane finally took off.

As we drove back to town, I said, "I hope they will be able to cure him."

"He will not be cured," Moczar replied. I looked at him in surprise. "There is no physical explanation for this ailment," he said. "He may think it is witchcraft, but I have talked with Africans. It is not witchcraft. It is not poison. It is an affliction of the mind. Medicine won't get rid of it."

"What are you getting at: that it's not real?"

"Of course, it's real," he snorted. "That man's in misery."

We drove on. "He has developed an allergy—to blacks," Moczar said. "Apparently it's his reaction to realizing that his servants were wearing his clothes. An unfortunate malady for one so heavily invested in the Congo."

"And what will happen?" I asked.

The doctor shrugged. "There will only be four of us left."

When Jamart did come back to town, it was to wind up his affairs. It was a difficult period. Jamart had everything tied up in his properties and, understandably, did not want to sell them. I agreed that he need not. Compassion required this concession of me, but it was not an important one. There were no buyers in any case. He asked me to manage his holdings for a percentage of the return. I had time, but not enthusiasm, for this project, and it would certainly earn me no money. But I agreed. What else could I do? Especially when, after making our final business arrangements, it became clear that he would not have the money to buy an air ticket to Belgium. I wrote out a personal check to cover this.

When I handed it to him, he would not take it. I laid it on the table before him, and he closed his eyes. Tears ran down his cheeks. "Who has done this to me?" he asked.

I could not answer.

"I worked to build this town," he said. "While others laugh at this country, I believe in it. When others ran from trouble here, I stayed. When others exploited the Congolese, I trained them." His voice broke. "Why has this happened?"

I did not know what to say. Moczar's answer was not one I could offer. I said nothing.

After Jamart left, we invited Van Belle to join us at cards, but he refused. We stopped meeting so often at the Cercle Wallon. There were evenings when Dieudonné was the only person at the club. Congolese friends began to drop by to see him. They played the phonograph—so loudly finally that one could hear it all over town at midnight. The Cercle became a kind of African dancehall/bar, with Dieudonné as proprietor. Pereira, Moczar, and I stopped going there altogether.

After several months Jamart sent me a query about his properties and a check to cover the air fare. He had found a job in a garage outside Charleroi, where his wife had family. "Good possibility," he wrote, "I can move up to foreman in two-three years. Proprietor's getting on. With luck I'll buy the business." Then he added, "Luck likes me here. The rash is gone. In Charleroi the weather's cool and we're beyond the range of juju." He finished with a postscript, "Miss our little corner of Africa. But regret the waste of years."

That's a long time ago now. I doubt that Jamart thinks very often of that wild continent. I do feel certain, though, that there are times when he plays cards or draughts at the bar he frequents in Charleroi when he grumbles about bad luck. Then he curses the money lost and years wasted in the Congo. I imagine he blames juju for those losses, never understanding that witch-craft is an excuse for something darker in his heart.

LENOIR

HE WAS ALREADY A LEGEND when I went out there and that was long before he disappeared. "History's a meat grinder," he once told me. "One turn the Belgians make mince of the Congolese. Next turn they make mince of us." When he said it, he had no idea how true it would prove to be. Neither did I. What did he know?

He was a scruffy Walloon peasant. A quarrelsome fellow. He couldn't get along with anyone. He was— I wonder how old. Not old, not young. He had thick black hair he never combed and a heavy beard that he sometimes shaved, sometimes didn't. He had a short, thick-set body that moved awkwardly and heavy shoulders and large, clumsy hands with stubby fingers. He owned a plantation near Boende on the north bank of the Tshuapa. It was the kind of place that never made him ten francs profit no matter how hard he worked it.

"Lenoir n'aime pas les noirs; les noirs n'aiment pas Lenoir." They always said that in Boende. "Lenoir doesn't like blacks;

blacks don't like Lenoir." And no wonder! He must have been impossible to work for. The grumpiness and complaints, the bad temper, they were the first things you noticed in him.

But the legend? I think that came from the mystery. No one knew anything about him: where he'd come from or why, how long he'd been there, how he'd gotten the way he was. No one had visited his plantation, not even the administrators—although everyone knew he was in debt. No one knew how he lived or with whom or even how he managed to keep the place going.

None of this was really surprising. He didn't go to Boende often and when he was there he talked a great deal, as lonely men do. But it was mainly complaints: about the blacks or the administration or the metropole. Usually about the blacks. His grumbling made him the butt of jokes. People mocked themselves by mocking him. His mystery enhanced the jokes and the jokes enhanced the legend.

Still, people accepted him when he came into town. He was white, after all, and before independence that was enough credentials. He stayed at Tslentis the Greek's place where they all played cards and draughts in the evenings.

I first saw him there my third or fourth visit to Boende. After sweating and slapping mosquitoes all day I'd come into Tslentis's place to have a beer before dinner. I joined the men there and while we drank, we heard a deep, angry-sounding voice from behind the faded curtain Tslentis used to separate the bar from the dining room. The voice was complaining about Belgium, about its small-mindedness, its commercial ethic, the stifling Catholicism, the pettiness and suspicion of the villages: in short, the things we all disliked about our homeland.

Then one of the men I was sitting with, a young patriot-administrator out on his first tour, yelled, "Enough, Lenoir! Shut yap!" He winked at the rest of us and settled back, watching the fan in the ceiling, waiting for the response.

"Is that Lenoir?" I asked the man beside me.

"That's him," he said. "The famous Lenoir."

Lenoir kept on talking as if he hadn't heard. The young man shouted again, "Put on the feedbag, Lenoir, and give us some peace!" The complaints continued. Finally the young man cried, "Enough, Lenoir. Tell it to your wives and *piccanins!* Don't tell it to us."

A chair scraped in the dining room. The curtain fluttered. Then Lenoir pulled it aside and stood, short but strong, his big hands clenched into fists. "Who says so?" he demanded.

Finally the young administrator answered, "I say so." His voice sounded less confident now that Lenoir was before him, giving off that strange, magnetic quality of impulsive passion being reined in.

"Say it again," Lenoir invited. The young man said nothing. "Say it again," Lenoir repeated. The young man would not look at him. Lenoir came and stood directly before him. "Children are to be seen, not heard," he said. Then he belched and laughed, and all of us laughed to dissolve the tension.

"Why do you denounce the most beautiful country in Europe?" the young administrator asked, petulant now.

"It's a foul place!" was the answer.

"You're homesick, Lenoir," the man beside me told him.

"Homesick!" Lenoir roared with mock laughter.

"You're like a man who shows his love for a woman by insulting her reputation," the man beside me said. "If you didn't love Belgium, you wouldn't talk about it all the time. You're homesick for your village."

"For little Suronne?" Lenoir asked, laughing too loudly again.

"With its eight detestable stores and its post office. I hate the place and it hates me." It seemed likely there was some truth in this, although it was difficult to guess just what.

"Take some leave and go home," the man beside me advised. "Visit your village so we can stop hearing how bad it is. Go and see what it's really like."

Lenoir looked oddly abashed. "I'll never go back," he answered gruffly. He returned to his dinner and complaining.

Later that evening when the card games ended, the same man drew him aside. "Take some advice, my friend. Leave here for three months and visit your home."

"The plantation's my home," Lenoir said.

"You want to go home," the other insisted. "You wear the longing like a skin." Then he said quietly, "You'd be happier when you came back."

"I don't want to go," Lenoir repeated. The man merely smiled. Finally Lenoir said, "I can't go. And why not is my business." He blustered through the screen door and walked out into the night.

"What is it?" I asked my companion. "Some woman trouble in the past?"

"I doubt it," he said. "What woman would love him?"

I shrugged. Men like that appealed to some women.

"Look at his hands," my companion said. "They break everything they touch." He shook his head. "It's no great secret why he can't go back. He'd have to sell out to pay the passage. It's as simple as that," the man said. He seemed certain that this explanation covered everything. I wasn't so sure.

I didn't see Lenoir again for three or four years. I knew he was still working the plantation because I heard jokes about him whenever I went to Boende.

Then I saw him again— When would that have been: '57?

Britain had just granted independence to the Gold Coast. Lenoir sat in the corner of Tslentis's bar, reading old copies of *La Libre Belgique*, swearing and muttering. "Within five years Brussels will do this to us!" he grumbled. Of course, we all laughed at him. The idea was absurd. We laughed so hard we could not properly bid our cards.

"You're a fool, Lenoir!" someone called. "The blacks can't govern themselves. They don't even want to. Everyone knows that!"

"The Brits don't know it!" he shouted back.

"Merde aux anglais!!" declared the patriot-administrator who was still in Boende then. "They care about power. We Belgians care about people."

"Merde à toi!" Lenoir retorted, his finger tracing the words as he read. We all laughed at him. "Brussels will abandon us to a government of messengers and postal clerks and waiters!" This made us laugh very hard.

"Look, wise man," the young administrator called at him. "The Belgians have a mission to civilize these people. Does it look finished to you?"

"You're a glorious fool," Lenoir said. "And you can afford to be. But what happens to people who've tried to build something in this miserable jungle? What becomes of us, eh, when Brussels abandons the Congo and the blacks chase us out?"

"Talk sense or shut up," someone said, tired of his complaints. "The blacks don't want us to leave. They'll beg us to stay."

At that time I too thought they would. Then I saw one of Tslentis's waiters, standing against the wall as silent and unmoving as furniture. He was following what we said with a look of unexpected intelligence. And I remember thinking, what do we really know of them? What would become of us if independence came?

Then within two years we saw what Lenoir had predicted about to befall us. Brussels capitulated at the Round Table Conference, and we were all worried. Riots in the capital in '59 showed the potential for violence. Still, I was working harder than ever. Buildings were being finished, both in Coquilhatville and Boende, and I had crews in both places, laying the wiring, installing fixtures, selling equipment. I was making three or four trips to Boende every month. I had never been so busy.

On top of everything my father fell ill. I was afraid he would die before I could get home to see him.

On my last trip to Boende before going home I had trouble with the pick-up. Nothing serious. The hose from the gas tank worked loose and jerked free bumping over a rut. In less than a minute I lost all the gasoline in the tank. I made the repair and put in my reserve, hoping it would get me to Boende. But it didn't. Shortly after I ran out, thinking I was in the middle of nowhere, an elderly African, a *tata*, came along the road and said there was a plantation nearby. It turned out to be Lenoir's.

I walked with the *tata* for almost an hour. Finally we came upon something that looked more like an African village than plantation buildings. There was a cleared area. Grass had once sprouted there, but now it was untended. Huts stood at the edge of this, mud-walled and thatched with palm fronds. Outside one of these a bare-breasted woman was pounding manioc tubers in a mortar, singing to herself, and wearing a light-skinned baby tied to her back. She did not hear us approach.

Other African women were sleeping on mats in the shade with their children nearby. Some were as dark as black coffee; others had the color of *café au lait*. When the woman at the mortar saw me, she screamed with fright, threw down her pestle, and ran off into the bush. The other women woke terrified and ran after her. It seemed unlikely that white men visited Lenoir very often.

The *tata* showed me a sturdy structure, built with home-made bricks and covered with a corrugated iron roof. Lenoir apparently used it as a storehouse. Across from it stood a second building, properly roofed but less well constructed: Lenoir's house. There were no windows, nor even a door. Most of the furniture stood under the roof, but in the open air. There was one lounge chair, a plain table with a stool beneath it, a rude armoire he'd obviously made himself, a kerosene lamp, and a large, heavy footlocker with a combination lock. Inside a brick-walled cubicle he had a hard-looking bed with patched mosquito netting over it. The place had only one embellishment: an old photograph, framed and set on the footlocker.

The *tata* went off after the women, hollering at them not to be afraid and to come fetch me some tea. I sat in the lounge chair, waiting a long time, and my eyes kept returning to the photograph. It showed a young woman, rather pretty, but sedate and shy. You could tell little about her except that she had probably doubled her age since the photograph was taken. I kept wondering who she was: a sister, a dead fiancée, someone else's wife? Who meant so much to Lenoir that after all his years in the Congo he still displayed her photograph?

After a while a very clean-looking child came walking with great seriousness across the cleared area. He was a mulatto boy of six or seven. *"Bonjour, Monsieur,"* he said. He extended his hand, as if he greeted visitors every day, and announced, "I will bring you some tea." Very soon he returned and served the tea gravely, saying, *"S'il vous plaît, Monsieur,"* as he extended the tray toward me. It shook a little from heaviness.

After he left, I wondered not only about the woman in the

photograph, but also about the boy. How, I asked myself, had Lenoir trained him to be the opposite of himself? And why had he bothered?

Finally Lenoir appeared. He parked his battered truck beside the storehouse and strode brusquely toward the house. He seemed intent on showing himself ready for confrontation if that was what so unusual a visit portended. "Oh, it's you," he said when he recognized me. "They said someone was here. The boy got you some tea?"

"Yes, thank you."

"Want some more?" he asked.

"All right. Will you have some?"

He shouted for more tea, but made no attempt to be sociable. He took a clay pot of water from the floor, stripped as I suppose he did every afternoon when he came in, bathed, rinsed himself and dried off with a dirty cloth. He slapped the dust out of the clothes he had been wearing and put them back on. Then he went to the footlocker. With unexpected gentleness he took the photograph and set it on the table.

"I couldn't help noticing that," I said, although he hadn't spoken the entire time. "Who is she?"

"A woman I once knew," he answered, busy with the lock. He took a short-wave radio from the footlocker and set it on the table. The child brought tea with the same grace and gravity as before. Watching Lenoir I could see that he adored the boy.

"He's beautifully trained," I said.

"You think so?" Lenoir replied, giving the boy no praise beyond the slightest twinkle of his eye.

"A lovely child," I said.

Lenoir only grunted. He turned on the news and we listened in silence. It was a broadcast from the capital, and when news of the imminent independence came, he began to mutter. "We've got five or six months left in this foul place," he said, as much to the sky and trees as to me. "And then it's flee or . . ." He made a sharp noise and drew his hand across his neck. "We've been betrayed as I always said we would be." I did not answer. He said, "Haven't we?"

"By history, perhaps," I said. "Or by our own expectations. A country like Belgium can't change history."

"History, that great meat grinder," he said and finished his tea. "We're here at the wrong turn of the handle. Admirable explanation. Only what becomes of us?"

"Will you go back to Belgium?" I asked.

He gave one of his extravagant, rhetorical laughs and shook his head. Then he asked, "Well, what do you want? You didn't come for tea."

In the end he came to Boende with me. He could sell me some gasoline, he said, but his stocks were low and needed to be replenished. But this was only an excuse. He wanted company. He wanted to know what independence would mean, wanted to talk to people about it. Naturally that was all anyone talked about in Boende those days.

Lenoir received no more respect there than before, even though he had predicted the course of events. Respect still flowed to the doctor, the administrator, the lawyer. In a hushed voice in Tslentis's bar the lawyer assured us it would only be a paper independence; the Belgians would still control things. Our interests would remain safe, he said, and the administrator nodded ever so slightly in agreement.

Lenoir challenged them. "You have a saying here," he shouted. "Lenoir doesn't like the blacks. But I know them, and you do not. I know this: the blacks are not fools. They know us better than we know them. They will take what you claim is a paper independence. Then they will force us to honor it. They will risk chaos for this. The Belgian government will run from chaos!"

Of course, they laughed at him and shouted him down. A fight almost broke out. I was embarrassed that we had come to Boende together, embarrassed that, because Tslentis's place was full, we had to sleep in the same room.

I woke in the night having dreamed that my father died. When I lit a cigarette, I saw Lenoir sitting in the corner of the room, watching me. "You aren't asleep," I said.

He only grunted, sitting in his undershorts, his chest black with hair.

I asked if he wanted a cigarette. He muttered an assent and I tossed him the pack and matches. When he brought the match to his mouth, I saw that his face was the color of ashes. "Are you ill?" I asked. He shook his head. "What's the matter then?"

"Worried," he said.

"We're all worried," I replied and lay down again.

"But you can sleep," he said.

"You want a pill?" I asked. I had some with me.

"Trapped men don't sleep," was all he said.

"Aren't we all trapped?" I asked.

"You'll escape," he said. "I can only hide." Finally he added, "I'm watching my life go by, my hated, wasted life."

I didn't want to talk, but the tone of despair awakened my compassion. "How did you happen to come here?" I asked.

He ignored the question. At long last he said, "It all turns to gall. You come to the earth's most God-forsaken corner. You spend twenty years on a wretched plantation, thinking, Here at least I'm safe. But it turns to gall in your mouth."

I drifted off to sleep, but it couldn't have been much later when I woke again. I sensed Lenoir awake still in the corner. I struck a match. He appeared not to have moved. I offered him another cigarette and he took it. After a while I asked, "What are you thinking about?"

"Suronne," he said.

"Your village?"

"Yes. A place that hurt me so much I wish it had killed me. I'd like to burn it to the ground." Then he added, "But there isn't a day in the twenty-three years I've been in this cursed Congo that I haven't thought of it."

"Maybe it's changed," I offered.

"I'll never know," he said. "I'll never go back." He said nothing for a long time. I could hear him breathing hard, working himself up to something. At last he said, "I killed a man there."

Suddenly I felt very awake. I listened closely, aware of his bulky form in the chair across the room. I said nothing.

Finally he asked, "Did you hear me?"

"Yes," I said. Even though I was curious, I did not want the responsibility of his revelation. He was still breathing hard.

"He was a doctor," he said at last. "He was a young fellow, tall and handsome. From Brussels. He was getting the experience of practice in a village. He had been to university. He was the kind of man who had never lived in our village or in any village that we knew of. Because of him all our yearning bourgeois saw themselves as burghers. He could do no wrong.

"Before long half our women were in love with him. They took him eggs and soups and pastries. They imagined pains and went to see him." Suddenly Lenoir cursed. "We had a pack of filthy bitches in Suronne!" he said. "They all swooned over his delicate hands that had never known a blister—not like the rough peasant hands we had. They would cut themselves or twist their ankles or dream up tumors in their breasts just so the doctor would touch them with his slender, healing hands.

"The young doctor was no fool. He knew a good thing when it came chasing him. So he serviced half the women that ran after him. I didn't blame him for that. But he bothered women who did not chase him, too," Lenoir said, old anger echoing in his voice. "He came after my wife to seduce her."

The sober, shyly pretty face in the photograph appeared immediately in my mind. It had worn no trace of flirtation and, frankly, it did not seem the sort to attract a seducer.

"She wasn't the kind to chase him, eh?" I said.

"No," he declared firmly. "She was pure, a virgin to her wedding day. She had not even let her suitors touch her much. In fact, it took us three weeks after we were married to manage things." Lenoir said nothing for a long time as if stopped by memory. Then he said, "We had been married only four months when the doctor came after her."

"There were no medical reasons?" I asked. "Sometimes—"

"There were no medical reasons," he answered flatly.

"She wasn't pregnant?"

"No."

"But why should the doctor take an interest in her?" I asked. "Especially if other women were chasing him?"

"She was beautiful and indifferent," said Lenoir. "This was a city man who had never seen real modesty. My wife's modesty, her purity, they attracted him. I had seen him watch her at dances. But my wife had frivolous friends. They saw the doctor's interest. They considered me crude and rough, stupid, a primitive peasant. They advised her not to miss her chance."

"Women!" I sighed—just to let him know I was listening.

"She took sick—or so she said—sometimes in the morning,

sometimes in the afternoon, but always when I was gone. The doctor came to see her at the house."

"She wasn't pregnant?" I asked again.

"No!" Lenoir insisted. "I told you that." Then, "I wanted her to be. I'd have gone crazy with joy over a child. It's the first thing she would have told me."

He fell silent. I said nothing more. I lay in bed thinking. These did not seem to me reasons to kill someone. But, on the other hand, it was his wife and his village and a doctor he knew. Probably the wife had been unfaithful to him—and not without her reasons. He was rough and awkward and may have hurt her without knowing it. Maybe after four months of marriage she wanted something different, something tender.

Still, I had the feeling that part of it was the young Lenoir's astonishment at being happy. Perhaps he had not realized that such things were for all men, doctors and peasants alike. I wondered if, instead of thanking whoever he prayed to for it, he hadn't simply convinced himself that his happiness was counterfeit and had to be destroyed.

"So I killed him," he said after a while. "I followed him one morning after he left our house. I hid in some woods near the house where he made his next call. When he came out, I shot him twice with my hunting rifle. He fell dead."

Having finally told the story, he panted with relief and fatigue. "I hadn't planned what to do afterwards," he said. "I expected to give myself up. But instead I ran. Finally I came here, to this ghastly stretch of jungle.

"I've never seen my wife again," he said. "I've never written. I've wanted to send her money, but I've never had any to spare. She probably doesn't think of me anymore. But I think of her every hour."

After a while I asked, "Why have the police never found you here?"

"I changed my name," he said. "Le Noir was a nickname of mine in Suronne. Because of my hair. My real name is Masure." Then he said very tiredly, "Perhaps the police know I'm here. My plantation is a worse prison than anything they have in Belgium."

With great suddenness he fell asleep. His last cigarette was still burning. I had to get out of bed and take it from his hand. He was still asleep in that chair when I came back from breakfast. When I returned for lunch, he was gone.

During the rest of my stay in Boende I wrestled with feelings of guilt. Should I tell the police what I knew? In the end I did nothing. I was unwilling to betray Lenoir.

When I returned to Coq, there was a cable saying that I should fly to Belgium immediately. My father died three or four hours after I arrived. That experience shattered me. To comfort my mother I stayed a week. But I knew hardly anyone in the town anymore and I was restless and lonely. I spent several afternoons driving around the countryside by myself.

Toward the middle of one cold, gray afternoon I passed a sign to a place called Suronne. I must have driven five kilometers before realizing that Suronne was Lenoir's village. Without really knowing what I intended to do, I turned back and drove into its little square.

It was a tiny place, no different from hundreds of other Walloon villages, and I walked from one end to the other. That took about ten minutes. I felt certain that people were watching me from behind their curtained windows. I still had no exact idea of why I had come, but it seemed pointless not to inquire.

I went to see the postmaster. He was at his desk, a newspaper spread before him, and he was leaning over it squinting to read in the half-light. He tilted his head up toward me when I entered, but neither sat up nor made any welcoming gesture. In fact, his manner reminded me a bit of Lenoir. I wondered if everyone in Suronne shared the same lack of sociability. I asked if there was a Madame Masure in the village.

"Who wants to know?" the postmaster asked, looking back at his newspaper.

"I have a message for her from the Congo," I told him.

"Where?" he asked with a frown. I told him again. "The Belgian Congo?" he asked as if it were Mars. He inspected me with the small-minded suspiciousness that Lenoir reviled and said no more.

"I wonder if you could tell me where Mme Masure lives," I asked very calmly, very politely.

"She doesn't know anyone in the Congo," he said.

"How do you know?" I asked.

"There hasn't been a letter from the Congo through this post office in twenty-five years," he said.

"I would still like to say hello," I explained.

He merely shrugged and looked back at the paper. I went over to his window and looked out at the village. Some children were crossing the square, all huddled against the cold.

"It's a nice village you have," I said. The postmaster grunted. "Anything ever happen here?"

"Nothing extraordinary," he replied without looking up.

"You must have a murder now and then," I suggested, half teasing him.

"A murder!" He looked up and laughed. "A murder in Suronne!" He fell over his paper in genuine amusement. I could see he would have a good time telling this one over dice games at the village bar.

"But there was a doctor killed here twenty or twenty-five years ago," I said.

"No one's ever been killed in Suronne," he retorted.

"This was a young doctor from Brussels. He started a practice here just out of medical school. A tall man, handsome. With delicate hands."

"You mean Dr. Anciaux?" he asked. "He did have a practice here once. He teaches medicine now in Liège."

"No doctor here has ever been killed?" I asked.

"No." He went back to his newspaper. Then after a moment he said, "Wait now." He looked at me curiously. "Anciaux was once shot at, I believe. I think that's right. He hadn't been here long. I was a young man at the time, in and out of the village. I hardly remember the incident." He scratched his head as if to stimulate his memory. "A hunting accident, I think."

"Was the doctor badly wounded?" I asked.

The postmaster frowned. "Perhaps," he said. "But I don't remember that he was wounded at all. Seems to me he heard a couple of shots. He fell to the ground as any sensible man would and that was that." He shrugged. "A hunting accident. Such things happen."

He looked at me for a long moment, then said, "You don't get too much sun down there in Africa, do you?" We laughed at this village witticism and talked about the Congo for a while. I don't think he had ever met anyone who had been there. Finally he declared, "You want to see Mme Masure, eh?"

"Yes," I said. "I'd like to deliver these greetings."

"Congratulations, I suppose, on the daughter's wedding," he said.

"Yes, that's it," I told him after a pause. "Exactly when was she married?"

"Four-five months ago," he said, giving the date. "She married a university graduate. Suronne is very proud of her for that!"

"How old was she?" I asked.

"Twenty-two," he said. "A lovely girl, beautifully trained. Mme Masure deserves a lot of credit. It has not been easy for her."

At last he gave me her address. I had no business visiting her, of course, but I did not want to return yet to the house where my father had died. I found the address and knocked at the door. Finally she came, the woman in Lenoir's photograph two decades older.

She seemed a gentle person, still serious, still pretty, though more from good nature than from intelligence. She had an attractive figure and handsome carriage; they helped explain Lenoir's jealousy. It seemed surprising that in the intervening years she had not found another man. Village life had pinched her mind closed, though. When I mentioned the Congo, she seemed unable to comprehend that other Belgians, people she might know, actually lived there.

Standing on the stone steps before her door, I told her that a Congo friend of her husband, a man named Henri Lenoir who had a plantation near Boende in the Equateur Province, had heard about her daughter's marriage. He had asked me to convey his greetings if I was ever near Suronne. She frowned. She asked me to repeat his name. She said she was sure she hadn't known any Lenoir, but that she hadn't known all her husband's friends as they had not been married long.

I could see that she was a good Belgian and would not invite me into her house. So I shivered exaggeratedly, explaining that we of the Congo lost our tolerance for Belgian weather. At last she invited me inside.

Once I sat down, I said that this Lenoir was a man of some mystery, but had known her husband well. We were none of us certain just why Lenoir had come to the Congo, I told her, but rumors said that he had killed a young Brussels doctor who had made advances to his wife.

She shook her head at this. "Jean-Luc Masure had many friends," she said. "But he was careful about which ones he presented to me. I'm sure I never met this one."

"Do you remember the murder?" I asked. "I understand it occurred right outside Suronne. A young Brussels doctor."

"That could only be the good Dr. Anciaux," she said. "He who delivered my baby all these years ago. He's a famous professor of medicine now in Liège."

"Lenoir doesn't understand what happened to your husband," I told her. "I'm sorry to inquire, but he asked if I would."

"It's all right," she said. "It used to hurt me to think of it, but it doesn't anymore. He was killed in a dreadful train accident not far from Namur. He had gone there looking for a better job. That was not unlike him. Scores of people were killed. Jean-Luc was one of them. They made an identification from clothes and shoes which satisfied the courts. For years I wouldn't believe it. I prayed every night for his safety, wherever he was. Finally I realized that I must accept the truth if only for the child's sake.

"He wanted a child so much," she said. "I should have told him that I might be expecting. The good Dr. Anciaux was making tests and I was afraid of disappointing him. Dr. Anciaux confirmed the pregnancy the very day of the train accident. Jean-Luc never knew."

She blinked, looking down at her hands. "I blamed myself for a long time," she said. "I kept thinking that if I had told him about the tests, then he might have waited that day for the news."

She said nothing for a time, then went to get a photograph. "Here we are together," she said, handing it to me. There was a younger Lenoir smiling at the woman in the photograph he kept on his footlocker.

"You look very happy," I remarked.

"We were very different," she said. "He was a little on the rough side, a bit frightened of the gentleness inside him. I was the only person he ever revealed that side of himself to. Perhaps that's why I married him. That gentleness surprised him; he didn't know what to make of it. We could have been very happy."

"And you've been alone all these years?" I asked.

"No, no. There was our daughter. She's gone now."

At last she smiled secretively, with a surprising girlishness. "I am marrying again a week from Saturday," she confided. "To the postmaster. He lost his wife two years ago."

"Ah ha!" I said. "He was very suspicious when I inquired for you."

She laughed. "He telephoned to warn me. You see he takes very good care of me already!" I realized that she was very fond of him. "I have been lonely, yes," she admitted. "But it has all come right in the end."

By the time I visited Boende again Lenoir had told his story to others. Perhaps he enjoyed the notoriety and supposed that with independence the administration would not bother him. His story came up for discussion the first night I was there. Tslentis's bar was jammed with people; there were more diners than the cook could feed. When I sat down for a beer, the habitués started to tell Lenoir's tale. The bar grew hushed as everyone waited to see how I would react.

I don't know why I didn't keep my mouth shut. Perhaps it

was that they were all so pleased that they knew something I didn't. I had to show them they were wrong. When they came to the climax of the story, I said, "He never killed anyone."

A hush fell across the bar.

"He never killed anyone," I repeated.

"What!" A voice shouted from the dining room, behind the curtain. Silence fell across the room and I wished I had not spoken. Then a large hand ripped the curtain aside. There stood Lenoir. A chicken leg dangled from his fingers.

"What?" he shouted again.

I said nothing. He walked to where I was sitting and stood right before my chair. "You've been to Suronne?"

Finally I nodded. He glared at me. At last I asked, "Was the doctor's name Anciaux?"

"Yes," he said in a hush, almost afraid.

"Anciaux teaches medicine at Liège now," I said. "It seems you may not have even wounded him."

"No!" he shouted. "No!"

I could not look at him. But he wanted more. He crouched down before my chair and took my wrist. "What else?" he asked. I said nothing, but his pressure on my wrist was so great I thought he would stop the blood. He repeated, "What else?"

"He went to your house that day to tell your wife she was pregnant. She was afraid to tell you until she was sure. The baby was a girl."

He held my wrist ever more tightly. "And? And!" he demanded.

"She was married five months ago."

Lenoir closed his eyes. He covered his face with a massive hand, slowly shaking his head.

"The villagers have finally convinced your wife that you died in a train crash," I said. "She wouldn't believe them for years."

"How is she?" he whispered.

I could not look.

"Tell me," he insisted.

I said, "She married the postmaster three weeks ago."

He gave a cry. It grew into low, wretched sobs. People turned away. He stood and passed through the bar, groaning like an animal. He went outside. We could hear him moving up the street, his sobs tearing the night.

When I went out to find him, he had gone. I looked for him again the next morning, but I couldn't find him.

When I drove back home several days later, I stopped at his plantation. The buildings had been burned to the ground. His women were wailing and raking through the ashes with palm fronds. As I watched them, the *tata* appeared. He said that Lenoir had taken the boy and the truck and had gone. He vanished from the Equateur as completely as he did from Suronne.

I left that country years ago, but I suppose somewhere, hidden in its vastness, Lenoir and his son are still there.

ELIZABETH WHO DISAPPEARED

WHEN I AGREED TO ACCOMPANY George Templeton into jungle a thousand miles west of Nairobi, I did not imagine that I would meet Elizabeth, who at fifteen was about to marry a missionary doctor, or that she would vanish from among us. The job was presented to me simply as a week's gig helping a man fly a plane to a mission station. Since my teaching job had ended for the year and I was idle, I was glad to sign on.

Ordinarily George traveled with his wife. But she wanted no part of the trip. She had come to Africa to watch animals, not to inspect mission stations. George, however, wanted something from Africa that was more than counting lions and giraffes. But I'm not sure he knew what that something was.

He seemed to have everything: pots of money, a beautiful and intelligent wife (though maybe not a beautiful marriage; there were no children and maybe not much intimacy), a phenomenal house in Santa Barbara, another at the Smoke Tree Ranch in Palm Springs, and a third on Vancouver Island, and he had no need to work. He loved flying. After graduating from Yale in the '50s he'd gone to the Northwest Territories of Canada as a bush pilot. There he'd built an airline that had been bought a year or two before we met by Air Canada. Now he was a multi-millionaire with time on his hands. The thing he had lived for most of his life—his airline—had been taken from him. But he still had a questing spirit and a desire to do things that counted.

The Central African Mission had a string of twelve stations in the old Equateur Province of what was then Mobutu's Zaire. It also had a long shopping list of equipment needs. As an important contributor to the denomination, George knew of these needs. His first full day in Nairobi he went out to Wilson Airport and rented a plane to look at the country. Apparently this was how he always oriented himself. He found a used Cessna for sale, checked it over carefully, took it up and liked it. He mulled the matter during the week of game-viewing, then decided to buy the plane and donate it to the Mission. He would fly out there, visit stations in a CAM vehicle he could leave in Kisangani, and then hop a plane back to Nairobi.

Mrs. Templeton did not want George to fly long distances over Africa alone. That prospect didn't bother him; he'd landed in dozens of unlikely places bush-piloting in the Northwest Territories. But he agreed that it was not wise to drive very far alone; no telling who might commandeer the vehicle. Local missionaries would have been happy to accompany him, but he did not want to make a donation to their work that resulted in keeping them from that work. So it was decided that he would take a companion along. The companion turned out to be me.

I had been teaching English at a secondary school in Nanyuki. I'd signed a contract to teach a second year, largely because I did not want to return to a job market in America that would put me behind a counter at McDonald's. So I had a few weeks to kill. George asked around for someone who might accompany him into the jungle. My name was mentioned; he sought me out. I gave him references, and he invited me to dinner at the Norfolk Hotel. The fact that I had been living in Kenya, traveling about when I could, provided proof of an independent spirit. While we were having after-dinner coffee, I excused myself, ostensibly to take a leak, but actually to give them time to discuss me. When I returned, I had passed muster with Mrs. Templeton. George offered me the opportunity, agreeing to pick up all the expenses and offering a small salary, and I signed on.

We flew west-southwest for three days. Over open savannah the first with herds of zebras and gazelles sometimes visible beneath us. Across the Rift Valley early the second day and over dense forest. More forest the third day, even denser, with some treetops seeming to reach into the sky almost far enough to touch us. The air grew more humid; it began to have a physical weight on your skin. The dense canopy of trees produced a kind of green gloom on the jungle floor. Now and then through foliage we caught glimpses of river surfaces coruscating in the dappled light. These were old rivers. They meandered across the jungle floor, discarding horseshoe lakes, curling back on themselves in long miles of s-shaped squiggles.

The farther we flew, away from his wife, away from telephones and fax connections to the world, the more relaxed George became. I asked about his bush-piloting days in Canada and he told me story after story as we sat above the green landscape passing below. George asked what my plans were. When I said I expected to stay in Kenya to escape the uncertain job market at home, he said, "You've got a sense of adventure. And I've got contacts. What sort of job would you like?" His question so caught me by surprise that I did not know what to say. It struck me that George was a man who'd had an airline and perhaps wished he'd had a son.

"Something that would let me see the world," I finally replied. "And make some contribution to it."

"I'll make some inquiries when we get back," he said.

My father was a man who'd had sons—three of them, in fact—and perhaps wished he'd had an airline. The middle of the three chips off his Midwestern block, I'd never felt close to my father. It always seemed that he showed his love for me by criticizing what I did. I was half-aware that I might be in Africa partly to distance myself from that kind of affection.

"If I could get a career-path job," I told George, "I'd be ready to go home tomorrow."

"You might be able to assist me," he said. "I've got some investment schemes and could use some help."

"Thanks," I said. I had never thought I'd find a mentor two thousand feet over rain forest.

We found a road and followed it to Bololo station: church, school, hospital, homes with wide screened porches, all roofed in corrugated metal. We buzzed the place. As we circled back, you could see people, black and white, running from all ends of the station toward the landing strip. We were greeted a little the way Lindbergh was received at Le Bourget. People I never did meet embraced me. They used Christian phrases and spoke in born-again jargon that I did not fully understand. They clustered around the new-to-them plane, touching it with a gentleness that made it seem alive. Behind this cluster of greeters stood a congregation of Africans, mainly children, but including some adults, who simply stared. There was also a quiet, remarkably beautiful girl with dark hair, fair skin, and blue eyes that observed everything. Standing in the crowd of milling people, she smiled at me. I heard people call her Elizabeth and wondered why in the world she was here in the remote reaches of the jungle.

That evening at the meeting hall there was a "social," a large gathering of missionaries and African brethren. First, the new plane had arrived. Second, with it had come guests from the outside world, one of whom was giving the Central African Mission a handsome gift. And, third, there was soon to be a wedding on the station. A missionary doctor whose wife had died, leaving him with two small children, was marrying the only daughter of a missionary family. When the bride-to-be was presented to us, I recognized her as Elizabeth who had welcomed me with a smile at the landing strip. So she was to be the doctor's wife.

Standing together, she and the doctor did not seem to have much rapport. Elizabeth was very shy with him. Probably with reason. Tall, balding at thirty-five, and with metal-rimmed glasses, the doctor seemed that odd combination, a cold fish in a warm climate. Still, I noticed that when he took her hand in his to cut a cake together, his touch was gentle. I felt that he was both clearly pleased with what Providence had sent his way and that he meant to be good to her. His exterior was obviously not the best way to judge him. Even so, she stood beside him as if he were her schoolmaster, not her husband-to-be. His name was Dave Roberts; she called him "Doctor Dave."

The doctor escorted George and me to the guest house when the party ended. "Would you fellas like to see some surgery tomorrow?" he asked. "I know I've got operations skedded." George said he'd like to watch. I wondered if the doctor had wooed Elizabeth with such an invitation. What constituted a big date on a mission station?

Fresh water supplies were tight at Bololo; everyone bathed in the river. Since I was awake at first light, I slipped out of the guest house across the landing strip to the river, shucked off the shorts I'd slept in, dipped myself into the water naked, and soaped my body. Africans appeared out of nowhere to watch. It turned out that you weren't supposed to wash in the buff. The missionaries bathed regularly in swim suits.

With the shorts on again, I started back across the landing strip, my entourage of watchers following. Then I stopped. I observed an African woman approach the parked and inanimate plane as if it were a living creature, as if it might waken and turn on her. Tall, probably in her thirties, she moved on long legs, watched from a tattooed face, and had scarification designs on her back. Braids of tight-coiled hair stuck out all over her head like antennae. She wore nothing but a loincloth. She moved toward the plane in a manner that suggested not so much shyness as an instinctive animal reluctance to draw near to the incomprehensible and unknown. Arriving, she stood with one foot resting on the opposite ankle, her long arms folded across her body, one hand in her armpit, the other in her mouth. She watched the plane, absolutely motionless. Then she reached forward, her breasts hanging like wide, thin flaps almost to her waist. She extended an arm and lightly laid her hand on the skin of the wing, ready to dart away if the creature should move. But it did not move. Neither did the woman. She stood there, almost more animal than human, her hand resting on that white and yellow metal bird which would always remain inexplicable to her. In evolution she seemed a million light years away and I was close enough to touch her.

As I watched this pristine savage in my undershorts and sandals, towel tossed over my shoulder, I noticed Elizabeth. She observed the woman from the door of the guest house George and I had slept in. She held a tray in her hands; on it sat a teapot cloaked in a cozy and two cups. Our eyes met. She smiled. I returned the smile, feeling more naked than I expected to, more naked than I needed to in this place where people lived so close to their native state. She waited for me.

"*Olecko, mondeli,*" she called. I frowned and came up to her. "'*Olecko*' means 'Are you there?' in Lonkundo," she explained. "'*Mondeli*' means 'stranger.' You answer, '*Olecko.*'" She watched me, waiting for me to answer.

"*Olecko,*" I said.

"That means, 'I am here. Are you there?' And I say, '*Oh.*' Which means, 'I am here.'"

"I'll try to remember."

She glanced again at the woman and said, "That's how I'll look if I ever go to the States again."

"You'll never look like that," I told her. "Not unless you've got scars all down your back." She laughed. I asked, "When were you in the States?"

"It was real long ago. I don't remember much. When Doctor Dave takes me back, I'll be more like her than like you." She handed me the tea tray. "This will help you and George wake up."

"Do you want to go to the States?" I asked.

She said nothing, but her eyes betrayed her eagerness to see a world that would be as strange to her as the plane was to the woman standing with one foot on the other like a water bird.

"How old are you?" she asked.

"Twenty-three," I said. "And you?"

"Guess," she commanded.

"Twenty, maybe?" She shook her head and seemed pleased to have fooled me. "Eighteen?"

"Fifteen."

My look said no-you're-not, but she nodded, insisting. When I kept looking at her, she said, "Doctor Dave needs help with his kids." I said nothing. She added, "Mutimba who I grew up with has two babies already."

"How did his wife die?" I asked.

"Childbirth." Then she added, "He wants me to replace the child they lost."

We looked at each other a long moment. "I'm sure you'll have lovely babies," I said. I pushed on into the guest house.

I set the tray down in the parlor and knocked on George's door. "Tea!" I called. I went into my room to throw on a tee shirt and fresh shorts. When I returned to the parlor, George had poured tea for both of us. I said, "That girl they're marrying off to the doctor is only fifteen."

George replied, "That's what I heard. Even missionary girls ripen fast in the tropics."

After having our tea George and I went to the surgery. Because the heat of midday made operating difficult, work there started early. An African nurse beckoned to us. She gave us caps and surgical masks, helped us put them on, and escorted us inside.

I had never entered an operating room before and felt a momentary vertigo brought on by the strong scent of disinfectant in the mask that covered my nose. The surgery was perhaps fourteen feet square, a well-made shed, clean but not antiseptic, the interior painted white with neon lights powered by a gas-driven generator that chugged away in a lean-to outside. In a rectangular pot off in the corner operating scalpels and tweezers were sitting in a boiling solution, being sterilized. Steam drifted out the sides of the gurgling box. Wearing a cap, mask, and smock, all clean but none of them ironed, Dave was already at work. Beneath the smock he wore no shirt, a pair of loose-fitting shorts, and Teva sandals. Assisting him were three male nurses, also in smocks, caps, masks, and the woman who had welcomed us, wearing cap, mask, and mammy cloth.

"Morning, fellas," Dave said without looking at us. "I hope the condition of our surgery doesn't put you off." He took instruments his African assistant handed him and continued to work. "Given the conditions we deal with out here, anything more elaborate doesn't serve our purpose."

The portrayals of surgery I had seen in movies and on TV where something dreadful was always at stake had never suggested that a surgeon could work and chat at the same time. But there was about Dave an aura of such unpretentious competence that I had no doubt that in real life this was possible.

"This is a hernia case," he told us. "You can come as close as you like. Just don't touch anything."

As we approached the table, I glanced at George. He seemed as reluctant as I was to get too close.

"We have a lot of hernia cases here," Dave went on. "My hunch is it's congenital with Bantus. If African medicine were better developed, we'd know the reason. But I do more hernias in a year than a Stateside surgeon sees in a lifetime."

The operating table stood in the center of the room. It was tilted, the patient's head downward, his arms flung out from his sides. He was conscious, anesthetized and feeling nothing, but looking uncertain, particularly at the sight of two unknown visitors gazing at his open abdomen. When Dave started to close the wound, I retreated. Partly out of deference to the patient, partly because I felt assailed by unusual sensations—the disinfectant clogging my nostrils, the sight of guts—and was becoming lightheaded.

"If you're having trouble," Dave said, noticing my retreat, "just put your head down between your legs."

"I'm okay," I replied.

When the operation was finished, the nurses righted the table, uncovered the patient, cloaked him with a mammy cloth, placed him onto a woven stretcher that had been brought in and took him out. Dave went to a sink, poured solution into a basin, and scrubbed his hands and forearms. "We don't do it the way they do in the States," Dave said. "We do them mass production here. If we had air-conditioning, maybe we could break between surgeries, but here we're trying to beat the heat."

"What if someone gave you an air-conditioned surgery?" George asked.

"We've looked into it," Dave said. "The question is: Could we keep it going? Or would it just break down the way everything else here does? You fellas live at the end of the twentieth century. In a lot of ways we live at the beginning of it. Our methods are decades out of date. We know it. What can we do about it? Not much. Air-conditioning won't change that."

A new patient was brought in, a man whose belly was badly swollen. As he was transferred from the stretcher to the operating table, I felt myself lightheaded again and left the surgery.

Outside I removed the mask and breathed deeply of clean, cool air. I pulled off my tee shirt and sat on the steps, my head between my knees. Inside I heard one of the nurses saying a prayer before the operation began. The dizziness abated and I felt annoyed with myself for having to leave. When I looked up, I saw the usual crowd of Africans watching the *mondeli*. I felt as disconcerted as the patient must have while George and I stared at him.

Sitting there, I was aware of the drone of Dave's voice chatting with George inside. Then there was silence. Tension flooded out the surgery door as strong as an odor. Something had gone wrong. I stood, backed away from the steps, and peered at the screen door. George staggered out, reeling as I had. There was blood on his cap and mask and shirt. I took his wrists and lowered him to the steps. He pulled off the cap and mask, wiped an arm across his eyes, and put his head way down between his knees. The crowd of children moved a little closer to watch the two white strangers.

Finally when he looked up, George said, "That patient? The swelling? It was internal bleeding. When Dave cut him open, blood sprayed out of him. Like a fountain. God, there was blood everywhere."

I fanned him with my tee shirt. "Things okay now?"

George shook his head. "I think he died."

We were to have breakfast at Dave's house. While George went back to the guest house to wash and change, I went over there. I climbed the steps and entered the screened porch, not quite sure what to do. An African servant, a man, peeked out at me, then disappeared. After a moment Elizabeth came onto the porch. We looked at each other. "He lost a patient, I think," I said. She nodded; she had already heard the news. We looked at each other a long moment, both a little alarmed. Then I did what seemed natural. I went to her and gave her a hug.

"What do I say to him?" she asked when I released her. "I don't know what to say to him."

Her lovely soft eyes looked at me with the frightened expression I sometimes saw on the faces of the youngest students in the school in Nanyuki, the ones who felt lost and had no idea what to do and were afraid.

"Can't you just hug him?" I suggested.

"He doesn't hug," she said.

"Then I don't know."

We looked at each other a long time. I felt sorry for her, the fifteen-year-old kid who was about to marry a man she didn't even know. When I realized that I was going to hug her again unless I got away, I said, "I'll be back in a while," and took off. I walked down by the river until the houseboy appeared to gesture that breakfast was served.

We hardly spoke while we ate. Elizabeth sat beside her husband-to-be, obviously uncomfortable. Occasionally she would look up from staring at her plate and glance at me as if for some kind of help. I did not know what to do. Instead of waiting for the servant to clear the plates, Elizabeth took them and disappeared.

"If you had modern equipment, would that have happened?" George asked at last.

Dave shrugged. "Maybe this region once seemed on the brink of joining the modern world," he said. "But today it's sinking back into a way of life no better than when the first explorers came through here. Leprosy's on the rise again."

The houseboy came onto the porch to pour us coffee. I looked about for Elizabeth, but she did not reappear.

"Tomorrow when you drive to Mondombe," Dave said, "you'll be on roads that were once so smooth you could zip along at sixty miles an hour. They were never paved, but they were well-maintained. Work crews cut the forest back ten-twenty yards from the road so that the sun dried the surface after a rain. That prevented potholes forming.

"You'll pass plantations that used to get their produce to markets on the rivers. Not anymore. Boats don't ply the rivers like they used to. Schedule? Why bother? Why stop at plantations that don't bribe the crews? So palm nuts don't get taken to market; they rot instead. If it's properly processed, raw rubber lasts indefinitely. But African-run plantations don't process it properly. The foreign-owned ones have all been driven out. So rubber decays on the docks or at the roadside. You'll smell it. The stench carries for miles."

Dave looked up at George, shrugged again and tried to smile. "Our water's uncertain. So's our electricity. Our gasoline. We don't eat much fresh food. Sometimes my wife used to cry at night." After a moment he said, "So what's the point of a modern surgery, complete with air-conditioning and the latest diagnostic equipment? We're in the midst of ten thousand square miles of jungle where nothing works."

"Why do you stay?" George asked.

"My wife used to ask me that. I promised her we'd get out when this tour ends." He stared, preoccupied. It was obvious that he was thinking about his wife. "I stay because the doctoring matters here. I handle it easily now. I don't spend time worrying about filling hospital beds and filing insurance forms or scheduling golf or dealing with patients who want surgery they don't need. After ten years out here I know the language and the customs. I like the people." Dave finished his coffee and pushed the cup away. "And maybe I stay," he said, "because no hospital in the States wants a doctor who is absolutely first-class in jungle conditions doing procedures that haven't been done in thirty years."

"I think I'll take the plane up again," George said. "You want to come along?"

Dave shook his head. "I'll come," I said.

Out of the blue Dave said, "There was a report of cannibalism last week at Bololo State Post."

George and I exchanged a glance. We looked over at Dave who was staring preoccupiedly again.

"Half a dozen women ate a six- or seven-year-old child."

For a moment no one spoke.

Then I asked, "That sort of thing really happens?"

Dave nodded. "We get inquiries now and then from people looking for a missing child. Or a young adult. They take them, too. In the newspapers from Kinshasa there are always headlines: *'On Cherche un Disparu.'*"

"I've heard of ritual cannibalism," George said.

"There's that," Dave replied, "but this is meat-hunger. Something we never think of. But Africans think about it all the time. We had a teacher go crazy at Monieka. He kept screaming, 'Don't let them eat me when I die.'"

I stood and gathered the coffee cups, took them into the house, and found my way to the kitchen. I saw Elizabeth out in the yard. In the African fashion she was stretching sheets over bushes to dry. I watched her, thought how beautiful she seemed, how great she looked reaching up on one foot to stretch out the corner of a sheet. It seemed a terrible thing to me that the next day she should be marrying this strange, good man in order to take care of his motherless kids and give him others. It seemed to me that in a way the missionaries were eating their own children. It wasn't just the Africans who were cannibals.

George took the plane up again, ostensibly to give the mission pilot a check-out, but really, I think, to put some air between him and the problems down below. I went along. We flew over the route we would drive the next day and I saw that the roads were, indeed, full of potholes. At one point a crowd of Africans was trying to get an old truck moving. They waved to us as if they thought we might stop to help. I wondered if we would encounter the same truck the next day.

Late that afternoon Dave drove over to Bololo State Post and invited me along. It was necessary that the mission maintain good relations with the Territorial Administrator, he said. The Administrator's teenaged daughter had recently come to him, complaining of stomach cramps. Examining her, Dave had found nothing wrong—although the girl insisted the pains continued. Dave had kept her under observation for a week, wanting to be sure there was nothing he could do to help her. "Elizabeth spent a lot of time with her," he said. "Prepared her food. Mutimba is Elizabeth's big buddy."

I nodded, remembering that Elizabeth had mentioned her friend Mutimba who already had two children.

"She really wanted to go to the witch doctor," Dave said. "So I needed to be sure there was nothing I could do. A witch doctor's expensive. And her father didn't want to give him a chance to seem powerful."

At the State Post the Territorial Administrator had liquor on his breath. When we appeared, he unleashed a burst of rage at a subordinate, designed, I was sure, to impress us with his authority. Dave invited both men to the wedding the next day. They made jokes and wished him well.

As the Administrator walked us to the vehicle, Dave asked after Mutimba. The Administrator said she still complained. "Did she go to the witch doctor?" Dave asked.

"Oh, you know how women are," the Administrator said.

We walked down the road to a one-room store and bought bottles of lukewarm beer. To drink it, we sat on stools under a canopy of banana fronds. "My fellow missionaries scold me for drinking this," Dave said. "I do it because there's so much we forbid Africans to do. They mustn't dance because we think that excites their lusts. Mustn't be idle. Mustn't go naked. I don't think beer will send 'em to hell."

I asked about the case of cannibalism he had mentioned. How had it come to light? How would it be handled judicially? He shrugged and muttered something about there being two systems of law just as there were of medicine, one trying to be modern, the other still traditional. He was not certain how the case would be handled, he said, and stared at the emptiness of the road.

Finally he said, "You must think it strange, don't you, that I'm marrying a girl who's even too young for you?"

"I guess girls get married young out here," I replied.

"It was Lucas Jenkins's idea," Dave said. Jenkins was Elizabeth's father. "Makes a kind of sense, I suppose. My kids do need a mother. But I'm still trying to get used to the idea that my wife is dead, not just on home leave."

I glanced over at Dave. He was staring at the road. It occurred to me that he needed someone to talk to in order to hear how the idea of his marrying Elizabeth sounded when it was put into words. Neither of us said anything for a while.

"Mutimba's father—he's both the Administrator and the local chief—went to Lucas and asked for Elizabeth. Did it in the old-fashioned way. He led a delegation of elders. They offered bride-wealth, the whole thing. He wanted Elizabeth for his oldest son. About your age. Likely to take over the chieftaincy."

Dave shook his head.

"Jenkins was flabbergasted. Almost apoplectic. He thought his daughter was still playing with dolls."

I laughed. So did Dave.

"The chief's son's not a bad kid. Went to our school. Did all right. He's not a Christian, but he agreed to be baptized."

Dave took a swallow of beer. And I smiled.

"This raises interesting problems for us," Dave said. "We talk about all being brothers in Christ. But we have a color bar. Lucas Jenkins can preach Christian brotherhood. But he sure won't let some black savage marry his daughter. No way!"

"What does Elizabeth think about getting married?"

"I don't know that anyone's asked her. She was supposed to finish high school out here—her mother teaches her the Calvert System—then go off to Bible college somewhere."

"What made Jenkins come to you?"

"Bad options. It was unthinkable that Elizabeth should marry an African in the tribal manner, go off to live in a hut some-where, and become an African. The guy could be baptized and join us, but we couldn't let Elizabeth join them. How would you like to think of your daughter bare-breasted and in a breech-clout pounding manioc in a mortar?"

I nodded, taking his point.

"The Jenkinses couldn't send Elizabeth home to finish high school. There were no relatives for her to stay with and no money to send her to boarding school."

"Why couldn't she just stay here?"

"Lucas was afraid the chief might harm her in some way. Kidnap her. Maybe worse. Such things happen."

"Couldn't the Mission Society help place her in a school in the States?"

"The truth is Lucas didn't want her in the States. We've got a little island of our own creating out here. If Elizabeth leaves our island in the forest with an African husband, she faces the deg-radation and reversion to savagery that's all around us. If she leaves our island for the States, she faces the corruption of America's irreligious, sex-crazed, immediate-gratification, drive-by-shooting society we all fear."

"Not an easy choice when you put it that way."

"No one thinks this is a paradise. It's just better than the other alternatives."

"Are you and Elizabeth friends?"

"I'm not great with people. Don't talk easily to women. The truth is: I hardly know her."

"But this marriage: it's what you want, right?"

"It looks good on paper. My kids have a mother. I have a companion. I don't have to leave our little island. And maybe it mollifies the Africans. They see that Lucas Jenkins had other offers for Elizabeth so they're not insulted."

"You 'don't have to leave.' You wouldn't have stayed out here unmarried? It just doesn't work for the kids?"

"Society rules. No unmarried male missionaries in the field."

I nodded.

"The body needs it satisfactions. We're not saints. I can tell you in confidence that I've seen African women who looked pretty good to me since my wife died."

"We're not talking intellectual companionship here."

"No." He smiled shyly. "I thought about marrying an African woman. Broached the idea to some of my colleagues. They all opposed the idea. "

"Why was that?"

"They wanted to know: Did I expect to take her back to the States when I went home? Would she adjust? What would people think? Then there was the problem of training an African woman to be the social equal of Ruthie Jenkins. It would've changed the way everything works here and I didn't have the time for it."

"Maybe marrying Elizabeth works out pretty well then," I suggested.

Dave shrugged. "I don't know that Ruthie has talked to her about what married life is like. I guess Mutimba has. We'll just take it slow. Eventually bodies do attract. That's why marriages work. You toil together, have children, get past challenges. After a while you find you love someone. Love comes slowly, but it comes."

That evening after dinner the Bololo missionaries gathered in the Roberts living room for a jungle-style wedding rehearsal party. George and I arrived in time to watch Reverend Jenkins, who had decided to preside at his daughter's wedding, tell Elizabeth and Dave and their two attendants how to manage the exchange of rings. Thanks to a radio net that linked the entire chain of stations, not unlike party line telephones of long ago, CAM missionaries along the river were present for the rehearsal. People chatted back and forth, gossiping, talking shop, and offering the couple congratulations. When Jenkins invited Dave to kiss the bride, someone shouted into the net, "He's gonna kiss her now!" People laughed. Elizabeth stiffened. Dave hesitated, then pecked her as if he were kissing his daughter. The missionaries laughed, whistled, clapped, and people on the net asked, "Did he give her a good one? Is she gonna want more where that came from?" Refreshments were brought out: Kool-Aid and cookies that Dave's children and Elizabeth had made that afternoon. I remembered Dave describing Bololo as an island that the missionaries had created. It struck me as a place that the long-departed Norman Rockwell might recognize.

By this time I rather liked Dave. I saw that he was still preoccupied, probably by the death of the patient on his operating table that morning. I wondered if he were also thinking of his wife, feeling confused at marrying again so soon. I watched him trying to join the spirit of the occasion, offering jokes to friends up and down the river. But the attempts seemed awk-ward; he really did lack personal warmth. Strangely, given the virginal setting, I hoped he was good at sex. It seemed un-likely, but doctors sometimes knew secrets. Since he was truly an admirable person, if he were also an accomplished lover, why shouldn't Elizabeth fall in love with him? I hoped she'd be happy. If she were, it would be because she had no idea of the possibilities that lay in the wide world beyond Bololo.

George offered the couple a toast in Kool-Aid. Dave and Eliza-beth stood side by side, not yet well enough acquainted to touch. While George spoke, Elizabeth kept glancing at me, sometimes smiling the way she had across the landing strip when I knew only that she was beautiful. I found the smile disconcerting. When he returned to the States, George promised, he would send as a gift the entire Disney Video Library. The missionaries cheered; it was the perfect gift for their island. George quaffed his Kool-Aid, kissed the bride and left. "We hit the road at first light," he reminded me. I nodded that I'd be coming soon and looked back at Elizabeth. Our eyes met. I wanted very much to kiss her. But I didn't trust myself doing that in front of a room full of religionists trained in detecting lust. So I clasped my hands above my head, signaled thumbs up to both her and Dave and left the house without looking back.

Once in bed, I couldn't sleep. George began to snore as soon as his light went out. The sound came from his room like a far-off sawing. Finally I crawled out from under the mosquito net and went to close his door. He did not stir.

Later I woke, sensing that someone had entered the room. I did not move, only opened my eyes. A figure came beside my bed, stared at me, then crouched. *"Olecko,"* it whispered.

I tried to remember how she had told me to respond, but I

couldn't. My heart was beating so fast and I had such a hard-on that it was pointless to think.

"*Olecko,*" she said again, looking down at me.

"What're you doing here?" I whispered.

"Can I come in?" she asked. She pulled the mosquito net out from under the mattress, slid beneath it, and slithered up onto the bed. She wore an old-time missionary outfit, a loose dress that fitted over her head and reached to her ankles. By contrast I was naked. I was lying without covers, wearing only boxers, boxers that looked more and more like a tent. I sat up, crossed my legs and arms before me and moved to the far end of the bed.

"What're you doing here?"

"You didn't say goodbye. Why not?"

"I waved. We smiled at each other."

"That's not the same as goodbye."

"Goodbye," I said. "There."

She looked at me—as much as that was possible across the darkness. "Are you looking at me?" She reached out and touched my face. "Why didn't you say goodbye? You were supposed to kiss the bride."

"I didn't want to kiss you," I said.

"Why not? I don't believe that." Her hand moved across my cheek.

Very softly I said, "Shhh. George is in the next room."

"Why didn't you want to kiss me? I know you've been watching me. I've felt your eyes on me." Her fingertips touched my eye sockets. Feeling her touch, remembering her beauty, I forgot for a moment that she was only fifteen.

"I was afraid to kiss you," I said, remembering her age.

"Why?" she asked.

"Because," I said.

"Because why?"

My excitement was slackening with all these teenager's questions. I took her hands in mine and kissed them. "There. I kissed the bride."

"Why were you afraid to kiss me?"

"Because I wasn't sure I could give you the kind of kiss a guy is supposed to give a missionary girl in front of her fiancé."

"Kiss me the way you wanted to. Right now."

I put her hands in her lap and released them. "I can't even see your face," I said.

Suddenly she rose on her knees, put her arms over her head and pulled off the dress. "Show me how to do this," she said. She crawled toward me. "I don't even know Doctor Dave. I don't want him to be the first man to do this with me."

"No," I said. I held her away from me. "In five years you're going to love him. If we do anything, you'll feel unworthy. You'll feel guilty all your life. You can't want that." I crawled out from under the mosquito net and tiptoed outside. I had gotten a good look at her crouching there and I needed to be away from her.

After a minute she came outside wearing the dress again.

"Have a good life," I said. I offered my hand.

"Please kiss me," she implored. "Please kiss the bride."

I leaned forward, my body well away from hers, and kissed her lightly on the mouth. "I know you'll be very happy," I said.

She walked off toward the houses. I went down to the river, shucked off my shorts and slipped into the water. Its coolness brought solace to my groin. The current was fairly fast; I could swim energetically against it and stay where I was. I swam until I was tired and rain was threatening. I walked back naked to the guest house, carrying my shorts. Damned if there weren't a couple of Africans gawking at me. I thought it was a good thing I had done nothing with Elizabeth. There were certainly Africans who would have been watching.

When George and I came out of the guest house with our duffels, dawn was just creeping into the sky. Rain had fallen heavily for an hour after I returned to bed, but the clouds had scattered and were clearing. We had tea and toast while CAM Africans loaded the rear of the Ford Explorer with gear and packages to be delivered to Mondombe. Dave shook our hands on his way to the surgery; he was operating even on his wedding day. I half-expected to see Elizabeth, but she hadn't appeared by the time we crept out of Bololo Station.

We encountered potholes in the road almost immediately. George took the first turn at the wheel. I was still tired from my long swim in the river, but it was impossible to sleep. Holes were hard to distinguish in the dawn half-light and once we hit a few of them, I scanned the road as intently as George did, pointing out trouble spots if I thought he hadn't seen them.

We made slow progress, passing occasional villages which all looked the same. In one of them men were pushing a derelict truck, hoping to get it started. I realized they were the same men I had seen the day before from the air.

The country was hilly and we drove up and down, up and down. From ridge line to swamp, ridge line to swamp. In the swamps the roads were sand. Moving up toward the ridge lines we would hit clay, wet clay where the wheels lost their traction. Although the rain had stopped hours before, in many places rushing water had cut gullies six to eight inches deep across the surface of the road. At the bottom of the descent from each ridge line, we encountered crude bridges over streams; they were merely a series of logs laid the same direction as the road. George was concerned not only about the vehicle slipping off the logs into the streambed, but about the condition of the logs themselves, and I regularly left my seat to test the strength and solidness of the logs, walking ahead of the vehicle. I signaled it forward when I felt sure the bridge could hold its weight.

We did not arrive at Mondombe until after dark. Instead of being greeted the way we had been at Bololo, everyone making a festive fuss about the presence of George, the Central African Mission's great benefactor, the mood was gloomy and depressed. Virtually all the missionaries were assembled in the living room of the home of Dr. Ronald Roberts, the older brother of Bololo's Doctor Dave. They crowded around the radio. Some sat on the floor; others stood with grave expressions on their faces. Doctor Ron shook our hands quietly and steered us into the kitchen. His once-pretty wife, her prematurely gray hair pulled back in a bun, her glasses askew where she had been wiping tears from her eyes, dished tuna casserole onto plates and handed them to us. Before we could thank her, she turned her back to us, overcome by tears. She moved into the pantry where shelves were stacked heavy with cans of tuna and vegetables. From the living room came the crackle of voices on the radio. As she stood in the pantry, her back to us, a handkerchief to her eyes, I felt the doctor's wife was listening to those voices.

"There's coffee here if you'd like some," Ron Roberts said distractedly. He gestured to a tall thermos and some mugs. "All kinds of confusion over at Bololo," he added. "One of the girls is missing."

George and I glanced at one another.

Then the missionary looked at us oddly. "You were just over there, weren't you?" he said, as if only then realizing where we'd come from. "Maybe you met her. Elizabeth Jenkins. My brother was supposed to marry her today."

"She's missing?" George asked, incredulous.

"People saw her at dawn—"

"We left about dawn," I said.

"She was around then," the doctor said, "but when she was supposed to be getting dressed for the wedding, no one could find her. Lucas and Ruthie looked everywhere for her. Thought maybe she'd turn up at the church—she's an independent-minded gal, mature for her age. That's why she'd make a good wife for Dave, despite the age difference." The wife emerged from the pantry, studiedly looking at the floor. She pushed past us and hurried into the living room. Ron Roberts ran a hand through his hair. "But she wasn't at the church. She's vanished."

Neither George nor I said a word. I had arrived at Mondombe feeling famished, but now my hunger disappeared in the same way that Elizabeth Jenkins evidently had. I put my plate on the counter and poured myself some coffee.

"There's two things could've happened," Ron Roberts went on. "Local chief over there could've had her kidnapped. He wanted Elizabeth for her son and Lucas Jenkins wouldn't hear of it. But I don't think that's it. He's always supported our work and Dave patched him up one time after he'd had an accident."

"Have they talked to him?" I asked.

"Yes. Talked to him. And his daughter who's a pal of Elizabeth. They say they have no idea what happened to her and Dave thinks they don't. Lucas Jenkins isn't so sure, but that's what you'd expect of him."

"Could she have run away?" George asked. "She was pretty young to marry."

"Where'd she have gone?" Ron Roberts asked. "She didn't take any clothes. Didn't take any money, not that she had much. Didn't leave a note."

There was a silence. For some reason I knew what was going to fill it. I took up my plate again and forced the tuna casserole into my mouth.

"The other possibility is—" Again the silence. It created a hollowness in me. Finally he spoke the words, "Cannibals got her."

George put down his plate. I did the same; it would have been a kind of sacrilege to touch food while these words hung in the air. Once more the silence. It slowly faded and I again became conscious of the crackling voices from the radio in the living room.

"These things happen," Ron Roberts said.

"But how?" George asked, his voice a croak, a whisper of astonishment. I glanced at him. He was appalled, but inclined to believe. I was not. Nothing was ever said about cannibalism in Kenya and I thought it was missionary juju. I turned away from them.

"Savagery's making a comeback out here," Ron Roberts explained to George. "This is one of the most savage places on earth. Read a little history. Read what the first explorers found when they came here."

"Read what the first explorers *did* when they came here," I interjected. "King Léopold and the Belgians. This place was worse than Auschwitz and Buchenwald." George turned to me, dismayed by my sudden vehemence.

Roberts regarded me patronizingly as if I were an ignorant anti-missionary liberal that hospitality required him to tolerate. "You're in denial, friend," he told me.

"Bullshit," I said.

"Stay calm," George advised. "I know it's hard to believe."

"We're tiny spots of light in this huge benighted jungle,"

Roberts informed George. "We made progress for a while. But since that kleptomaniac Mobutu took power, all our gains have been eroded. Savagery's on the rise again. Believe me. Our Africans know it; they don't much care. That's how bad the paralysis is." George nodded and we were silent a moment. Roberts shook his head. "If it turns out Elizabeth was taken by cannibals—" His voice faded on the air. "Well, I don't know what the next step is."

I could stand neither this talk nor the improbable thought of Elizabeth dead. I went outside. Everyone on the station seemed to be either in the Roberts living room or standing outside it. Africans stood there, crowding at the edge of the verandah in bewildered groups holding flashlights or kerosene lanterns. I hurried away from the house, feeling alone, feeling grateful that I was less interesting to the Africans than what was going on in the house. I went down to the river that flowed below the station. I stripped off my clothes and walked into the quiet and welcoming coolness of the water. Once I washed the day away and cleansed myself of talk of cannibalism, I felt sane again.

The night was very warm. The water soothed me. As I swam on my back, my feet kicking easily, my hands working lightly at my sides, I watched the thousands of stars and felt almost as if I were floating among them. Eventually people began to leave the Roberts house. I saw their feet lighted by lantern glow and flashlight beams. I left the water, moved to the pile of my clothes and wiped the river water off me with my hands. As I reached for my undershorts, I heard someone call my name. I looked around and through the darkness saw a figure moving toward me. *"Olecko,"* the voice said. It was Elizabeth.

Standing there, clad only in the night, I felt no self-consciousness. Only a profound relief that she was here and okay.

We embraced, holding each other tightly. When I looked at her for an explanation, she said only, "I couldn't marry Doctor Dave."

We embraced again and kissed fumblingly, awkwardly—she had not kissed much—our bodies pressed together. Lolling in the water I could not believe that she had been carried off, but the thought of that possibility made me wish I had obliged her the previous night when she came to my bed. Now my body was responding to her presence, her warm nearness. I released her. I turned away. Feeling suddenly confused, I did not want her, the mission station virgin, to see my arousal. I shucked on my jeans, slipped into my Tevas and picked up the rest of my clothes in my arms.

"How did you get here?" I asked.

She grinned. "In the Ford Explorer."

"With George and me?"

She nodded and gave a laugh which she immediately stifled, putting her hand to her mouth. "No one can know."

"But someone at Bololo must know," I said.

She gave me an impish smile. "I came to say goodbye to you," she explained. "I saw you talking to Dave." She took my hand in the darkness. "I knew that if I married him I would never see you again. Or anyone like you."

I felt apprehensive. Had she done this for me?

"Or ever have my own life." She shrugged. "So I jumped into the back of the vehicle and crawled under the tarpaulin. When Ndeki came with your duffels and the other gear I showed myself. I swore him to silence. He packed the gear around me so that I would be okay."

"Are you okay?"

"I'm stiff," she admitted. "And I'm famished."

"People are very worried about you. They think cannibals got you."

"Well, they didn't," she said. "Do you have anything I could eat?"

I went up to the station guest house where George and I were to stay. I found my duffel in the room where I would sleep, removed two Power Bars from my gear, and returned with them to the place where she was waiting at the river.

"There must be Africans who know you're here," I said. She nodded. "They won't reveal you're here?"

"They always know more than they tell," she replied. "Some may tell on me. But not until I have a chance to get away."

"Where are you going to sleep?"

"Can I come to your room?"

We agreed that she would not come until after the station generators cut off. I would leave the doors open for her and hope that George would be asleep. The driving had been long and hard; George had done most of it and I was sure he was tired.

When I returned to the guest house, George was reading a Bible in the living room. He glanced at me, then looked back at the book. "'Yea, though I walk through the Valley of the Shadow of Death I will fear no evil,'" he read, "'for thou art with me.'" He put the book down. "I know this disturbs you." I nodded. "Me, too," he said.

I waited on the narrow single bed under the mosquito net. Finally the generator cut off. Elizabeth would share the bed with me—sleeping outside the mosquito net was not an option—and so I wore my jeans. The room was very hot, so hot that at last I pulled off my jeans and wore only my shorts. George began to snore. I could hear the ebb and flow of his breathing and felt certain Elizabeth could hear it, too, all the way to the river. I fell asleep before she came.

As she crawled beneath the mosquito net, I woke. "I couldn't tell if it was you snoring or George," she said. She snuggled down beside me, wearing only underpants.

We lay side by side. I kept my arms above my head, seeking to elongate myself, trying not to touch her. But the bed was too narrow for two people, even slight young people, to lie side by side in it without touching. She lay completely still for a time, her hands folded atop her breastbone. When I glanced down at her, her lips were moving. "I was saying my prayers," she told me. She turned beside me. She had small breasts, but they touched my rib cage and burned there. She kissed my shoulder. "Thank you for rescuing me," she said.

We lay awake for a long time. I wondered if she knew that in the larger world beyond the island the missionaries had created men found the sight and feel of women's breasts arousing. When I finally slept, I did so fitfully for I feared that I would turn toward her while asleep, wrap my arms about her, and not be responsible for what happened.

I supervised reloading the Ford Explorer before dawn and did my best to make sure Elizabeth was comfortable on the floor beneath the tarpaulin. I drove off the station. George rode with Ron Roberts and an ancient African called N'Djoku, meaning elephant. They went ahead of me in a Land Rover that must have been given the station before independence. We drove east ten miles, then turned onto a track, two tire-trails with vegetation growing tall between them and scraping the undercarriage. It led deep into the jungle, the track all but disappearing. Finally Roberts stopped the Land Rover in an open space. He and George and N'Djoku left the vehicle. I parked the Explorer, feigned a chore in the middle seat, and told Elizabeth that I did not know where we were or why we had stopped or what we were doing.

When I joined the other men, N'Djoku led us along a trail so overgrown with vegetation that curtains of lianas hung from trees. Underbrush grew as high as our waists. The forest was dark and from the surrounding distance came caws and scratchy chirruping that gave warning of our approach, then fell into silence. We moved through a gloom that became silent all around us. I marveled at N'Djoku's knowing where the path led. Occasionally he would stop, as if listening. He would glance around, as if fearing danger, then move cautiously ahead. Finally he stopped. He and Roberts conferred in low tones. Then Roberts said to George and me, "We'll proceed alone," and he led the way.

Eventually we came into a sunlit, swampy area that opened onto a small lake. We stopped. "What was the matter back there?" George asked. "Why wouldn't your friend come any further?"

"Spirits," Roberts said. "There are powerful spirits in this part of the forest. Don't you feel them?"

George and I glanced at one another.

Roberts laughed. "Here's a metaphysical conundrum for you," he said. "If you are told that spirits exist, but the only evidence you have of them is the effect of their belief on the people who tell you about them— Well, do they really exist?" He sighed and led us along the edge of the swamp. The earth was so soft that we squished through it, wetting our feet. "Once you've worked that one out," Roberts went on, "let me know. Because I'm still working on it."

Quite suddenly we came onto a cairn made of what appeared to be cannonballs.

"What's this?" George asked.

"A place of powerful spirits," Roberts said mysteriously. "Bad spirits. N'Djoku knows it's here, but he won't come up with *mindeli*."

"I don't feel the spirits," George said, "but it's nice to be back in sunlight."

Roberts walked over to the cairn and nudged it with his foot. "You guys ever heard of Patrice Lumumba?" he asked. We nodded. "Well, I hadn't," he said, "when I got out here fifteen years ago. First prime minister of the independent Congo. A rabble-rouser. A Communist." He looked at us again, enjoying being mysterious. "You're standing over his bones." He nudged the cairn again.

No one spoke. Finally I ventured, "Historians claim he was assassinated in Katanga."

"Western historians," Roberts said scornfully. "What do they know? I can't keep all the politics straight," he went on, "but here's what went down. An enemy of Lumumba named Kalonji, a politician Lumumba had crossed, bought Lumumba from the Katangese. Lumumba had ordered the massacre of some of Kalonji's people; I believe that was it. Kalonji had connections with the diamond mining consortium in the old Kasai. He acquired Lumumba for a fabulous sum of money."

I glanced at George Templeton, wondering if he believed this tale. He was staring at the cairn.

"Kalonji brought him here," Roberts went on. "He was accused of the massacre and condemned for it. They told Lumumba they were going to eat him. Which terrified him, of course."

"What happened?" asked George.

"He was killed right here," Roberts said. "And eaten. What was left was buried under the cairn."

George said nothing.

"Who told you this?" I asked.

"A chief who attended the ceremony," the missionary replied. "A venerable guy. I didn't believe it. But I got to know him quite well. He's never lied to me."

Roberts went on, "This is why Mobutu surrounds himself with fellow tribesmen. This is why he lives on that yacht on the river off Kinshasa."

George frowned at the doctor, not following his logic. "He's afraid his enemies will eat him," Roberts explained. "They're all afraid of that. I get terminally ill patients whose greatest fear is that they will be eaten when they die."

"You think Elizabeth was taken by cannibals?" George asked.

Roberts shrugged. He would not say that this was his belief, but why else had he taken us to this remote spot in the jungle?

Once we got back to the Ford Explorer, George drove without speaking for many miles. He would stop at bridges and I would get out to inspect them, waving him slowly forward, and then return to my seat beside him. This would happen without a single word passing between us.

Finally I said, "Here's a metaphysical conundrum for you. If you are told by missionaries that cannibals exist and snatch children and young adults, but the only evidence you have of them is the missionaries' belief in them— Well, do they really exist?"

He was silent for a long time. Then he said, "You don't believe it."

I shook my head.

"Then what happened to Elizabeth?" he asked.

I ignored the question. "For some reason we are willing to believe that Africans are capable of unspeakable depravity," I said. "Whites come into this country. They want raw rubber and ivory and they murder and enslave the populace to get it. Lop off men's hands. Starve them. Put them in stockades. Eat them every way except factually—and yet somehow it is still the Africans who are thought to be so depraved that they feed on their own kind."

Neither of us spoke for a long while. Finally George said, "I want to get out of this country."

"This benighted country," I said. "The heart of darkness. Which is reverting to savagery at the speed of light."

"You don't believe it?" George asked.

"I don't know what to believe. Except that it's a contention which very conveniently feeds the martyr complex of missionaries. Who are well-intentioned—even truly good—people. They just cannot believe that doing things any way but their way could possibly be okay."

When we stopped for lunch at the side of the road, we had not encountered a single vehicle. George set the cooler on the hood of the vehicle; someone at Mondombe had made sandwiches for us. I opened the rear of the Explorer, pulled our luggage from it and set it on the road. When I rolled back the tarpaulin, Elizabeth stared at me with frightened eyes. "It's all right," I said. I helped her onto the road.

When George saw her, he almost overturned the sandwich cooler.

"Not eaten," I said.

"Hasn't eaten," Elizabeth corrected. "I'm starved."

George laughed heartily and handed her a sandwich. He listened without comment to Elizabeth's account of why she was with us. He nodded when she explained that she had not been consulted about marrying "Doctor Dave," that she had not been asked for her consent even in the way an African girl was asked for it in a form of marriage that her parents regarded as akin to selling girls. She said that she did not consent to spending her life having babies and making meals for a man—however good he was, however important the work he did—whom she did not know. Her decision to flee had been sudden, but it was irrevocable. "Please don't send me back," she said.

"You better have something to eat," was all George said. He spoke hardly at all the rest of the day. We spent the night drawn into the yard of a derelict building with half its corrugated iron roof pulled off. George and I took turns sitting guard in the Explorer. When half a dozen warriors carrying hunting nets discovered us and drew near shortly before dawn, I honked the horn. They jumped, whirling as one man, and raced off into the gloom.

We reached Kisangani late the next afternoon and stayed three days waiting for a plane to Nairobi. It was clear that Elizabeth had not been in a real town in a very long time. She looked at everything with her intelligent and eager curiosity, but she also held onto my wrist or hand wherever we went, wanting to make sure that she never got separated from me. George put us up in the best hotel, a room for him and one for Elizabeth and me. When people stared at Elizabeth, we realized reports were circulating of a missing girl fitting her description. When George contacted the local missionaries who would look after the Explorer until CAM missionaries could fetch it, they wanted to know all about the mission girl who had vanished. Was it really cannibalism? George suggested, "You better stay with her. Keep her out of sight."

So while he arranged our flight and made the payoffs necessary to get proper documents for Elizabeth, I tended her—

babysat her really. She was like a precocious child. Questions popped into her head about the most improbable things: What became of refuse when you flushed a toilet? How did vending machines work? Why were buildings built so tall? Did they often fall down? When I assured her they did not, she became intrigued by elevators; it seemed magical to her that you could enter a room on one floor and leave it on another. She wanted to see everything in the town, but, of course, was forbidden to do so. So she spent hours gazing from the balcony of our room, asking questions about everything she did not understand. If she was partly a child, she was also partly a woman. The room had two queen-sized beds, but fearing perhaps that I would leave her, she insisted on our sleeping together.

As a young woman who had almost gotten married, she also wanted to know about sex. Against my better judgment, we began to make love. For my judgment proved much weaker than the power of biology. Our first lovemaking was not a success. "Why does everyone make such a big deal about this?" she asked. "Mutimba says it's wonderful, but it hurts." However, the hurt wore off and she thought we should keep trying.

When I told George that we had become lovers, he gazed at me as if he were severely disappointed. I asked, "What happens to her when we get to Nairobi?"

"I've been wondering," he said. "I'm sure I can get her a passport."

"Can you take her to the States?"

He shook his head. His wife who had stayed watching animals would be with him. They could not appear to be trying to slip a young woman out of Africa against her parents' will. "Can she stay in Kenya?" he asked. "Can you look after her?"

"I'm a school teacher," I said.

"Can you get her into the school?" he asked. "I'll take care of the expenses."

Once we got to Nairobi—and before his wife flew in—George succeeded in securing Elizabeth an American passport. The deputy headmaster assured me that an exception could be made; she could enroll in the school where I taught. When the Templetons left, Mrs. Templeton assuming that Elizabeth was the daughter of American expatriates in Kenya, everything seemed to have been worked out.

The next week, however, the Kalenjin headmaster overruled the decision of his Kikuyu deputy. In what seemed a matter of tribal one-up-manship, I was informed that Elizabeth could enroll only if she were my wife. In which case, of course, she would be living with me. When I explained this to Elizabeth, she burst into tears. She was still very dependent on me; she refused to go into Nairobi streets alone. "I should have obeyed my parents," she cried. I shook my head. "Well, will you marry me then?" she asked.

I went to the Kenya Marriage Registry office. I ingratiated myself to a clerk, gave him one hundred dollars American and received in return a certificate affirming that Elizabeth and I were man and wife. But were we married? It was one of those metaphysical conundrums. I tried to explain it to Elizabeth. "We are not married," I told her, showing her the certificate. "This paper says we are. But we aren't really."

She nodded, looking at me with huge eyes.

"I mean we haven't exchanged vows."

"But we love each other," she said. "We do love each other, don't we?"

I assured her we did. "But it isn't the kind of love married people feel."

"Let's say vows," she suggested.

I did not want to exchange vows and stalled. "We'll have to think about the kind of vows we'd make."

That night when we were in bed together, holding one another, she said, "I love you. I always will. That's my vow."

"I will not let you make that vow at fifteen," I said.

"What kind of vow can I make? Will you make a vow?"

"I vow," I said, "always to be your friend. To love you as a friend." I could feel that she might cry and I began to laugh. "And," I added, "I will take care of you until you finish high school."

She repeated this vow and we kissed and made love. "We are getting better at this," she said. "I understand why Mutimba thinks about it so much."

"Do you think about it a lot?" I asked.

"Hmm," she replied drowsily. "Do you?"

Elizabeth completed her third year of high school in Nanyuki. She lived with me as my wife. When my teaching contract was not renewed, we returned to the States with George Templeton's help. He found me a job in San Jose and we established residency so that when Elizabeth finished high school the following year—as she did—she would qualify for a resident's admission to the University of California system. I repeatedly suggested that she tell her parents where she was, but while she was still in high school, she refused. When she won admission to UC Davis, she rented a post office box, informed her parents that she was alive, and suggested they write her there.

Although she was "married" in high school, she went off to Davis as a single woman. We agreed that she must have a life independent of me. No one at the university was to know that the law had ever considered her married. Or that she might have considered herself married. I moved to Sacramento so that she would not feel abandoned. I was less than an hour away if she needed me.

Our being apart seemed right to me. A mentor should not be sleeping with the woman he mentors. A young person coming of age should not keep trying to please the person who has parented her.

She is now in her fourth year at Davis. She expects to graduate in June. I am back in Kenya, teaching at a secondary school in Nairobi. George Templeton has promised Elizabeth a trip to Africa when she graduates: to Kenya to see me, to the Congo to see her parents who write to her that Kabila's takeover of the country has speeded the reversion to savagery. Cannibalism is once more on the rise.

Elizabeth writes me she has had boyfriends; she even lived with one man for a while. She knows there is a Kenyan woman whom I see. She writes that she loves me, in fact has *always* loved me since the night she came to my room in the guest house at Bololo. She claims that when she is with other men there is always a withholding. The withholding is about me. She cannot give herself fully, she says, to any other man.

Her letters perplex me. How can she love me? Isn't it just a matter of my having romantically imprinted on her at a moment of emotional susceptibility?

Yet strangely I, too, feel toward her an emotional— Connection? Attachment? Commitment? I'm not sure what. Is it possible that I love her? When I met her, I was a man. She was only fifteen—and a mission kid. And yet . . . There is also a withholding in me. When I am with women, Elizabeth is always there, too. Can this be love? Perhaps we'll find out when she comes to visit in June.

Africa, Africa!

THE TWO FAMILIES CROSSED OVER FROM DOVER on the morning hydrofoil. In Ostend they found drizzle in July. Belgium was showing its northern European face. As they drove through flat Flemish countryside to Bruges, Derek acknowledged that he had visited the town before. Couldn't remember much about it, he said; there were museums and a market square. Was there a belfry?

The families checked in to their hotel. After lunch in a café, they donned raincoats and walked to the old market square. Derek's memory was correct; there was, indeed, a glorious belfry. To get out of the weather, they visited the Groeninge Museum, admired its finely wrought masterpieces curiously known as "Flemish primitives." They made the requisite turn around the cathedral. Now the drizzle was lifting. There was even a bit of sunlight showing through the overcast. Each couple had a teenaged son, born within a year of one another. The boys wanted to return to the belfry and conquer its circular stairway.

"Back to the market square then?" asked the other husband. He and Derek had become friends years before when they worked as correspondents for the same paper.

The others were ready to start off, but Derek hesitated. Just across the street was a hospital. A woman he had known long ago was there. He wanted to see her—and wanted to see her alone.

As a young man he had lived in Belgium. He had dated an American girl who was studying there on a Fulbright scholarship. They had toured museums together, and they had discovered it was not difficult to distinguish a van der Weyden from a Brueghel, a van Eyck from a Rubens or a Bosch.

He and the girl had visited Bruges. They had happened into the hospital which was, in fact, a museum. It owned an exquisite collection of the works of the Flemish primitive artist Hans Memling. Among other paintings, they saw a Madonna holding an apple in her left hand and the Christ-child in her right. They were amazed by the painting, by the deftness of its brushwork, by the specificity and demureness of the Madonna's characterization, by its timelessness that was, even so, definitely of its time.

Derek could not take his eyes off the woman. Later she came to mean a great deal to him. She became his friend.

In June of that year Derek and the American girl took a farewell trip together. He was being sent to the Congo; she was returning to Illinois. They wandered through northern France in Derek's car, through Normandy and Brittany. The girl was ready to resume the course of her life, to see once again the "sort of" fiancé to whom she had been "sort of" faithful in a way that made it possible for her and Derek to "sort of" talk about getting married. At the Gare St. Lazare, Derek and the girl had an emotional parting. But once the boat train left, Derek wondered if he would ever see her again.

He wondered, too, about the Congo, then only three years into its bloody and chaotic independence, about the people he would meet. There had been girlfriends in Derek's life ever since high school. Now most of his friends were getting married. Would there be a woman for him in Elisabethville, where he was being transferred? If not, would he survive? Well, probably. Elisabethville was a real city and he was a survivor.

When Derek arrived in the Congo, he was not sent to Elisabethville. He went instead to Coquilhatville in a region called the Equateur. During his first weeks there he was unspeakably lonely. Then a month or so before Christmas an advertising brochure arrived in the mail. Inside was a reproduction of the Memling Madonna. Derek cut it out and mounted it on cardboard. He placed her in his house where he could look at her often. In his bathroom, in fact. He sometimes talked with her, joked with her. He teased her with irreverent nicknames. She turned out to be his girlfriend in the Congo.

Now Derek wanted to see his friend again. He wanted to stand beside her alone. When he did, he would not say anything—at least not audibly. That had always been their way. He wanted to look again on her flattish, long-nosed face. He wanted to see the special modesty of her eyes, to feel once more the virtue her manner and presence exuded.

Virtue. Not a quality that most men prize in the women of their pasts, especially when they have married it, as Derek had done. But virtue was the special characteristic of this woman. She and Derek had shared hardships. Her goodness had assuaged his loneliness and helped to carry him through difficult times.

They had been together in Coquilhatville for seven or eight

months. During that time the Congo flared into rebellion. Civil war started in the country's southeast and eventually threatened Derek in the northwest. When that happened, he found it wonderful to have the woman with him. As the conflict grew more violent, he frequently sought solace in her tranquillity. Derek would gaze at her for long moments and he would feel strangely reassured.

Finally, when the rebel army was only a few hours outside of town, most foreigners fled. Derek packed hurriedly. A United States Air Force C-130 evacuated him and he lost track of his belongings. They stayed in storage for months. Eventually he left the Congo. He changed professions. He married and had a son. During that time he came upon some forgotten Congo possessions. Among them, in an envelope, he found the reproduction that he had mounted on cardboard. He displayed it on a shelf in his office and called to his wife, "Look what I found!" They laughed together about the woman he'd lived with in Coq.

Now being so close to her, just across the street, Derek wanted to see his friend. He might never return to Belgium. If he did not visit her now, he might never see her again. Derek told the group, "I'm going over to St. John's Hospital." He spoke the words as if the idea had occurred to him that very moment. "It's just across the street."

"You all right?" asked Derek's colleague.

"It's a museum. I visited it when I lived here."

"Not another museum!" said the colleague's wife.

"Memling," explained Derek. "Another primitive."

His colleague shook his head; he'd had enough fifteenth century Flemish art.

"If we don't hurry, the belfry's gonna close," prompted Derek's son.

"Go on," Derek urged them. "I'll catch up with you."

His wife understood where he was headed. She smiled at him and moved off with the others.

Inside the hospital Derek made his way through dark, cold, pre-modern hallways. Finally he found the gallery and entered it. Derek glanced about and there she was, across the room. He approached.

He stood close before her, examined her minutely. Her lashless, thin-browed eyes were downcast, as they always were. In his mind he said, "Look at me! Look at me!" But she would not; she never had. Derek thought, "I know, I know. It's all right." He felt once again the sense of peace he had always known with her.

Derek smiled at the sight of her tiny mouth, her delicate but quite long nose, at the hint of the double chin. He remembered the open window behind her with its view of the northern Europe of Memling's day. Derek remembered the circular mirror and how it provided a rear view of the woman and a glimpse of the room she faced—although, of course, Memling and his easel were not there. Derek delighted once more in the long-fingered delicacy with which her left hand offered the apple to the Christ-child. The woman enchanted him, seeming hardly older than twenty. But he'd always had reservations about the Christ-child. Derek thought the child looked like a babyfied Hanseatic merchant. Being held, he did not cuddle against his mother as real babies cuddled, as his own son had cuddled against his wife. Instead he seemed to float.

Derek stood before the painting for long moments. Then he moved off to observe the other Memlings, those consummately sophisticated "primitives." Before leaving, he glanced again at the painting. He crossed the gallery to bid farewell.

Then suddenly he and the woman were back together in the

Congo, during that terrible time. He could feel the coolness of the nights after the heat of the long days. Once again the African humidity lay moist on his skin. He tasted papaya; he had often eaten slices of it before turning in. He heard the night stillness broken by that patter of droplets that turned to rain battering on the metal roof. Quite unexpectedly he experienced a flutter in his heart, a pang of nostalgia for Africa. It had been a terrible time. But had he ever felt more alive?

"Went through a lot together, didn't we?"

Derek studied his friend. Demurely she watched the apple, for his rhetorical questions never received answers. Derek thought the words a man always wants to say to the women from his past, "Thanks for all you gave me."

Leaving her, returning through the cold hallways, Derek felt a curious dizziness. He placed his hand against a cold wall to steady himself. Africa, Africa! Nostalgia for Africa. It was something you never got over. A little like malaria. It hit you—sometimes predictably, in certain weathers, in certain places; sometimes unexpectedly—and all you could do was suffer through it and let it pass.

Outside the sky was clearing. On the sidewalk before a shop selling souvenirs Derek caught up with his wife and the other couple. The boys had gone on to the belfry. His wife smiled and asked, "How was she?"

"She still doesn't talk to me," Derek said.

His wife clasped his hand for a moment and smiled. Then she went into the shop with the other couple to look at souvenirs.

Derek stayed alone on the sidewalk for a long time.